AMBER

He brushed to the rh teased h curled an trying to slow the blood rushing through his veins. It didn't help. The air was filled with Amber's scent.

"Clay?"

The sound of her voice was like a caress. "Hmm?"

"There's something I want for my birthday, and I was wondering if you'd give it to me."

He'd give her the moon if he could reach it. "What's that, sweetheart?"

She paused, then whispered softly, "A kiss."

**Books by Sue Rich**

The Scarlet Temptress
Shadowed Vows
Rawhide and Roses
Mistress of Sin
The Silver Witch
Wayward Angel
Aim for the Heart
Amber

Published by POCKET BOOKS

# Sue Rich

# Amber

**POCKET BOOKS**
New York   London   Toronto   Sydney   Tokyo   Singapore

An *Original* Publication of POCKET BOOKS

POCKET BOOKS, a division of Simon & Schuster Inc.
1230 Avenue of the Americas, New York, NY 10020

Copyright © 1997 by Sue Rich

ISBN: 0-671-00044-6

First Pocket Books printing February 1997

10  9  8  7  6  5  4  3  2  1

POCKET and colophon are registered trademarks of
Simon & Schuster Inc.

Cover art by Vittorio Dangelico

Printed in the U.S.A.

To my mother-in-law, Agnes Rich, and to my niece, Amber. This one's for both of you.

To my editor, Caroline Tolley. Thanks again.

And, as always, to my understanding other half, Jim Rich.

# Chapter 1

*Someone was going to die today.*

Clayton Cordell bolted upright in bed. The vicious clenching in his stomach made it hard to breathe, and he broke into a sweat. Not again. Please, Lord. *Not again.*

"Clay? Is something wrong?" Clarissa Demoine asked from beside him. Her long nails trailed along his arm. A smooth bare leg slid between his thighs with a familiarity only a mistress could execute.

What could he say? That he knew someone close to him was going to die? That he could *feel* it? That he'd experienced the eerie sensations since he was a child? She'd be convinced—like everyone else—that he was unbalanced. Hell, it had taken him weeks to assure her of his sanity. Again he cursed himself for losing his temper and taking a strap to a nobleman in front of so many people.

Tossing back the silk coverlet, he rose and strode naked to a chair near the armoire, where his breeches had been tossed earlier that day.

1

The unearthly feeling gripped him again, snatching his breath, and he immediately thought of his mother's second husband, Robert Frazier. His fingers bit into the fine linen. *Please, not him.* Suppressing his mounting fears, Clay glanced at the beautiful brunette lying on the bed. "I just remembered an appointment," he lied as he pulled on his clothes.

She arched a brow, clearly indicating her disbelief. "If you have another rendezvous, Your Grace, simply say so."

Even though he was lying, it irritated him that she didn't believe him. He'd never lied to her before. "If I planned to bed another woman, you'd be the first to know." He stomped into his black, knee-high boots and drew on his shirt. "I believe I made that fact clear from the onset."

"So you did."

Although her tone was unruffled, he didn't miss the relief in her eyes. But he knew it wasn't because she feared losing his affection. She was simply worried about her station as the duke of Westshire's mistress . . . and the numerous amenities that came with that position.

Gathering his hair into a queue, he tied the unruly strands with a leather strip as he headed for the door. "I don't know when I'll return," he said noncommittally, but he knew it wouldn't be soon. His time with Clarissa was at an end. Like so many before her, she had become tiresome.

Leaving the brownstone on Downing Street that he kept for his rendezvous with Clarissa, he took the front steps two at a time. The odor of rotting fish and wood smoke wafted from the docks, and he turned away from the disagreeable smell. He gave St. James Park across the street a momentary glance, then headed toward the alley where he kept his mount.

Wishing he'd taken the time to hire a groom, he

sprinted into the stables, then grabbed his saddle, and tossed it over his thoroughbred, Sundial.

The animal pranced and leather creaked as Clay settled himself in the saddle. Unexpectedly, the tension in his stomach tightened into a searing knot, and a rush of urgency swept him. He kicked Sundial into motion.

Carts, vendors, and Londoners draped in capes and cloaks against the fall chill crowded the streets, making his harried ride through town take forever.

At last he made it to the tree-lined road leading to his stepfather's country estate on the outskirts of London and was able to urge Sundial into a gallop. The roadway was littered with fall leaves, their golden shells scattering in the cool breeze.

He leaned low over the animal and urged him into a faster pace, hoping the feeling in his middle wasn't meant for Robert. But who else could it be? Dust and leaves exploded beneath him. The afternoon sun blinded him. The wind stung his cheeks, but he refused to slow. If there was any way he could stop what was happening, he would.

Leaping from the saddle before his horse stopped, he charged up the brick steps and burst through the double doors of Ainshall Manor—and collided with his stepfather's butler, Liberty.

The elderly, stick-thin figure grumbled as he smoothed out his black knee breeches and a matching tailcoat.

Clay gripped his shoulders. "Where's my father?"

The frail man didn't bat an eye. He'd been in the Ainshall household since before Clay was born, and he wasn't in the least concerned by the urgency in Clay's voice. "I believe you'll find the viscount in his study, Your Grace."

Clay ran.

Robert Frazier, Viscount Ainshall, looked up from

the *London Gazette* he'd been reading. A thin line of smoke snaked upward from a cheroot resting in a tray by his hand. Steam hovered over a cup of tea on his other side. "Well, I see you saw fit to visit at last," Robert teased, knowing full well Clay had been there just two days ago.

"Are you all right?"

Gray brows lifted over Robert's clear blue eyes, then understanding dawned. "The 'feeling' again?"

"Yes." Rubbing the nape of his neck, Clay sank into a chair. "Damn it. Why does this keep happening to me?"

"Your mother, God rest her soul, blamed it on the Captain's heritage," Robert said in a quiet tone. He never called Clay's sire by name, only the Captain. "She told me he was half Irish and half gypsy—and his mother was a soothsayer."

Clay studied the man he'd called Father until he was twelve years old—until the day the Captain abducted Clay and took him aboard his pirate ship. Clay hadn't known until then that Robert wasn't his father.

The Captain had explained everything to Clay that first night. He'd said Clay's mother had been on a voyage to Spain when the Captain and his crew attacked her ship. The Captain had taken one look at Elaina Wingate and had fallen in love with her. He abducted her and made for open waters. They married, his mother quite willingly, less than a fortnight later, but Elaina hadn't been able to adjust to life away from London. By the time Clay was three months old, she'd left the Captain and returned to England. She'd even risked scandal by petitioning the king for a divorce.

Recalling Robert's comment, Clay returned his gaze to his stepfather. "Well, gypsy blood or not, I detest these feelings."

"They're a part of you, son. There's nothing you can do to change that." Robert drew on his cheroot and leaned back. Through spirals of smoke a beam of sunlight slipped in between the drapes to touch his gray-streaked brown hair. "Don't you remember the day your grandmother's heart failed when you were six? You came to me, telling me something was wrong. Something bad was going to happen."

"I remember." It was impossible to forget. The pressure in his chest had been so bad, he'd had to fight for breath. "It was the same four years ago when Mother drowned in the lake out back, and last year when my friend Joseph was killed in a duel. And when the Captain—" He swallowed. "Damn, I hate this."

"I know, but you have to accept it. It's part of you." He set his cheroot down and folded his hands. "Who do you think it is this time?"

"I thought it was you."

Compassion touched Robert's eyes. "I'm not going to leave you for a long time." A dimple appeared at the corner of his expressive mouth. "Besides, Morgan is one up on me. I couldn't possibly *retire* until I've evened the score."

Clay's younger brother, Morgan, Robert's true son, had been in a contest of practical jokes with Robert for as long as Clay could recall. Trying to outdo each other had become a Frazier ritual. "What did he do this time?"

"Posted a note in town for the sale of my prize stallion . . . for ten shillings."

"My God! The horse is worth a thousand times that amount."

"I know. I had a devil of a time warding off the herd of would-be purchasers, too."

Clay could just picture the utter chaos that must have abounded in Ainshall after that prank. "Some-day one of you will go too far."

"It's clean fun. Don't begrudge us that. Besides, we received enough warnings and dire predictions from your mother to last a lifetime."

"I can imagine."

"Your lordship!" A fist pounded on the door. "Come quick. There's been an accident!"

A surge of panic shot through Clay. He met Robert's eyes for an instant, then they both bolted for the door.

"What is it, Liberty?" Robert demanded. "Speak up, man."

Liberty gestured to a winded, disheveled man standing behind him. Their neighbor's driver.

Clay felt the blood leave his face. Ah, God. *Not him.* "Has something happened to William Sinclair?"

"Yes, Your G-grace," the driver acknowledged on a labored breath. "The carriage o-overturned 'bout half a mile down the road. The master, he—he's pinned beneath it."

Terror held Clay motionless for a heartbeat, then he burst into action. "Liberty, get all the men you can find to help." Racing out the door, he leaped astride Sundial and kicked him into a mile-eating gallop.

Within a few moments, Robert's animal pounded behind him.

The mile between Ainshall and William's estate, Markland, was a winding, wooded lane with deep ravines on either side. Patches of browning grass forced its way between the trees to make small clearings.

Clay saw the carriage horse first, lying in a ditch on its side, kicking and squealing, jerking against the harness that still bound it to the overturned coach. Blood mingled with dirt on the animal's once white coat. Its eyes were wild with fear.

Urgently, Clay motioned to Robert to release the animal then leaped down from his own horse. As he hurried to the upside-down coach in the ravine, he noticed a girl lying near the road. His step faltered. Amber? Another knot of fear tightened his middle, and he started toward her. He had to make sure she was all right. The squeal of the Markland pacer halted him. *William was pinned beneath the carriage.*

Torn, Clay gave a quick, silent prayer for Amber's safety and hurried down the side of the ravine to William. Birds fluttered overhead. The scent of blood and dirt permeated the air, but he couldn't see the extent of the damage until he reached the bottom. William's entire lower body was crushed. Blood spread out from his sides in crimson pools. His once handsome face was gray and deeply grooved by lines of pain.

The coil in Clay's stomach snapped. Frantically, he grabbed the edge of the coach and strained to lift it.

Robert was beside him in an instant, and together, they were able to raise it high enough to free William. Clay held the vehicle in place with desperate strength while Robert pulled him from beneath it.

"See about Amber," Clay instructed as he tore off his shirt and pressed it to his friend's bleeding abdomen. Cold air brushed over his bare shoulders and chest, and he gave a light shiver that had nothing to do with the cold as he slipped an arm beneath William's shoulders. His back was warm and wet, and Clay didn't have to look to know it was covered in blood. Doom spread like a thick cloak. "William? Can you hear me?"

There were several seconds of silence, then the older man's lashes fluttered open. "Clay? That you?" He coughed, and blood trickled from the corner of his mouth. "What happened? Where's Amber?"

"There's been an accident, but Amber is fine." *He hoped.* "Don't talk now. Save your strength. The others will be here soon, and we'll get you to a physician."

"No accident," William wheezed.

Clay brushed a lock of graying blond hair from his damp brow. "I saw the broken axle."

Sinclair rolled his head from side to side. "Someone's t-trying to kill my daughter."

"What? For God's sake, why?" William must have injured his head, too.

The ailing man closed his eyes. "I don't know why. I j-just know it's happening."

"Surely you're mistaken."

"No." William lifted a shaking hand and placed it on Clay's arm. "T-This was the third time." He coughed again, and more blood dribbled down to his chin. "You've got to protect her, Clay, until my investigators learn who—" His words were silenced by another spasm of coughing.

Clay felt the constriction in his own chest, then overwhelming anger. Someone had done this deliberately.

"Promise me," William gasped, "you'll take her away from here."

"You're going to be al—"

"We've never lied to each other, b-boy. Don't start now." He tightened his fingers on Clay's arm. "Promise me, damn you."

"I give you my word, William. I'll protect her with my life."

Sinclair drew in a raspy breath and nodded. Another wheezing convulsion gripped him, and he began gasping for air. His skin grew pale, and Clay knew in that instant that his friend wasn't going to make it.

William knew it, too. He lifted his tired blue eyes to Clay, the lines around his mouth deepening with pain. "T-Tell Amber . . . not to mourn me. Tell her not to wear black." A watery gasp rattled up his throat, and he began to choke.

Clay knew how much William hated somber, depressing mourning clothes that went so against his belief in a wonderful world beyond life, and he knew those words would be William's last. He drew him closer, feeling a rush of blood down William's spine, the raspy jerk to his chest. Clay held him. He prayed. He tried to breathe for him. Tried to stop the bleeding—but nothing helped.

With a long, anguished wheeze, William at last slumped lifeless in his arms.

The loss was unbearable. For several minutes, he stayed with his friend, cradling him, letting the tears fall freely. William didn't deserve to die like this.

"Son?" Robert touched his shoulder. "You can't help him any more, but we need to get Amber home and summon help. She's unconscious, and a wound on her head is bleeding. I think it needs stitching."

*Amber needs me.* The thought was almost laughable, considering their last parting. Clay swiped at the tears on his cheeks and again glanced at William's lifeless form. He would get the bastard who did this. By all that was holy, he would. Taking deep breaths to soften the ache in his throat, he slowly came to his feet. "William said this wasn't an accident. He thinks someone's trying to kill Amber. I'm hoping he was talking out of his head, but I can't take any chances." He nodded toward the top of the ravine. "Would you take her home to Markland while I bring William?"

"Of course." Robert kneaded Clay's shoulder. "I'm sorry, son. I know how close you were."

Unable to speak, Clay could only manage a dip of his head in response.

The ride to the Sinclair's estate was long and painful. Time and again, Clay's gaze drifted to William's body cradled in his arms, to the blood dripping onto the saddle, to the blood dampening his own bare chest. The urge to avenge his friend—*to kill*—was so strong, he trembled with it.

Desperate to turn his thoughts from William, he focused on Robert riding ahead of him. He was holding Amber, but Clay couldn't see more than the flutter of lilac satin draping the side of the horse. He hadn't seen her in four years, and he wasn't sure he wanted to see her now. Not after what happened last time.

But he would have to see her . . . and talk to her. Soon. He slowed his mount, suddenly needing to prolong the meeting as long as possible.

When he reached Markland, Robert had already taken Amber inside, and Clay carried William to a bedchamber on the lower floor. The sound of sobbing servants echoed through the house as he stared at his friend's pale body stretched out on the bed. Sweet Lord in heaven, he couldn't take the pain.

"Your Grace?"

He turned to see one of William's relatives, his wife's cousin Georgina Becker. At least two score in years, she was a pretty woman, slim of stature, with sand-colored hair and hazel eyes. She stood behind him, her attention fixed on William.

Clay cleared the grief from his throat. "Yes? What is it?"

The woman dragged her gaze to his and held up one of William's shirts. "I thought you could use this."

Having tied his own shirt around William's middle, Clay gratefully donned the garment. "Thank you, Mrs. Becker," he managed through a tight throat, then William's scent drifted up from the material, and another wave of grief swept him.

"Dr. Baldwick has come to tend Amber, but he should be finished soon. If you'd like to speak to him, you can wait in the parlor." The woman gave him an understanding smile. "There are spirits on the sideboard that might be beneficial at a time like this."

Clay didn't need further urging. He headed for the parlor. With numb hands, he poured a healthy shot and downed it in one gulp. The liquid seared his throat, and he waited for the burning to subside, then poured another and stared at the richly furnished room. He remembered the day William's late wife, Victoria, had ordered it redecorated. She had just returned home from a visit to Italy and had tried to duplicate the Italian flavor in the parlor with bold silk colors, candelabrum dripping with crystals, heavy, ornately carved furnishings, and oil paintings of Venice. The overall picture was a little too dramatic for him, but Victoria's London friends had been duly impressed.

The thought of all the London pomp made him ill. Even though he was a peer of the realm himself because he inherited his maternal grandfather's title, he wasn't one of the elite. And he didn't want to be. During his days aboard the *Black Wind,* he'd learned about real people and real life. In fact, he couldn't wait to begin a 'real' life of his own in the Colonies, in a lush valley near his friend Bragen Alexander. It was a raw, pure land where titles meant nothing, and a man was judged solely by his actions.

"Your Grace?" A rotund man in spectacles came into the room, but he didn't approach Clay. In fact, he kept a healthy distance from him.

Clay wasn't surprised. Over the last year, he'd received that type of treatment often—since the day he lost control when he stopped a nobleman from whipping his servant in the marketplace.

He should have stayed out of it, but the action had hit too close to home. In his mind he had seen Miranda—and this time he hadn't been helpless.

Clay shook the thought away. "How's the child, Dr. Baldwick?"

"She is still unconscious."

A new spark of fear shot through him. "Is she going to be all right?"

The doctor removed his eyeglasses and placed them in a small carpetbag he carried, still maintaining his distance. "The wound appears superficial and not at all extensive. Of course, I will not know for certain until she rouses. In the meantime, someone must stay with her at all times. I will return on the morrow to check her progress, but if she awakens before then, send for me immediately."

The thought of spending time alone with Amber ignited an unwanted memory, and Clay downed his drink and set the glass aside. "She needs her family at a time like this." *Anyone* but him. Besides, the little social butterfly needed a chaperon to protect her all-so-important reputation. Pushing aside the uncharitable thought, he tried to remember where her kin were. Her mother was dead, and the Becker woman was only a distant relation. William's brothers were somewhere in the Colonies.

"The Chatsworths are her godparents. If you send a message, I am sure they will come straightaway."

He'd forgotten about the haughty couple and their son who lived just beyond Markland. "I'll send a footman." He opened the door for the physician. "Who's going to tend to . . . William?"

"Lord Frazier. He is with him now."

"I see." The ache in Clay's throat returned, but he would be eternally grateful to Robert for his thoughtfulness.

After showing Baldwick out, Clay went in search of a boy to send for Amber's godparents. He found him outside the chamber where William had been taken.

The young man glanced up as Clay approached, his eyes red, his cheeks wet. A kerchief was knotted between his fingers. "M-Master Sinclair, he was a g-good man."

Clay felt the boy's anguish. "Yes, he was, and you'd do him a great service if you'd help me care for his daughter during this time."

"Me? How?"

"She needs her godparents, the Chatsworths."

The boy straightened. "I'll go for them immediately."

Clay watched the lad sprint toward the front door, then numbly mounted the stairs to check on Amber.

The room on the second floor was dim, with a beam of light squeezing through the pulled drapes. Golden candlelight flickered over the satin walls and delicate furnishings, yet shadowed the heavily draped bed.

Georgina Becker was sitting in a high-backed chair at Amber's side, holding her hand.

Not wanting to disturb her, he moved silently to the foot of the four-poster and peeked through a part in the sheer netting. Then stared. Amber was beautiful. Even more so than he remembered. The square bandage covering one temple was surrounded by a wealth of shimmering gold curls. Her blood-stained dress had been replaced with a nightgown that laced to her throat, but the garment did nothing to conceal the alluring curves that truly proclaimed her a grown woman—not the fifteen-year-old child he remembered.

The realization sent a rush of unwanted feelings through him. Feelings he'd spent years trying to subdue.

He inspected her delicate bone structure and nub of a nose, her full lips, and the smooth line of her jaw that hinted at a trace of stubbornness. A trace, hell. He remembered exactly how stubborn and willful and hard-headed she was. No, he amended. That was the way she used to be. According to William, over the last years she'd become entranced by the London social whirl—just as her mother had. *As his own had.*

Not wanting to think about how much Amber's activities bothered him, he shifted his gaze to her closed eyes, to the thick lashes making tiny crescents on her porcelain skin. Even though he couldn't see their color, he remembered well. Her eyes were deep, deep violet.

She was so lovely. Why would anyone want to hurt her?

"Did you need something, Your Grace?"

He glanced at Georgina. "Er . . . yes. I've sent a message to Amber's godparents, and I imagine they'll need a room. You might have a maid prepare one."

"Of course. How thoughtless of me." She rose but was hesitant to leave.

"Don't worry. I'll stay with her."

She still appeared uncertain, then at last nodded. "I won't be long."

When the door closed, Clay turned the chair around and straddled it, bracing his arms on the back. His gaze again drifted over Amber. She was going to be devastated over her father's death. They'd always been so close. He dreaded the time when someone would have to tell her.

He fingered one of her long shiny curls, remembering the first time he saw her. The Captain had allowed him to leave the *Black Wind* for a visit home when he was sixteen. William and Robert had been at the docks to greet him, and William had been holding the hand of an adorable five-year-old child in a lacy white dress. Amber Victoria Sinclair, heiress to the earl of Markland's fortune.

Other images of Amber rose to mind. The mischievous child in ringlets. The impish smile and flashing violet eyes when he brought her a present, a ritual he'd adhered to on every visit—even during the last years when they'd avoided each other.

He recalled the reckless way she raced horses. The daring way she fenced with her friend Albert Chatsworth. But most of all, he remembered the last time he saw her. The time he'd deliberately hurt her.

"Father?"

Clay moved to sit beside her on the bed. "Shh, sweetheart. It's all right."

She blinked those lovely eyes and stared at him. "Clay?" Her voice came out in a breathy whisper, and a warmth like he'd never seen turned those shimmering violet pools to liquid. She opened her mouth as if to speak, then suddenly clamped it shut. Her lips drew into a hard line, and he knew she'd remembered their previous encounter.

He wiped a streak of blood from her cheek. "How are you feeling?"

"What are you doing in my room—on my bed?"

"Sitting with you."

"I don't want you here."

"You did before." The words came out before he could stop them.

Her hands trembled, and she gripped the quilt. "I knew you were cruel, but I never realized how much."

"You were damn cruel, yourself. You just didn't know it."

She lifted her chin. "There's no need to swear, Your Grace."

"Do excuse my manners, *Lady Sinclair,*" he returned in the same stiffly formal tone she'd used.

Their eyes met, and hers were as cold as a frozen pond. "Where's my father?"

Ah, damn. Not now. He wasn't ready for this. Without answering, he went to the door and opened it. "Mrs. Becker! Send someone for Dr. Baldwick. Amber is awake."

A distant gasp, then the sound of hurried footsteps was his answer.

Knowing he couldn't put off the inevitable any longer, Clay closed the door and faced the woman on the bed. "Do you remember the accident?"

"What accident?" She touched the bandage on her temple and frowned. "How did I get—*there was an accident?*"

"What's the last thing you recall?"

She furrowed her brow, as if trying to remember. A golden curl toppled onto her forehead, and she swept it back. "Father and I were taking a basket of cakes and scones to Robert. I'd returned from France two weeks ago but hadn't had a chance to see him yet with all the unpacking and catching up at Markland to do." Her gaze drifted past him to the door. "What's this about? Where's my father?"

Clay sat on the edge of the bed and braced himself as he lifted her hands. "He's gone, Amber."

She stared at him in confusion. "Gone where?"

"He's . . . dead."

"What? How? When?"

"The carriage accident."

"No!" She jerked away from him, her eyes wild as she scooted to the head of the bed. "You're lying! You're lying!" She tried to get out of bed, but he caught her around the waist.

She clawed and kicked and cried. "No! Let me go. Father! Father, help me!"

"Amber, don't . . ." He pulled her into his arms and pressed her cheek to his shoulder. "He's dead, sweetheart. No matter how much we both wish it isn't so, it is. He's dead."

"Noooo. Oh, God, *please,* no." She clung to him, her nails digging into his shoulders, then she began to cry. Deep, anguished sobs that cut into his heart.

Clay buried his face in her hair and held her, fighting his own tears and wishing he could absorb her pain.

He drew her closer, massaging the small of her back, talking to her in quiet, soothing tones. He didn't know what he said or how long he held her before he became aware of another presence in the room.

Keeping her face against the curve of his neck, he turned his head to see the physician pouring laudanum into a spoon. He met Clay's gaze, then nodded silently to Amber.

Clay eased her away the slightest bit, then took the spoon. "Here, sweetheart. Take this. It'll dull the pain." He touched the spoon to her lips, then slid it between them.

As soon as she swallowed, she again buried her face in his shoulder. Her sobs had grown quieter now, but they were just as heartbreaking.

Within minutes the drug began to take effect, and she grew limp in his arms. He continued to hold her, though, telling himself it was because she needed comfort—not because he enjoyed the warmth of her body nestled against his.

When the physician cleared his throat, Clay felt heat move up his neck and very gently laid her down.

The doctor waited for him to step aside before he approached the bed and lifted one of her eyelids, then the other. He removed the bandage and inspected her wound before replacing it. "As I suspected, the wound is not serious." He pulled the covers up to her chin. "She should remain asleep until morning, but I still want someone to sit with her tonight."

"I won't leave her." He couldn't—and not only because her life was in danger.

The door latch clicked, and Georgina came into the room. He noticed that she, too, didn't venture too close to him. For the hundredth time, he cursed his temper.

"Your Grace," Amber's cousin said quietly, "the Chatsworths have arrived. They're in the parlor."

*Your Grace.* He wasn't anyone's *grace,* he was just a man. And, damn it, he wasn't insane, either. "I'll be down in a minute."

When she left, Dr. Baldwick put his spectacles into his bag and snapped it shut. "If Lady Sinclair stirs before morning, give her another small portion of the laudanum, but no more than one dose. Is that clear?"

"Yes."

The doctor hefted his bag and hurried to precede Clay out the door.

Clay wanted to gnash his teeth at the man's wariness. With a sigh, he gave Amber one last glance before joining the physician.

She looked so beautiful and peaceful. So untroubled. He hated to see the time come when he'd have to tell her that someone had murdered her father.

# Chapter 2

Concerned for Amber, and wondering if she knew about the threat to her life, Clay strode toward the parlor to greet Ellison and Katherine Chatsworth.

Seeing both standing anxiously in front of the fireplace, he schooled his features to keep his distaste for the haughty couple from showing. Ellison Chatsworth was knighted by the king for his service to the Crown, but by their arrogant attitudes, one would think they were related to George himself.

Clay quickly explained what happened—and William's insistence that the accident had been deliberate.

Katherine, a slight, attractive woman who didn't look as if she'd quite reached forty, sank down onto a settee. Her milk white skin appeared gray against her green dress and dark hairpiece. "He is dead?" A slim, bejeweled hand encircled her throat. "William is truly dead?"

"I'm afraid so."

Ellison, his gray hair visible at the edges of his wig,

shoved his hands into the pockets of his redingote and stared at the carpet. The gold color reflected on his stockings and in the shine of his buckled shoes. His heavy jowls quivered when he spoke. "How is Amber?"

"Devastated."

Katherine surged to her feet, causing her tall hairpiece to sway. "I am going to her."

"She's sleeping."

"I will sit with her."

"No, Mrs. Chatsworth. I'll stay with her tonight, but I believe Mrs. Becker has had a room prepared for you."

Realizing she'd ventured too close to him, Katherine took an anxious step backward but managed to bristle. "You will do no such thing, Your Grace. Why, the very idea! I simply will not allow you to ruin that sweet child's reputation. Why, the *ton* would—"

"Madam. I don't give a damn about the *ton*. Amber's life may be in danger, and William entrusted her care to me. That's the end of it."

Katherine flinched at the sound of his voice, and glanced anxiously to her husband for support.

Ellison looked as if he wanted to run, but he held his ground and puffed out his chest. "You are mistaken, sir."

"You have absolutely no rights where my goddaughter is concerned," Katherine insisted. She gripped the folds of her skirt to hide her shaking hands. "She is fully within our control."

Clay stared directly into her angry blue eyes, wondering how she could be so nervous, yet stalwart at the same time. "Until I discover who is trying to harm Amber, *no one* is going near her."

"Surely you don't suspect us," Ellison said, trying to force outrage into his quaking voice.

"No. But whoever attempted to murder her may try again, and I'm going to be there to stop him." Tired from the long, grueling day, he turned for the door. "I'm sure a maid will see you to your room shortly. Now, if you'll excuse me, I'll say good night."

Snatching a bottle of brandy from the sideboard, he made for the stairs. *Gossip* and protocol were the beginning and end of all existence to them. Damn, he couldn't wait to leave England.

When he reached Amber's chamber, only a low-burning fire now lighted the room, its glow dancing over the delicate angles of her beautiful face.

Her cousin was reluctant to leave but frightened to be in the same room with him, and as the manor's only hostess, she had no choice.

Clay poured himself a glass of brandy and sat at Amber's desk, recalling that day in the marketplace last year. He and Morgan had gone to the docks to oversee the cargo being loaded on Clay's newest ship, the *French Maiden*. It was a hot day, so on the way back, they stopped by the marketplace to buy a lemonade for the ride home.

Clay could still recall the fury he'd felt when he saw the baron Solcrest strip a young female servant and beat her mercilessly because she'd dropped a jar from the heavy box she'd been carrying.

The cries from the girl, who couldn't have been more than twelve, had somehow transformed into Miranda's cries, and Clay had exploded with rage. He took the strap from the baron and turned it on him. It had taken Morgan and three other men to stop Clay.

Word of his actions had spread like a brush fire through the *ton*—and, like most gossip, became exaggerated. The next he'd heard, he was supposed to have tried to cut the baron's throat with his cutlass. Then he'd heard the name Captain Cutthroat whispered with awe among the servants.

His gaze drifted to Amber, and he wondered if she'd heard—*and believed*—the exaggerated gossip. He recalled her expression when she first awakened.

He'd seen something warm and welcoming, then anger, but he hadn't detected fear.

She either hadn't heard the tales, which was unlikely giving her involvement with the *ton,* or because she knew him so well, she didn't believe them. He hoped it was the latter.

Staring at the woman he'd vowed to protect, unbidden memories of that last year before their volatile parting came to mind. It was the year the Captain was killed in a battle, and Clay had inherited the *Black Wind* and her crew. They had buried the Captain at sea, then Clay had returned to London. Being aboard the ship had become too painful, and Amber had helped him through his grief with a compassion and understanding that went far beyond her fifteen years.

It was during that time that he started getting too close to the child he had known since she was five.

*"Awk.* Clay is a fool. Clay is a fool."

Startled, he whirled around and spotted a cage on the bureau he hadn't noticed earlier. "Poop Deck? Is that you?"

*"Awk.* Ahoy, mate. Ahoy mate."

"Well, I'll be damned." Approaching the cage, Clay was amazed that Amber still had the brightly colored rainbow lorikeet he'd given her eight years ago—a young parrot he'd captured in Asia and who'd learned to talk listening to the crewmen of the *Black Wind.* "It's good to see you, Poo. You look like you've fared well." He opened the metal door and lifted the bird onto his finger, wondering if Amber had kept his other presents, too.

Poo hopped onto his shoulder. *"Awk.* Need a wench. Need a wench."

"After eight years, I imagine you do."

A beady eye, surrounded by light blue feathers, blinked rapidly. He was a beautiful bird, and true to his breed, he did resemble a rainbow with his blue face, green back, yellow crown, and red chest.

*"Awk.* Clay is a fool. Clay is a fool."

"You could be right about that." Smiling, he returned the bird to his pen and shut the door, wondering who had taught the parrot that particular phrase. He glanced at the bed where Amber lay . . . and he knew. The little witch.

"Your Grace?" Georgina opened the door but stayed in the threshold. "Mrs. Chatsworth told me about the danger to Amber and your insistence to watch over her, so I've had the maid prepare the adjoining room." She gestured to a pair of double doors. "I thought you might rest easier—and still be able to keep an eye on Amber."

Clay was touched by her thoughtfulness. Georgina had always been considerate. She was a family outcast William had taken in when she was barely eighteen, and because of his kindness, she had always gone out of her way to please. "Is my father still here?"

"No. He sent some stable hands to bury William's carriage horse, then Lord Frazier said he was going home. He did mention that he'd return in the morning with fresh clothing for you, though."

"I'm grateful—"

*"Awk.* Fire on the bridge. Fire on the bridge."

"Oh, hush, now," the woman scolded, but she still didn't venture all the way into Amber's room. "He's always noisy after his pen is cleaned. If you cover his cage, he'll be quiet." She sidled over to the adjoining doors and pushed them open. "I've laid out a dressing gown for you." She gestured to a burgundy robe draping the foot of a massive bed. "Do you want me to have your supper sent up before I retire?"

"I'm not hungry, but I think I will explore William's library for something to read."

"There are several newly published volumes you might find interesting."

He didn't comment, yet he wondered at her thoughts. She was such a private person, always in the background, never drawing attention to herself. He wondered at her fall from grace so many years ago. He'd heard it had something to do with a stable boy.

When she slipped out the door, Clay let his gaze drift back to Amber. He'd promised William he'd take her away from London. If he was going to do that, he had to make arrangements.

*"Awk.* Man the sails. Man the sails."

Smiling, Clay covered the bird's cage, then strode to the desk and located a piece of parchment and a quill. He penned a quick note to Miranda at his coastal estate, Westshire. He hadn't seen her during the last few years, but he could imagine her delighted reaction to his instructions.

After summoning a footman, he headed for the library, returning moments later with *The Marriage of Figaro.* He changed into the robe and opened the book to read.

William's scent again enveloped him, and he fought a burning sensation behind his eyes. Determinedly forcing his grief aside, he began Beaumarchais's comedy.

Loud voices in the hall surprised him, then the thunder of heavy footsteps.

Clay had almost reached the door when it burst open.

A tall, well-built man stood in the opening, his tricorne askew, gray eyes bright with determination. He glanced at Clay with distaste, then started for Amber.

"Who the hell are you?" Clay demanded as he stepped into his path.

The younger man stopped but didn't cower. He simply glared at Clay.

Georgina and a butler came bustling into the room. "We tried to announce him, Your Grace. Truly we did."

Clay waved a dismissing hand, his eyes never leaving the stranger. "I said, *who are you?*"

The man gave an arrogant smirk. "I'm surprised you don't recognize me, Your Grace." His hostile gaze drifted over the dressing robe Clay wore, then Amber. "And what the hell are you doing in Amber's bedchamber?"

Clay stared hard at the young man. "Albert? Albert Chatsworth?"

"So you do remember me."

*All too well,* Clay thought with irritation. This boy and Amber had been inseparable as children. Amber had always adored him. They were so close, Clay didn't doubt that one day they would marry. The thought sent a stab of jealousy through him that he had no business feeling. He motioned to the butler. "Show Mr. Chatsworth to the parlor. We'll talk there."

Leaving Georgina with Amber, he headed downstairs.

Chatsworth was sprawled in a chair near the fireplace, his legs stretched out in front of him, his dark blue clothes a diabolical shadow against the brightly colored furniture. He held his tricorne in one hand, a goblet filled with port in the other.

His insolence set Clay's teeth on edge. "You've changed over the years, Albert." The last time Clay had seen him, he'd been close to sixteen, short, slight, and possessed a head full of thick, white blond curls. But the stranger sitting across from him was a man. A young one, but no doubt still a man.

"We all grow up, Your Grace." His gaze was filled with hatred as it met Clay's. "But few of us forget a wrong that was inflicted on those we love."

So Amber had told him what happened. Of course she had. Still, Clay wasn't about to defend his actions. If he did that to anyone, it would be Amber. "We also never forget when someone inflicts an injury on those we care about."

Albert's face lost some of its color. "You bastard. You know that was an accident. I'd never deliberately hurt Amber."

"Neither would I," Clay countered in a hard voice.

Albert set his glass aside and rose, not in the least intimidated by Clay, which was a refreshing change. "That's not the way I remember it, Your Grace." He strode to the door and opened it, then leaned out and shouted loud enough to wake the household. "Georgina! See a room prepared for me!"

Clay was annoyed by his high-handedness. "What makes you think you're staying?"

Chatsworth leveled a steady gaze on Clay. "What makes you think I'd leave Amber in your care again?"

He didn't know whether to be angered by Albert's remark or pleased by his concern. He couldn't change what had happened four years ago. "Chatsworth, if you're going to stay, leave off the remarks about what happened between me and Amber."

"I will unless it happens again."

*There wasn't a chance in hell of that.*

Albert leaned against the doorjamb and crossed his arms. "And if it does, this time I'll see you on the field of honor."

Clay arched a brow. The strutting peacock was getting too big for his breeches. Still, Clay was too tired and worn out to argue the point. "Fine. We understand each other, then."

"Precisely."

"So be it." Striding past the arrogant puppy, Clay marched up the stairs, wishing he could dislike Albert Chatsworth for caring about Amber.

Amber climbed through layers of thick fog to reach coherency. The pain of her father's death stabbed her with the viciousness of a dull dagger. He was gone. He was truly gone.

Tears slipped down her cheeks. Oh, God. *Why him? Why now, when he'd finally found love again and planned to marry?* Merciful heaven, what was his intended, Sara Lawrence, going to do? Father's death would destroy her. Sweet Lord in heaven, how would either of them cope? A moan worked its way up her throat.

In the darkness, warm, strong arms encircled her. "Go ahead, sweetheart, cry. Let the tears wash away your pain."

Clay's soothing voice, and the way he held her, cut into her like a razor. How many times had she dreamed of being held by him? Why did her father have to die to make it so? The emotions inside her collided, and she broke into wrenching sobs.

She didn't know how long she cried, or how long Clay held her, but one moment she was in his arms and the next he was gone.

"Here, take this."

She opened her eyes to see him leaning over her with a spoon. A small glow from a single candle illuminated his eyes, and she saw the compassion in them—the pain. Her own deepened, and she shifted her gaze to his dark hair. It was tousled, as if he'd repeatedly raked it with his fingers. Clay only did that when he was worried. The knowledge touched her in a way she didn't want to be touched. Not by him. She glanced at the spoon. "What is it?"

"Laudanum. The physician said to give you another dose if you woke before morning."

"I don't want that."

"Yes, you do." He cupped her cheek with one hand and placed the tip of the spoon against her lips with the other. "Open your mouth for me, sweetheart."

"Don't call me that—"

He slid the spoon into her mouth, and she was forced to swallow. Through her sputters she managed a glare.

His thumb stroked her cheek. "I figured you'd have outgrown that stubborn streak by now."

The warmth of his hand, the rich, salty scent of his skin, and the low vibration of his voice sent hot tingles racing through her. She had to struggle for words. "I . . . I'm not stubborn."

He smiled and brushed a curl away from her forehead. "Get some rest, Amber. The next few days are going to be rough."

The next few days. . . . She couldn't think about that yet. She closed her eyes, letting the laudanum do its work, and as she'd done since she was a child, she sank into comforting daydreams. She pictured a beautiful white beach, playful waves, and miles of blue ocean. On the horizon a sleek black ship glided toward the shore, and she knew he was coming for her. . . .

A horrible throbbing in Amber's head forced her awake the next morning. Placing her fingers on the square patch on her temple, she stared at the sheer gold canopy above her bed, wishing with all her heart that the events of yesterday had been nothing more than a nightmare. But she knew they weren't.

"Do you want some tea?" Clay asked from across the room.

Amber rolled her head to the side and saw him sitting at her desk, gesturing to a tray. He was wearing clean clothes, and his hair glistened from a recent washing. In full light he was even better looking than he had been last night—than he had been four years ago.

A queer flutter tickled her chest, and it angered her that he could still affect her. Curse it all, why didn't he have scars on that hard, tanned jaw, or have to wear a patch over one of those brilliant green eyes? Maybe if he wasn't so tall, or his shoulders so broad, or his hair so silky, she could forget her childhood crush on him. Forget the way she'd envisioned him standing on the deck of the *Black Wind,* legs spread, a gold earring glinting in his ear, a cutlass dangling at his side.

It was a sharp contrast to how he looked now sitting behind her dainty writing desk. Another flutter wiggled through her, and she had to force herself to speak. "No, I wouldn't care for anything."

He filled a cup from the silver tea service and carried it to her anyway. "You need your strength." He slipped a hand beneath her shoulders and raised her into a sitting position, then wrapped her fingers around the cup. "Now, drink."

She clutched the china with both hands. "Why are you here? Where's Georgina?"

"She's busy with the guests, and I'm here because your father asked me to be."

Another pound was added to the weight of her sorrow. He wasn't here because he wanted to be. "What guests?"

"Your godparents and Albert."

"Where are they?"

"I believe your cook is serving them breakfast."

She set the cup aside. "Would you excuse me while I dress? I should see them."

Concern filled his thick-lashed eyes. "Are you sure you're up to it?"

"Yes."

He hesitated briefly, then turned for the adjoining doors. "Let me know when you're ready, and I'll escort you downstairs." He closed the door so quietly, she barely heard a sound.

*"Awk.* Walk the plank. Walk the plank."

Amber glanced at Poo to see him prancing back and forth across his perch. Someone had uncovered his cage that morning. But the parrot had the right idea.

She'd rather walk the plank than be escorted anywhere by Clayton Cordell.

Giving the bird a piece of biscuit she kept on the bureau, she gave the bell pull a yank to summon her maid, then walked to the armoire and located the black silk day gown that she'd worn to her mother's funeral three years ago, the one her father hated. She held it up for inspection. The billowing skirt and wide, muttonchop sleeves had a few creases, but it would do . . . again.

The door swung open, and Clay glanced at the dress she held. "No black."

"But—"

His jaw hardened. "Your father said no black, Amber, and you're going to abide by his wishes."

"But—"

He closed the door.

Amber stared through her tears. Her father must have known he was going to die. Why else would he say that? She dropped the gown as if it burned her.

Swallowing to ease the tightness in her throat, she remembered how her father had always hated anything to do with mourning. He had a dogged belief that there was a wonderful, magical place waiting for him after death—a place that should be celebrated, not mourned.

Wishing with all her heart that it was so, she returned to the armoire. Her gaze drifted over the silks and satins lining her wardrobe. Most were pale blues, greens, and golds that she preferred, but none were suitable for today.

She touched the soft velvet sleeve of a burgundy gown she'd worn to a recital at Miss Renee's School for Young Ladies. It was a simple, elegant dress with a high collar and long sleeves that drew into a point over the backs of her hands. The open skirt revealed a ruffled pink satin underskirt.

Dreading her godmother's response to her choice of

clothing, and knowing how she would be scandalized by such a lapse in decorum, Amber laid the dress on the bed and waited for her maid.

Once her hair was styled around her bandaged temple, and she was decently clothed, she silently slipped out the door and went to greet her guests.

"Oh, Amber." Katherine leaped to her feet and hugged her fiercely. "I am so sorry about William." She stepped back and glanced at the gown Amber wore, then her own black taffeta, but she was kind enough not to say anything. Instead, she squeezed Amber's hand in compassion. "I had hoped I would never have to exercise my rights as your godmother."

No one could have hoped that more than Amber. She blinked back tears as she returned the gesture to the neighbor she'd known her entire life. Her parents and the Chatsworths had been friends even before Amber was born.

Ellison drew her into his arms. "If there is anything I can do to make this time easier for you . . ."

"You're being here is enough." She remained in his embrace a second longer, then asked quietly, "Has anyone told Sara Lawrence yet?"

He lowered his arm and stepped aside. "Yes. I'm afraid your father's betrothed took the news rather badly."

Her heart ached for the woman who would have soon been her stepmother. "Is someone with her?"

"A neighbor."

Her gaze drifted to Albert, where he stood by a window, downing a glass of spirits. She knew he was fortifying himself. Albert didn't handle awkward situations well.

When he set the glass aside, he strode across the room and stopped in front of her. He opened his mouth as if to speak, but quickly closed it. With a soft moan, he pulled her into his arms. "I'm so sorry, angel. So damned sorry."

She touched his soft hair, a mixture of ash and sunlight, then hugged him tighter. "I'm glad you're here."

"I'll always be here for you. That's one thing you can count on."

"Mr. Chatsworth, if this is the type of behavior you allow under your guardianship, then I'm extremely glad William left Amber's care to me."

Amber whipped her head toward Clay. Her father did *what?*

Clay approached Albert. "You have two seconds to remove your hands from my charge."

Albert's eyes narrowed.

"One . . ."

Amber jerked away. "What do you mean my father—"

"The duke is right, Albert," Ellison interrupted. "You are no longer children and should not take such liberties with Amber."

Albert sent his father a furious glare, then headed for the sideboard. "Of course, Father. How foolish of me."

Amber was still trying to grasp the fact that somehow Clay was in charge of her.

Clay took her arm and led her to the table. "You haven't had your tea."

She was too shocked to comment. How could her father have left her in Clay's care? He *knew* she despised him.

"Have any arrangements been made for the funeral yet, dear?" Katherine asked as Ellison helped her sit.

"What?" A surge of grief crashed over her, and her hands shook as she reached for the teapot. "I-I don't . . ."

Albert let out a harsh expulsion of breath, then tossed down his drink.

Clay filled her cup and set it in front of her. "I

believe my stepfather has instructed the servants to see to the matter, Mrs. Chatsworth."

"When—"

Amber couldn't breathe. She couldn't talk about this, and she couldn't accept that her father had placed her in Clay's care. Pushing away from the table, she came to her feet. "Excuse me. I'd . . . like to get some fresh air." She hurried through the doors to the veranda, praying Clay wouldn't follow her.

The cool morning air soothed her raw nerves, and she leaned against one of the towering pillars supporting an overhead balcony. Dear God in heaven, why would her father do this to her?

"I'll run him through if it'll help," Albert offered as he stepped out to join her.

Warmth filled her, and she smiled at her dearest friend. "It might make me feel better, but it wouldn't help."

"That's reason enough."

She took his hand as he approached. "Why don't we just walk instead."

As they moved down the path, Amber let her thoughts drift over her relationship with Albert. She couldn't explain it, even to herself. She had no romantic feelings toward him whatsoever, but there was a warmth, a love, that she couldn't begin to explain. And she knew Albert felt the same way. They hugged, and they held hands, but never once had he attempted to kiss her. Perhaps, she decided, that's simply the way true friends are toward each other.

They took a path through rows of her mother's prized rosebushes that in the spring burst forth with every possible color imaginable. And the fragrance. Oh, that was heavenly.

The loss of her father merged with the recent loss of her mother only three years ago. They were both gone. The people she'd loved most in her life were gone.

A tear trailed down her cheek, and she thought of that magical place her father believed in. If it existed, maybe her parents were there together. She could almost imagine them strolling hand in hand through fields of wildflowers, laughing and smiling . . . gazing at each other in that special private way.

Another tear fell, and she wondered if she'd ever experience those special moments with the man she would someday marry.

Albert squeezed her hand. "If you keep crying like that, you'll unman me. You know I can't tolerate a woman's tears."

She smiled up into his handsome face. "Far be it from me to 'unman' one of the most sought-after bachelors in London."

"You've got the wrong man, angel. I'm too poor to be included in those ranks."

She knew he was referring to the dire financial straits his father's estate had fallen into. "I'm sure next year's barley crop will flourish and set things to right again."

"What difference would that make? My father will continue to manage the estate as poorly as he has in the past. Damn it, if only he'd let me—" He clamped his mouth shut and turned away. He was silent for several seconds, but when he spoke again, none of the passion of moments ago could be detected in his voice. "I think I'll go for a ride to clear my head. This wretched situation is tarnishing my otherwise sterling character."

She smiled at his droll remark, knowing he considered himself to be about as sterling as a rusty nail. "I'd come with you, but I know there'll be guests arriving soon."

A tinge of sadness touched his gray eyes. "Maybe I should stay."

"No. Enjoy your ride for both of us. I'll be fine."

He still hesitated, then at last gave her a quick hug and sprinted toward the stables.

Amber turned around and dragged herself up to the privacy of her chamber. She felt numb and drained. So very tired. But her thoughts raced. They leaped from the accident to the funeral ahead to what would happen to her and the families who depended on Markland for survival. If what Albert thought was true, Ellison could ruin Markland. Her concerns and fears were overwhelming. Not even trying to hold back her pain and anger, she smashed her fist into a pillow and began to cry. "He can't do this. Father can't die and leave all of us to this uncertainty."

Through her grief she thought she heard a door open, and she lifted her head just as a gentle hand touched her back. "It's going to be hard for a while, sweetheart, but the pain will fade eventually."

She turned on Clay. "When did my father hand me over into *your* care?"

His throat worked. "It was his dying wish."

"I don't believe you."

"Amber . . ."

"He knew how I felt about you. How much I detest you. Why would he force me to—"

"The whole Continent probably knows how you feel about me, Amber. But your father also knew if I gave my word to protect you, I would."

She scoffed. "Always a man of honor. Well, tell me, Your Grace, where was your honor four years ago?"

His jaw hardened. "I thought I handled that situation in the most honorable way possible."

"It didn't appear that way to me."

He rose from the side of the bed and brought a hand to the nape of his neck. "I'm sorry I hurt you, Amber, but at the time you didn't give me much of a choice."

She opened her mouth to argue, but a knock on the door silenced her words.

"Your Grace?" a servant called. "Lord Frazier would like an audience with Lady Sinclair."

Clay sent her a searching glance. "Do you want to talk to him?"

"I can't." She knew Robert wanted to discuss the arrangements for her father's funeral, and she just couldn't do it.

"Then I will."

When he opened the door she stopped him. "Clay?"

"Yes?"

"Tell Robert my father looks good in b-blue."

He closed his eyes for a second, then nodded and quietly left the room.

Amber rolled onto her back and stared at the canopy overhead, letting the tears fall as pain and confusion churned through her. Her whole life was falling apart, and she couldn't do anything to stop it.

Massaging her sore temple, she wished with all her heart that the events of the last day were only a dream. A horrible nightmare.

"Amber?" Georgina called out as she came into the bedchamber. "Miss Lawrence has arrived."

Sara. Oh, God. Did she have to face her now? Wiping her eyes, she sat up, knowing that prolonging the inevitable would only make it worse. "I'll talk to her in the study." She didn't want to have to deal with the others in the parlor at the same time.

When the door closed, Amber splashed water on her face and straightened her hair, then braced herself for the meeting with the woman who would have been her stepmother.

# Chapter 3

Sara stood behind William's desk, with her back to the room, staring out the window. Even though she was in her fortieth year, she looked like a child with her round, cherubic face and auburn curls.

Distantly, Amber noted that the black skirt and matching waistcoat she wore weren't part of the trousseau William had bought her. He hadn't purchased anything for her in black. He never would have. . . .

Drawing in a breath, Amber closed the door as silently as she'd opened it. "Hello, Sara."

She didn't turn. Instead, she gripped the window ledge and lowered her head. "How are you doing, Amber?"

Sinking into an armchair, Amber brushed a curl off her bandaged temple. "I've been better."

Sara still didn't turn. "I-I want to take you in my arms and hold you, but if I do, I know I'm going to fall apart."

"Then don't. I'm on the verge of shattering, myself. Just talk to me."

"What do you want me to say?" She turned, and her red-rimmed eyes met Amber's. "That you'll get over this? That would be a lie. You won't. I know. I buried both my parents and a husband. Believe me, honey, the hurt never goes away."

Amber stared at her tear-stained face. Sara was holding on to her composure by a thread as fine as a cobweb. Amber's heart went out to her. "I'm sure the hurt will ease. It eventually did after Mother died, and it did for Clay after the Captain was killed."

"*Clay?* That wretched pirate. After what he did to you, I hope he grieves forever."

She tried not to smile at the vehemence in Sara's tone. Sara had been there for her four years ago when Amber had sought the closest comfort—her mother's widowed friend. Sara had held her, cried with her, and cursed Clayton Cordell. "He's not a pirate any-more."

"Oh, honey. When will you ever learn? A jackass does not change its color." She sat down and folded her hands on the desk, her gaze fixed on Amber. "Do you need anything?"

"Yes. I need you beside me during the f-funeral."

Tears trickled down Sara's cheeks. "You know I'll be there. I love you both."

Amber burst into tears.

Sara came to her, embraced her, rocked her, and talked to her through her own heartbroken sobs.

When they were finally able to compose themselves, Amber had a maid show Sara to a bedchamber to rest.

Amber felt drained. All she wanted to do was go to her own room and lie down—and erase the world. Gathering the folds of her skirt, she started upstairs.

Katherine stopped her halfway up. "Amber, I obtained your uncles' addresses in the Colonies from William's solicitors and sent word to them, but I wanted to know if there was anything else I could do for you? Not with the funeral or minister or anything, but personally? I mean, well . . . if you just need to talk."

Her heart warmed for the woman who'd been like a second mother to her. "I'd like that very much—at another time. But right now I feel as if I've been trampled, and I'd just like to rest."

"Then I'll escort you to your room," Clay's voice drifted from the dining room doorway.

Amber turned to see him standing with his arms folded over his chest, his shoulder braced against the jamb.

"That won't be necessary."

"Yes, it will." He shoved away from the door and strode toward her, then took her arm. "You will excuse us, won't you, Mrs. Chatsworth?"

Without waiting for Katherine's response, Clay led Amber up to her room.

She pulled free of him the second they were inside. "Must you be so abrupt with my friends?"

"That particular one, yes. She irritates the hell out of me." He filled a glass with brandy and handed it to her. "Here, drink this. It'll help you rest."

"Where did that come from?"

He shrugged. "I brought it up last night."

When she hesitated, he wrapped her fingers around the glass. "Drink. And don't worry about anything else today. I'll help your godmother tend to the arriving guests and take care of any problems that might arise." He raised her hands and tipped the glass to her mouth.

The fiery liquid took her breath, and she sputtered, trying to breathe. Finally, when the burning passed, and a relaxing warmth moved through her, she didn't protest when Clay urged her into bed.

She stared up at him. "You know, for a jackass, you're not a bad sort."

"You're not either . . . for a vixen."

Giving a most unladylike snort, she closed her eyes and allowed the soothing warmth of the alcohol to consume her. She thought of Sara, of the people who were depending on her, and of white beaches and miles of blue ocean, and a black ship. . . .

When she next opened her eyes, Georgina and a maid were bustling around the chamber getting Amber's clothes ready. "What time is it?" she asked, sitting up.

"One." Georgina smoothed a wrinkle from the skirt of her black silk gown. "His Grace sent us to wake you so you could dress for dinner."

She stared at the black gown. "I'd rather wear the dark blue silk I wore to the Washburns' party last week." She glanced at the adjoining door. "Where's Clay?"

"He and Lord Frazier are . . . on the knoll."

The knoll. The graveyard where the Sinclair family vault stood in marble splendor beneath a canopy of elm trees. Swallowing a lump in her throat, she rose and allowed her cousin and maid to help her dress, but inside she felt dead.

The next two days passed in a blur of tearful greetings, awkward conversations, and endless condolences as her father's friends filled the house. But the worst part for her was the worry and concern she saw in the eyes of her father's steward, Beau Franklin. Like her, Beau was apprehensive about Ellison taking charge.

Clay stayed by her side, and, even though they had their differences, she was grateful for his steadying presence. Somehow, he gave her strength.

When she finally retired the night before the funeral, she was exhausted and eternally thankful to him for politely but firmly removing her from the gathering of sympathizers and ushering her off to bed.

Still, as she lay in the dark, she couldn't put her thoughts to rest. Seeing Beau Franklin had brought back her greatest fears. Under Ellison's poor management, how could they survive?

The answer came to her with the swiftness of a plunging knife. She would have to marry.

Clay escorted her to the carriage the next day, and they rode in silence to the knoll. It was a lovely spot, with a small white picket fence and towering trees. The view was beautiful. It overlooked miles of rolling green hills. Distantly, Amber imagined it must be a lot like the wonderful place her father believed in.

She glanced at the sky, noticing the clear fall day. Somehow, that didn't seem right. Why wasn't it raining? Or foggy? Or overcast? They were burying her father. It wasn't supposed to be pleasant.

Clay left her beside Sara and went to say something to Robert and the minister. Through a haze she stared at the sea of faces filing past her father's coffin. His friends, their wives, the tenant farmers, aristocrats, his solicitors, members of his club, and business acquaintances. All were paying their last respects.

Last respects. . . . The words sent chills through her.

Her gaze drifted to the Chatsworths as they approached. Ellison stood stiffly beside Katherine as she bent over William. For the first time since Amber had known her, Katherine lost control. She began weeping openly, deep harsh sobs.

Albert was in line behind them, his mouth tightly clenched as if he was struggling for control.

Amber couldn't see her father, and she didn't want to. She couldn't bear to look at his cold, still features, to be forced to accept the finality of his death. But the last of the mourners passed, leaving him in full view. She saw his beloved face, the blue satin coat. . . .

Sara clutched her arm and began to cry.

Amber held herself rigid, She would not break down in front of her father's friends. *She would not.* He would want her to be strong. She tried to focus on happy times, but all she could think of was how she'd never hear his laughter again, see the way his face lit up when he danced, hear his comforting voice when her day went badly, or feel his arms surrounding her in warmth and love. Oh, why had she gone to that finishing school in France and spent so much time away from him? If only she could relive the last years, there were so many things she'd do differently.

Her hands started to shake, and she knew in that instant she wasn't going to make it. She was going to disgrace herself. She could feel herself falling apart, piece by piece. Her breath came in quick raspy pants. A wave of dizziness swept over her, and she swayed.

An arm caught her around the waist. "Hold on, sweetheart," Clay said softly. "You can do it. Just a few more minutes, and it'll be over."

So grateful for his calming strength, she leaned into him, but she couldn't stop the tears. Everything receded into a blessed fog. Even the minister's voice grew distant.

At long last, it was done, her father was sealed in a marble tomb next to her mother . . . for all eternity.

Clay remained beside her as they returned to Markland and joined the mourners in the great hall, where the servants had prepared enough food to feed the king's army.

She tried her best to be congenial, to accept everyone's sympathetic remarks without crumbling, but the satin-draped walls were starting to close in on her, the cloying scent of cheeses and melons and toilet water and candle wax were smothering her, and she knew she had to get out of there.

In silent understanding, Clay squeezed her hand. "Go on, get away for a while." He moved to intercept a group of people headed her way.

Thankful for his insight, she edged toward the glass doors and slipped out.

The evening air was cool and blowing softly across the torchlit gardens. She inhaled deeply, clearing the scents of the ballroom from her head, then lowering her gaze to the acres of gardens, she moved down the steps. Dying leaves rustled in the breeze. The flowers were gone now, but their absence didn't detract from the magnificence of the golden red foliage spilling over the grounds.

Its serene beauty was like a soothing balm. She walked to the gazebo her father had designed and took a seat on one of the many cushioned benches hugging the curved wall. Torchlight danced over the wood framing. Straightening her skirt, she folded her hands and leaned her head against a post. The silence felt wonderful.

She gazed lovingly at the gazebo, remembering the hours she and her father had spent planning the decor. She'd chosen the soft earth colors to blend with the gardens, no matter what season. She'd suggested a fire pit in the center for comfort on chilly days. But the sailcloth had been her father's idea. When one wished for privacy or escape from blowing wind or rain, they merely had to lower the rolls of sailcloth down from the roof to cover the sides.

It had been a brilliant idea. One that had been extremely welcome during the long, cold, foggy winters. The gazebo wasn't a place only for summer lounging anymore but one she could treasure year-round.

Suddenly, irrationally, she was angry at her father for destroying the carefree life she'd known. It wasn't fair.

"Amber?"

She jumped at the sound of Clay's voice, then rose as he came up the steps. "Yes?"

"I thought I'd find you here."

He looked magnificent in dark green, she thought distantly. "What is it?"

"We need to talk."

There was something in his tone that sent a trickle of wariness down her spine. "What's left to discuss? The reading of the will? If so, there's no need. I know Father provided for me."

"That's not what I wanted to talk about. I want you to tell me about the day of the accident."

She didn't want to *think* about it, much less discuss it. "I don't want—"

"Was anyone near the carriage before you left?"

"Why?"

"Just answer me."

Rubbing her upper arms, she resumed her seat and stared into the darkness, trying to remember. "Several people were at different times that day. Katherine came that morning to get the shawl she'd left on our last outing, and Ellison looked at Father's new carriage horse while they were there. Albert came shortly after his parents left to see me, then he harnessed the team because Whitcomb, our groom, was ill. And Georgina put a basket of scones and jam on the seat for us to take to Robert right before we left. Now, what's this about?"

He hesitated, then let out a thick breath. "I'm taking you to Westshire."

"You most certainly are not."

He braced his hand on a post, pulling the sleeve of his coat up over his cuff. Moonlight touched a dark lock of hair falling on his brow. "I promised your father I would."

"Why on earth would you do that?"

"To keep you safe."

"From what?"

"From whoever is trying to kill you."

A jolt of fear streaked through her, and she brought a hand to her throat. *"What?"*

"Because of everything that's happened, I've put off talking to you about it, but I can't any longer." He rubbed the nape of his neck and studied the cold fire pit. "I had hoped you already knew, but I see that wasn't the case. When the carriage overturned, it wasn't an accident. The axle had been sawed almost in two."

"But my father—"

"Believed someone was trying to kill you."

*"Me?* Who? Why?" A knot tightened in her chest. "I swear to you, I've never hurt anyone. I haven't given anybody a reason to want me dead."

"I know you haven't. You may be a termagant at times, but you've never been malicious. But we can't deny the facts, either. I spoke with the investigators your father hired, and they told me about your riding accident shortly after you arrived home from finishing school. Someone had placed a nettle under your saddle blanket." He gestured to the gazebo steps. "When you slipped on one of those last week and you almost broke your neck, they discovered somebody had smeared lard on the steps. Whether you want to believe it or not, someone is trying to kill you."

"Investigators?" Father had hired *investigators?* Waves of fear and guilt crashed over her. Someone wanted her dead. The accident was her fault. Her father had died because of her. . . . Oh, merciful God. "What am I going to do?"

"Come with me to Westshire and let William's investigators do their job."

"But—"

"No buts. The matter is settled."

Everything was happening too fast. She couldn't think. "What about the estate? I can't leave. Ellison can't take care of two estates, and our steward couldn't handle everything on his own. We have to notify the buyers when the harvest will begin and—"

"I'll send someone from Westshire."

"But—I can't stay in your house without a chaperon." She didn't trust herself. Her attraction to Clay was a force she'd never been able to control. Besides, she didn't want to go. She had to discover who was trying to kill her.

"Your godparents will be with us."

That gave her a fleeting second of relief, but she'd be hard pressed to find a husband at Westshire. "I'm not going."

"The hell you're not."

She was getting desperate. "I'm staying here until the person who murdered my father is apprehended." Images of the people at the funeral came to mind. Was one of them responsible for this? Had one of the friends she'd known and loved most of her life killed her father? The thought was as devastating as her father's death.

"You are not staying." He said each word slowly. Clearly.

"I'll be careful." There were too many things she had to do.

Clay's mouth drew into a hard line, and he looked every bit the dangerous pirate she'd fantasized about. "You're going to Westshire if I have to throw you over my shoulder and carry you."

She'd fantasized about that, too. The image caused shivers to skitter along her flesh. She crossed her arms over her middle, knowing she should keep her mouth shut and not challenge him. He may appear to be a gentleman on the surface, but his pirate blood made him unpredictable. Yet, no matter how hard she tried, her tongue wouldn't be silenced. "You can't intimidate me the way you do your crew. I'm not afraid of you."

His gaze locked onto hers, and she saw the slight flaring of his nostrils. "You should be," he said in a soft voice.

Keep your mouth shut, her common sense warned.

For heaven's sake, don't push him. But when had she ever listened to her better judgment? "You can't force me to go," Amber insisted.

A muscle in his jaw began to throb, and his eyes darkened. He gripped her upper arms and pulled her hard against him. "Can't I?"

# Chapter 4

Let go of me," Amber hissed.

Clay ignored her as he marched her toward the house and the roomful of people who'd attended her father's funeral.

"Clay, *please*. Don't do this to me. Not in front of my father's friends."

He hesitated, then damned himself for allowing her plea to affect him. He eased his grip on her arm but couldn't bring himself to release her. He searched her delicate face, her wide violet eyes. She looked so small, so vulnerable. Just like the child she'd been four years ago. He let go of her. "You're going to Westshire."

Uncertainty clouded her features, and she rubbed her arm. Uneasily, she glanced around. "Is it truly necessary? I mean, surely my servants—"

"I promised your father I'd take you away from London."

"We're not in London."

"Five miles is close enough."

"But—"

"I'm not giving you a choice, Amber."

She looked as if she wanted to argue, but she didn't. She made another anxious sweep of the area, then sighed. "All right. Under one condition."

"Which is?"

"Albert goes, too."

"No."

Her eyes darkened, and with a determined set to her jaw, she raised her arm, inviting him to take it again. "Then you might as well humiliate me and get it over with, because I won't go willingly."

Frustration tightened the muscles in his hands. "Why do you want him along?"

She started to say something, then clamped her mouth shut and turned away from him. Several seconds passed before she spoke. "He's my friend, Clayton." Her chin raised just the smallest bit in challenge. "One who has never let me down like— Well, it doesn't matter. I want him with me, so, either he goes or you may carry on with your barbarics."

For the barest instant, his long-dormant pirate's blood demanded he do just that, but he crushed the urge. She'd suffered enough. He wouldn't add to her grief. "All right, Amber. You win. But I strongly suggest you keep Chatsworth as far away from me as possible." Torn between jealousy of her friendship with Albert and his own erratic emotions, he strode into the house.

Amber watched Clay's departure with mixed feelings. She truly did want Albert along, but she couldn't tell Clay it was because she was going to make Albert a marriage proposition. Although they didn't love each other in that way, Albert had always wanted his own estate. Their friendship would make their marriage of convenience a successful one.

"Amber?"

Her nerves jumped at the sound of her name, then

she turned to see Robert standing on the pathway. He was a big man, yet he looked so tired and worn, she wanted to throw her arms around him and cradle him like a child.

As if he sensed her thoughts, he pulled her into his embrace. "I wanted to let you know I'm leaving for Ainshall in a few minutes, and I'm going to see Lady Lawrence home while I'm about it. She's nearly reached her limit of endurance."

Amber knew that for certain. She'd seen how pale and drawn Sara had become during the day, how withered, like a drooping flower about to lose its petals. "Thank you. We both appreciate your thoughtfulness."

He kissed her cheek, and gave her a last hug. "If there's anything I can do. . . ."

"Just take care of Sara. She needs someone so much right now."

"I'll take care of her as diligently as my son will take care of you." He gave her a half smile. "Which, by the way, has already started on his part."

"What do you mean?"

"He sent word to his steward to come to Markland, and he's ordered his field hands to Westshire manor. He plans to use them as guards until your father's murderer is apprehended."

"It's a wonder he didn't enlist Morgan's aid."

"Morgan is away, otherwise, he'd have been here today. But he's due anytime, so I'm sure he'll go to Westshire as soon as he arrives. I may even go with him."

"I'll look forward to seeing both of you." She took his hand and squeezed it. "Tell Sara I'm not up to saying good-bye to her tonight. Like her, I've overtaxed myself, but I'll write to her soon from Westshire."

"I will—and I'm sure she'll understand."

With a heaviness in her chest, Amber watched him walk away.

When Clay told her the carriages were readied the next morning, Amber hated to leave, even though her life was in danger. Her friends were here. Her home. Everything she held dear. And she couldn't shake the worry that Clay's steward might need guidance just like hers. Well, she consoled herself, at least Clay's man is accustomed to raising grain, even if Clay's fields *were* rye rather than barley.

Knowing all her concerns wouldn't change the inevitable, she gave her hair a final inspection, wishing she could remove the bandage on her temple, but the physician had asked her to wait a couple more days. Wishing she could turn back the clock and prevent everything that had happened in the last four days, she then went to join the others on the front veranda.

As she opened the door, she scanned the trees lining the cobbled drive, wondering if someone might be lying in wait for her. Who? her mind cried. Who would want her dead? And why?

Knowing the answers wouldn't come soon or easily, she lifted her skirt and stepped onto the brick porch. A gust of cool wind hit her. The sky was filled with thick gray clouds, and she knew the weather would soon turn nasty.

Remembering her thoughts on the weather yesterday, she lowered her gaze to the drive. To her surprise—or maybe not—she saw Clay and Albert standing near a carriage with the Westshire crest boldly displayed over the door. They were glaring at each other.

"What's wrong?" she asked Katherine as she walked up beside her.

Katherine's mouth thinned in disgust. "It seems His Grace is bent on being difficult again."

"What is it this time?"

"He takes exception to Albert's wish to accompany you in the carriage during the journey." She gave her black gloves a firm tug and readjusted the strap of her head scratcher dangling from her wrist. "In fact, he insists that Albert share our conveyance—if he goes at all."

Amber peeked at Clay. He stood with his legs apart as if he were standing on a ship's deck. His tight brown breeches hugged his firm buttocks and long legs, then disappeared at the knees into his boots. He said something to Albert, then crossed his arms, stretching the material of his coat across his broad shoulders.

Whatever he said angered Albert. He glared furiously, then stormed away.

Clay bent to inspect the underside of the vehicles, making sure the carriages hadn't been sabotaged.

Katherine sniffed. "It appears, His Grace is once again the victor."

Georgina shuffled up behind Katherine, carrying Poo's cage and trying to corral a sandy curl that had slipped from beneath her bonnet. "Since you insist on bringing this pound of prattling feathers, where do you want me to put him?"

"He can ride on the seat next to me." *Since Albert apparently wasn't going to.*

Ellison emerged from the house, looking quite smart in his satin waistcoat and breeches. He wore a conservative brown that enhanced his mature, gray-haired countenance.

"All set?" Startled by Clay's voice, Amber turned to see him standing at the foot of the steps, gazing up at her.

She couldn't resist the urge to find out what had transpired between him and Albert. "Where is Albert going to ride?"

"With his parents."

She was sure Albert would rather have walked than journeyed in close quarters with his father. "I'm surprised he agreed to that."

"He didn't." Without further explanation, Clay motioned for the footmen to help the others to their vehicle, then offered her his arm. "Your carriage awaits, milady."

The way he flashed that lethal smile made Amber's heart beat an odd tune, but she couldn't help scanning the trees again.

As if Clay had read her thoughts, he leaned close. "We searched them this morning. I wouldn't have let you out of the house, otherwise." He gave her another smile that not only reassured but brought back unwanted memories of how that beautiful mouth had felt against hers.

Her stomach tightened, and she stumbled.

With a steadying hand, he helped her regain her balance, then waited until a footman saw Georgina to her seat before he set her in the carriage, his palm lingering a little longer than necessary on her waist. Once she'd settled herself on the cushioned seat, she became aware of the scent of newly cleaned leather and axle grease.

Georgina had taken a place beside her and set Poo's cage between them, leaving Clay to occupy the opposite side by himself.

The vehicle lurched into motion, and Poo flapped his wings. *"Awk.* Damn me eyes! Damn me eyes!"

"Poo. For goodness' sake, stop cursing," Amber scolded.

The bird blinked and sidestepped along his perch until he was next to the bars. Showing his profile, he studied her with a single eye, then grabbed a thin metal rung in his beak and began to gnaw vigorously.

Clay watched with amused interest. "I believe he's hungry."

Taking a biscuit that she'd brought for the bird

from her reticule, Amber broke off a small portion and fed it to him. "How far do you think we'll get today?" she asked.

"I doubt if we'll make it farther than Lutton. The weather won't hold off too long."

"You sound very sure."

"I've spent the last eighteen years aboard ships, sweetheart. I had to learn to read the weather in order to survive."

"Well, I certainly hope there are suitable accommodations for Amber in that wretched farm country," Georgina huffed.

The way her cousin worried about her comfort made Amber feel like a child. "It's a well-traveled route. I'm sure there are several acceptable inns."

*"Awk.* Clay is a fool. Clay is a fool."

Georgina sucked in a horrified breath.

Amber's gaze flew to the opposite seat.

Clay's eyes were dancing with cynical amusement. "I wonder who taught him that?"

Flames of humiliation burned her cheeks, but she refused to cower. "Someone who was displeased with you, no doubt."

"No doubt," he returned in a quiet voice.

Georgina clucked her tongue and covered Poo's cage.

Amber parted the curtains and stared out the open window. She didn't want to look at Clay. Didn't want to know what he was thinking.

Several miles passed without any of them speaking. The rumble of the wheels on uneven ground, the squeak of carriage springs, and the monotonous rocking motion combined with the dreariness of the day soon lulled Amber into thoughts of last night. The parting with her father's friends had been painful and tearful, but nothing had compared to the empty hurt she felt when she had stood before her father's tomb later and told him good-bye. . . .

She blinked away tears and turned her thoughts to the journey ahead. Although she'd never tell Clay, she'd always dreamed of going to Westshire. Before their falling out, Clay had talked about the grandeur of his grandfather's estate with a fondness that bordered on reverence. Now he was the master. . . .

An explosion shook the carriage.

Georgina screamed.

Amber stifled a cry of terror and pressed back against the seat. Only then did she realize it had been thunder instead of a gun blast.

Poo squawked wildly.

The horses gave frightened shrieks, and the carriage careened wildly as the team veered sharply.

Rain swept in through the window, and Amber grabbed frantically for the flapping curtains.

Clay lunged across her and jerked them closed, then quickly fastened the bottom corners, not even aware that his arm had grazed her breast.

Georgina took care of the opposite curtains, then removed her shawl and handed it to Amber. "Here, love. Use this to dry yourself."

Swiping at the water staining her dress, and hiding a blush at the tingling sensation in her breast, she shook her head. "I'll do no such thing. Now put that back on before you catch a chill. For goodness' sake, I'm not made of sugar. I won't melt."

"If you do, I'll sop you up and mold you back together," Clay said, his eyes dancing with amusement. Then his gaze lowered to her breast. "Although I doubt I could do as good a job as nature did."

So the brush of his arm against her breast hadn't gone unnoticed by him. Amber knew she should at least act affronted, but she just couldn't. This was the rare side of him she adored the most. The gentle, teasing one.

Georgina harrumphed and pulled her shawl around her shoulders.

Clay held Amber's gaze for a few seconds longer, then collected a book from his portmanteau and leaned into the cushioned leather to read.

Her cousin unearthed her knitting.

Amber waited for her heartbeat to return to normal, then folded her arms and stared at the wet stain spreading on the gold velvet curtain. Rain beat down on the roof of the carriage, the wind howled. The curtain fluttered, and the carriage rocked and slowed as the horses began to struggle in the deepening mud.

"I figured you'd have outgrown that habit by now."

Her gaze flicked to Clay, and she saw that he'd set the book aside. "What habit?"

"Chewing on your lower lip when you're bored." His gaze lowered to her mouth and grew warm. "I used to watch you do that when discussions turned to hunting."

She never thought he'd noticed her. Guiltily, she touched a tender area at the corner of her mouth with her tongue.

He fixed on the movement. "You used to crease the hem of your skirt to resemble a folded fan, too."

"Fortunately, I've outgrown that habit."

"Now she fantasizes," Georgina piped in.

Clay leaned forward with interest. "You do? What about?"

There was no way she'd tell him.

"Pirates," her cousin supplied.

His green eyes crinkled with amusement. "You don't say?"

Amber wanted to sink through the carriage floor. "I do not."

Georgina glanced up in surprise. "You do, love. Why, just last week you told me you imagined a dashing pirate, dressed all in black, came into your room and threw you over his shoulder, then swept you away to his ship and—"

"*All right.* Maybe I do fantasize—sometimes." One

of these days she was going to fantasize about strangling her cousin, too.

"Do you still ride?" Clay asked.

Glad for the change of topic, she nodded. "As often as I can. I didn't get much of a chance in Paris, though. I was too busy with my lessons."

"Did you board at the school?"

"No. I attended Miss Renee's School for Young Ladies, and they don't have the facilities." Even now, she could see the thin, sour-faced woman slapping a measuring stick against her palm. "I stayed with my friends, Fiona and Pierre Desmound."

"You stayed with Bragen Alexander's sister?"

"I thought his name was Stanfield."

"Actually, it's Bragen Alexander Stanfield, but he went by Bragen Alexander for several years in the Colonies, and the name stuck."

When Amber returned from France, the first piece of gossip she'd heard had been about Clay's friend being charged with the murder of his wife—only to learn his best friend had done the deed. Bragen's murderous friend had also been Clay's and Morgan's. "How's your brother?"

"Morgan is fine. He was in Bath, but he should be on his way home by now."

"What's he doing there?"

"Finalizing the sale on one of his holdings so he can purchase my freighters. He's decided to try his hand at sailing."

She recalled how he'd dry-docked the *Black Wind* after the Captain died and purchased several freighters to become an 'honest' seaman. "How many ships do you have now?"

"Six."

"Are you selling him the *Black Wind,* too?" She tried not to show how much his answer meant to her.

"No."

Feeling ridiculously pleased, Amber smiled. The

carriage lurched as the horses slowed even more, and she placed a hand on Poo's cage to keep it from toppling off the seat. "I used to envy you so much going off with the Captain on that vessel. I envisioned fierce battles, cannons roaring, sword fights, and, of course, bulging chests of gold."

Clay's mouth twitched. "You forgot ravaging women."

"That aspect didn't interest me in the least. Besides, I don't believe those tales. No gentleman would—"

"Pirates aren't gentlemen."

She shifted against the hard seat, trying not to remember the times she'd wondered about his amorous activities at sea. "Are you saying—I mean, those women, did you . . .?"

"Yes." His gaze was steady and direct.

Georgina sputtered.

A rush of fear shot through Amber. He couldn't have been that ruthless, could he?

He gave her a wicked smile, then abruptly changed the subject again. "What did you study in France?"

She released her grip on the cage. "Etiquette, of course, and the finer aspects of running my future husband's household." Her heart was pounding so hard it scared her. The man was unprincipled and immoral, and he completely unbalanced her. She sent him a wary glance and was surprised to see a frown tightening his mouth.

Georgina sniffed and parted the curtains to look out. Another strand of hair slipped from her bonnet as she tilted her head. "There's a town ahead."

"That should be Lutton," Clay surmised. "We're going to stop there for the night." He glanced pointedly at Georgina. "There's an establishment called The Three Knights Inn—which I'm sure will meet with your approval."

Georgina put her knitting away. "My approval

doesn't enter into it. It's Amber's comfort that matters."

"I stand corrected."

Amber closed her eyes in resignation. Georgina made her sound so spoiled and pampered.

Clay leaned out the window and told the driver to stop in Lutton, then he resumed his seat and brushed the droplets from his hair and shoulders. The frown remained on his mouth, and she knew he was displeased about something, but she had no idea what. Georgina's insistence on her comfort? Or was it something more?

When the carriage rolled to a stop in front of the inn, Clay caught Amber by the waist and lifted her to the ground. Their bodies were so close, she could smell his clean ocean scent, and his hands remained on her for several seconds. Uneasily, she felt her heartbeat quicken.

Servants emerged from the inn carrying umbrellas. One held the shield over Amber and Clay while the others helped Georgina and the Chatsworths.

"Amber!" Albert called as he sprinted through the rain toward her.

Clay muttered something under his breath. "I'll see about the rooms." He strode inside before Albert reached them.

"Are you all right?" Albert asked he ducked under the umbrella, his blond hair dripping with water. He took her hand. "I know how frightened you are of storms, and I was so worried. . . ."

Amber hid a tolerant smile. "I outgrew my fear of storms years ago. You just haven't noticed."

He gave her a slanted grin. "I guess I still think of you as that little imp who always clung to me when the wind howled or the clouds roared."

"Well," she admitted. "Sometimes I do cling to my pillow."

He threw his head back and laughed, a deep rich sound that mingled with the patter of rain.

"Albert, do stop dawdling and see to our rooms," her godmother said as she approached them, tailed by a harried servant trying to keep the umbrella over her head. She shook her skirt to dislodge beads of water. "I am drenched to the bone."

Albert rolled his eyes, then winked at Amber and dashed through the rain toward the doors.

"I dare say, child, Albert thinks a great deal of you." She swept her with a critical eye. "But I do hope your friendship has not overgrown the bounds of propriety."

If anyone else had insinuated something like that about her and Albert, Amber would have become furious, but she knew Katherine wasn't being malicious. She was simply concerned about their reputations. For a fleeting second, she thought about telling Katherine about the proposition she intended to make to Albert, then decided to wait until she'd talked to him. She gave her godmother's hand a gentle squeeze. "There isn't—and never has been—anything improper between us."

She took Amber's arm and led her toward the inn. "I am sorry if I sounded as if I were making accusations, but I am only concerned for your welfare, as William would have been—God rest his soul."

At the mention of her father, an ache tightened Amber's throat, and she lowered her head.

"Katherine? Amber?"

They stopped inside the door and turned to see Ellison coming up behind them, tapping the rain from his tricorne. He gave them a smile. "I wonder if my two favorite ladies might like to take a stroll this evening—if the rain lets up? After being in that cramped carriage so long, I know I could use one."

Katherine considered the idea, then nodded. "I would like that."

He grinned at Amber, then took his wife's arm. "Then pray for clear skies, madam."

Amber smiled as she followed them through the door. They were such wonderful people.

Now that she was away from Markland, Amber was more relaxed and able to appreciate her surroundings without fear. The inn was small, yet neat, the floors well polished, the rugs and drapery clean.

Her gaze drifted over a pair of striped settees that matched the decor, then to a counter at the rear of the room. Clay stood in front of it, his dark, smoldering presence an ominous contrast to the orderly room, his manner intimidating as he spoke to Albert.

Whatever Clay said infuriated her friend. Albert whirled around and stalked angrily toward his parents.

Amber had seen Albert angry many times, and she knew how mercurial his temper—and his tongue— could be. She moved protectively closer to her godmother.

"Whatever is wrong, son?" Katherine asked in a soothing tone, clearly wanting to calm Albert before his temper got out of hand.

The tendons in Albert's neck bulged as he fought to keep his voice below a roar. "Cordell has ordered Amber's trunk taken to his room. The unprincipled bastard insists she share his bedchamber!"

# Chapter 5

No, Chatsworth," Clay countered. "We're not going to share a room, but we will share adjoining chambers, just as we did at Markland—and her cousin is going to be with her."

Albert whirled around. "Why? There's no threat to Amber here. No. I think you have other intentions, and I damned sure don't like it."

"If I did, boy, I'd be a helluva lot more discreet."

"Why, you—"

"Your Grace, Albert is right." Katherine touched his arm. "Amber is surrounded by those who care for her."

Clay wasn't in the mood to stand there all day explaining himself—nor justify the need to keep Amber close to him. "What makes you so sure someone didn't follow us?"

"Well, I—"

"It's settled, madam. Either accept my terms or Amber and I go on alone." Ignoring Albert's glare and

Katherine's sputter, he took Amber by the arm and led her toward the stairs.

"Do you really think that was necessary?" Amber asked breathlessly, as he all but dragged her up the staircase and down the hall to their rooms.

"Probably not, but I'm getting damned tired of explaining myself."

She jerked away from him. "Well, I'm getting deucedly tired of your high-handedness. You have no right to be uncivil to my friends."

He gripped her shoulders, barely suppressing the urge to shake her. "I have every right. I gave your father my word that I'd protect you, and that's what I'll do if I have to insult every acquaintance you have."

Her violet eyes flashed with fury. "Let go of me, you barbarous jackanapes. I'm not going anywhere with you."

"Take your hands off her," Albert grated from the head of the stairs, "or, so help me, I'll call you out."

Clay swung his gaze to the Chatsworth peacock, then gave him a slow smile. "Swords or pistols?"

Amber shivered beneath his grasp, then wiggled out of his hold. "Albert, please. It's all right. The duke and I merely have a difference of opinion. Certainly nothing to duel about."

"That's a matter of opinion."

"Oh, for goodness' sake, both of you need a good thrashing. Stop this nonsense at once."

Clay didn't doubt for a second what she was up to. She was trying to protect her young friend. He envied the loyalty she bestowed upon Albert Chatsworth. "Anything you say, sweetheart."

Her eyes narrowed at the endearment, then she returned her attention to the younger man. "Albert?"

He hesitated, then sighed. "If that's what you want."

"Absolutely." She opened the door to the bedchamber. "Now behave yourself, and I'll see you at supper."

Clay followed her inside, but the instant the door closed, she faced him with her hands on her hips. "What is the matter with you, Clayton? Have you lost your senses? Or have you been a pirate so long you now think it's great sport to kill a mere lad?"

"I wouldn't have hurt him. Besides, he's not that young. He's older than you." His gaze lowered to the curve of her breasts. "And, believe me, sweetheart, you're not a child anymore."

A flush rose to her cheeks, and those firm breasts began to heave with her unsteady breathing. "I . . . I'm going to my room." Gathering her skirts, she hurried through the connecting door and closed it.

Clay chuckled. He never thought he'd see the day she'd be at a loss for words.

Amber was a mass of nerves by the time she joined the others for supper. She couldn't count the times she'd prayed that Clay would look at her as a man does a woman, but when he finally had, she hadn't known how to cope with the sudden onslaught of emotions. She was pleased and excited and anxious and scared, all at the same time.

Over and over again she had to remind herself of the pain of their last encounter. Of her own scandalous actions when she sneaked into Clay's bedroom in the middle of the night, his volatile passion, then sudden rage when he threw her out.

"Amber," Albert called out as she entered a long dining room. Several linen-covered tables were stationed around the room, centered by brass candelabrum. The light from their white candles danced over paintings that decorated the otherwise stark walls. The aroma of warm bread and cinnamon made the room feel welcome and comfortable.

"Come on," Albert said. "Sit here." He patted the

seat of an empty chair next to him. The other tables were filled with travelers who'd apparently sought shelter from the rain, as they had.

Clay, who was at the head of the table, tightened his mouth in disgust as Amber took her seat, but he didn't say anything.

When the supper of mutton, small potatoes, glazed ham, and sweetbread was served, she filled her plate, then remained silent as she picked at her food and listened to the conversations around their table.

Katherine was talking to Georgina about the embroidery on one of her gowns that had come loose, while Ellison and Albert discussed the length of their journey. Clay remained silent, but his gaze often drifted to Amber.

She concentrated on her meal, amazed by how normal everything appeared. Her father was dead, yet nothing much had changed.

An ache tightened her throat, and she reached for her wineglass. *Oh, God. Why did this have to happen?* She took a sip from the goblet, hoping to ease the hurt. It didn't help.

She forced herself to pick up her fork, but her stomach churned restlessly, and she couldn't eat. She pushed her plate aside. "I hope everyone will excuse me, but I'm exhausted." The churning in her stomach turned into a roll as she stood. She gave Ellison an apologetic smile. "I guess our walk will have to wait till another time."

He dabbed his mouth with his napkin. "It's just as well. The rain hasn't stopped."

Georgina glanced up from her half-full plate, then started to rise.

Amber waved her back down. "Finish your meal. I'll be fine." Placing a hand on her stomach, she headed for the stairs. She had just entered her room when the first bout of nausea hit her.

Frantically, she lunged for the chamberpot. Her

stomach gave up its contents but continued to convulse in dry, racking heaves. She doubled over as pain speared through her belly. What on earth was happening?

Perspiration beaded on her forehead, and she clutched her middle in agony. She rolled to the floor on her side, drawing her knees to her chest. Dear God. She'd never known such horrible pain.

Without warning, Clay was there, kneeling beside her. "What is it, Amber? What's wrong?"

"P-Pain," she moaned, curling into a tighter ball.

He carried her to the bed and sat beside her, then gently brushed hair off her damp brow. "I'm going to send for a physician, sweetheart. Stay as still as possible."

He was gone before she realized he'd moved.

A moment later, Georgina burst into the room. "Oh, love. The duke said—sweet Providence, what's happened?"

Katherine was right behind her. "Quick, Georgina. Dampen a cloth."

Within seconds, Georgina was at her side, bathing her face. Katherine unbuttoned Amber's high-necked blouse while Georgina swathed her throat, cursing herself the whole time for not retiring when Amber had.

Amber wanted to tell her it wasn't her fault, but her throat felt as if it were on fire, then everything became hazy and dark. . . .

*She was drowning. The sea was pulling her under, deeper and deeper, yet she could hear the crew of the Black Wind laughing, the creak of the wood as the ship rocked on the waves.*

*She clawed frantically at the water, trying to find the surface. Her lungs burned. Her chest clenched with the need for air.*

*Out of nowhere Clay appeared, pulling her onto the*

*deck of his ship. He lay her on her back and shook her roughly. "Breathe, Amber. Damn it, breathe!"*

*She wanted to speak, to tell him she was trying, but the words wouldn't come. She tried to fill her lungs, but her chest jerked spasmodically.*

*She heard his impassioned, "Oh, Jesus," then his mouth was on hers, his sweet breath forcing its way into her lungs. Again. Again. It felt so wonderful. So very wonderful. . . . She drew in great gulps. Then he was clutching her to him, his voice gruff as he whispered passionately, "Thank you, God. Thank you." He was shaking.*

*She wanted to talk to him, to tell him she was all right now, but she couldn't speak. She was drifting away on a black sea. . . .*

Clay eased Amber back onto the feather tick and brushed the hair out of her eyes. Every muscle in his body shook from fear and anger. Someone had given her poison—arsenic, most likely. He'd seen the results of arsenic poisoning before when one of the dogs the Captain liked to keep aboard the *Black Wind* got into the cargo hold and tore open a burlap bag filled with packets of the drug they'd stolen from a Boston physician. Clay had found the animal right after it happened . . . and had helplessly watched him die.

He studied her pale features, and he knew he was right. Another surge of anger hit him. Whoever had done this to her would pay.

He tried to remember if she'd appeared ill at the table. Vaguely, he recalled her taking a sip of wine, then shortly afterwards placing a hand on her stomach. He'd wager that's how she'd ingested it.

He turned on the women behind him. "Georgina, have the hotel cook brought in here. Mrs. Chatsworth, you stay. We're going to talk." He waved Amber's cousin out.

Katherine wrung her hands. "Is she going to be all right?"

"We won't know for sure until the physician gets here, but right now I want you to tell me who set Amber's place at the dining table."

"I have no idea. All the places were set when Ellison and I arrived."

"Was anyone else in the room when you got there?"

"Several people. Travelers mostly."

"Who poured the wine?"

"The glasses were already filled."

Clay rubbed the back of his neck and began to pace. Was it possible someone slipped the poison into Amber's glass with everyone milling around the room? Or perhaps before everyone arrived? But how would they have known where she'd sit? He frowned at Katherine. "Who arranged the seating?"

"I am not aware that anyone did. We simply sat where we wanted."

Clay thought for a second. "There were only two seats vacant when I came in—one at the end of the table and one between you and Albert—and the chance of me sitting beside him was about as likely as you appearing at supper naked."

*"Your Grace!"*

He waved his hand. "No offense. I was just pointing out how remote the chance of me sitting in Amber's chair would have been. No. Whoever poisoned her was very sure where she'd sit."

"But, who—"

The door opened and Georgina came in, leading a hefty man in a stained apron.

"This is Sanders, Your Grace. He prepared supper."

The man looked scared. "I heard about her ladyship, gov'nor. But, I swear to ye, I didn't put nothing bad in the food."

"Who poured the wine?"

"The kitchen maid. Put the bottle on the sideboard, she did. Ye can check with her if ye like."

"I already did," another voice announced. Albert came in, followed by his father. "I talked to her and checked the bottle and remaining food on Amber's plate, then her goblet. The wine in her glass was fouled."

Clay returned his attention to the cook. "Was anyone seen near our table?"

"None of us was in there the whole time, gov'nor."

"Your Grace?" the hotel clerk said from the doorway. "The physician has arrived." He gestured to a man in green satin. "Dr. Whitehall."

The physician glanced at Amber, then the others in the room. "If you would all be so kind as to step out, I will examine the girl."

Clay ushered everyone through the door, but he refused to leave, which caused Katherine to bristle and the Chatsworth males to curse. Not that he cared. He wasn't going to let Amber out of his sight again, no matter how upset they got.

Still, a few minutes later, he wished he hadn't been so adamant. The amount of flesh the physician exposed during the examination was enough to make him sweat.

He turned away and tried to focus on the danger at hand. Someone had tried to kill Amber, and he had a strong suspicion it was one of her companions, but he honestly hoped he was wrong—not because of any love he felt for the group but because those people meant so much to Amber. He hoped someone had followed them from Markland.

Someone his guards would spot when they arrived at Westshire.

When Amber opened her eyes again, she became aware of several things at once. Her whole body ached, it was night, and Clay was asleep in a chair beside her bed. In the dim glow of candlelight she could see a growth of black stubble along his jaw, and his hair was mussed as if he'd been running his fingers through it repeatedly. His shirt was unbuttoned and wrinkled, his boots lying beside the chair.

"Clay?"

His lashes flew up, and there was a moment of panic in his eyes, then he focused on her. His mouth spread into a beautiful smile. "Amber. . . ."

The warmth in that single word sent a wave of heat through her. "W-What happened to you?"

Self-consciously, he laced his fingers through his hair and rose. "Nothing." He appeared embarrassed. "Listen, I'm going to get Mrs. Becker." Before she could respond, he grabbed his boots and strode out of the room.

Seconds later, Georgina came bustling into the chamber, her grin as bright as a summer dawn. "Oh, love. We've been so worried about you."

"Why?"

She pulled the chair closer to the bed, then clutched Amber's hand. "Don't you remember?"

"Remember what?"

"Someone poisoned you, and the physician said he thought you'd be all right, but you wouldn't wake up, then the duke started worrying. We all did."

*"Poison?"*

"His Grace thinks a deadly potion was put in the wine you drank. Why, if it hadn't been for him, you *would* be dead. He breathed life into you from his very own mouth when your throat closed up, and he kept you breathing until you were all right, then the physician came and purged you."

Clay had saved her? Hazily, she recalled her night-mare about the *Black Wind*—and Clay. Then the realization hit her. *Someone had tried to kill her.* Fear tightened her flesh. "Did they find out who did it?"

"No, love."

"What kind of poison was it?"

"I believe His Grace said arsenic."

Amber closed her eyes. *Dear God.*

"If you'd taken a full swallow, we would have . . . lost you."

Amber had trouble keeping her voice from quivering. "Who poured the wine?"

"The kitchen maid. Young Albert questioned her straight away—His Grace did, too, and she said she opened a fresh bottle right out of the wine cellar. No one touched it."

Placing a hand to her forehead, Amber noticed her bandage was gone, and there was a small ridge of puckered flesh. "Who was the first person in the dining room?"

"His Grace asked that, too, and all the other questions forming in your head. There just aren't any answers, or I'd have told you immediately. But I know His Grace has been terribly upset. He's been worrying and studying on what happened for days."

"Days?"

"Yes, love. Three days."

"I don't remember any of them."

"It's just as well. You were in terrible pain, and His Grace never left your side the whole time. Everyone he questioned he had brought to your room because he was afraid you'd slip away if he wasn't here. He sent men out to search the roads for strangers, too. It was rather a lost gesture, though, since nearly everyone on these roads is a stranger."

She remembered his haggard appearance when she first woke, and a surge of joy infused her, but it quickly died. Clay had given her father his word to protect her, and Clay took his duties very seriously. Of course, he would stay with her. "Where are the others?"

"I believe His Grace is in the next room, taking a bath. The last time I saw Mrs. Chatsworth, she was talking to the inn's cook about what she calls a perfectly horrid menu, and the others, I'm told, sought the comfort of a tavern down the road."

Amber rolled her head to the side and scanned the room. "Where's Poo?"

"In the next chamber. His Grace was afraid the parrot's infernal chattering would disturb you, so he took the bird in there. Do you want me to fetch you some tea?"

She wasn't sure. Her stomach felt raw. "Perhaps a small portion."

When Georgina left, Amber weakly climbed from the bed and, after seeking the chamberpot, dragged on a silk dressing robe. She dropped down on the bed again in exhaustion just as her cousin returned with a tray sporting a china tea service. "Here we go, love. I had the cook make it weak so it would be easier on your stomach. He sent some biscuits, too."

Setting the tray on a small writing table, Georgina filled a cup and handed it to her, then returned to place two biscuits on a napkin.

Amber raised the cup to her lips.

"Don't!" Clay strode into the room and took the cup from her. His hair was still damp from his bath, his clothes immaculate. "Before you eat or drink anything, I'm going to sample it first."

Amber stared at the cup for a moment and felt a tremor run through her. Still, the thought of Clay . . .

"I was there the whole time, Your Grace, while the cook prepared the tea," Georgina said in an attempt to reassure him.

Amber felt some of the apprehension leave her. "I'm sure after what happened, the cook takes extra care to guard the food."

He ignored both of them and took a healthy drink of the tea. His eyes flew open. "Bloody hell!"

"What is it? Clay, what's wrong?" She lunged to her

feet. The room spun, and she grabbed a bedpost for support.

He waved her back down, grimacing as he wiped his mouth. "I'm all right. But I know that's got to be the worst tea I've ever tasted. What'd the cook use—one tea leaf in the entire pot?"

"Curse you, Clayton Cordell, don't you ever frighten me like that again."

"I apologize, sweetheart. I was taken by surprise and reacted poorly."

Georgina sniffed. "Now that you've completed your sampling, Your Grace, may I serve her ladyship another cup?"

"By all means."

"What about the biscuits?" Amber taunted. "Don't you want to taste those?"

He arched a brow, then walked to the desk and popped one in his mouth. He chewed thoughtfully for several long seconds, then his gaze drifted to hers, and he winked. "Not bad."

Amber clenched her hands to control the surge of pleasure that shot through her. When he was playful like that, he made her insides go soft. He was so charming and so approachable, she could almost forget what happened four years ago.

Almost.

## Chapter 6

Amber was bored. She'd spent the entire day in bed with Clay watching over her constantly. She'd counted the bricks on all four walls, the squares in the green chintz quilt covering her bed—and Georgina's—and the crystals on the chandelier centering the high scrolled ceiling.

But the worst part was with so much time to think, her thoughts kept wandering to that night four years ago.

She fixed her gaze again on the ceiling, willing her thoughts in another direction. But the memories of how Clay had kissed her so passionately and held her pressed so close to him swarmed her.

"Want to share your thoughts with me?"

About as much as she wanted a toothache. She rolled her head to see Clay sitting at the writing table, holding a quill poised over a piece of parchment. His broad frame looked huge behind the small desk. "I . . . was merely trying to figure out who wants to kill me."

74

He glanced down at the paper in front of him. "That's what I was doing, too."

"Any solutions?"

"Not yet." He set the quill down. "Tell me about your companions."

"Surely, you don't suspect them."

"I can't afford to discount them."

"I don't understand."

"It's possible that something happened in the past that could have prompted this, or that your death will benefit one of them in the future."

She eased her legs over the side of the bed and sat up. "Nonsense. Nothing happened in the past to warrant such a thing, and if I were to die now, everything I possess would go to Uncle Trace and Uncle Conrad in the Colonies."

Clay was staring at her strangely.

"What's wrong?"

He swallowed and looked away. "Cover yourself."

"What?" She glanced down. The white sleeping gown she wore had come unlaced, and a goodly portion of one breast was exposed. She jerked the gaping neckline together. Flames of embarrassment warmed her cheeks, and she wanted to sink through the floor. Then the irony of the situation struck her. At one time, she had exposed a great deal more to him than that.

"If you're thinking what I *think* you are, don't say a word about it," he warned without turning. "It's an extremely dangerous subject at this moment."

Amber wasn't sure what he meant, but his softly spoken threat was enough to stop anything she might have wanted to say about their previous encounter. "I . . . um . . . was just wondering when we're going to leave here."

"The physician said you should be well enough to travel by tomorrow." His gaze drifted toward her, then down to the hand clutching the front of her gown. His eyes darkened to the color of a shaded forest, causing a ripple of fear—or was it excitement?—to spread through her.

She tightened her fingers on the material, only then realizing the gown was drawn taut across her breasts. She could feel her nipples pushing against the fabric. She didn't know what to do. Any movement on her part would surely draw more of his attention than she already had.

He took the matter out of her hands by rising abruptly. "Get dressed, and I'll take you for a short stroll. The fresh air will do us both good." Without waiting for an answer, he disappeared through the adjoining doors.

Amber didn't waste a single second. The next time she saw Clayton Cordell, she wanted to be fully clothed. Selecting a dark brown skirt and matching blouse, she discarded the idea of trying to squeeze into a corset and dressed. She buttoned on the corresponding waistcoat with weak fingers, then set a brush to her hair. While she was about it, she walked over to the desk and glanced at the paper Clay had been scribbling on. It was a list of her friends.

Shaking her head, she continued brushing her hair, but without help, she couldn't style the heavy mass, so she left it down, drawing it away from her face with a dark ribbon. She had just finished pulling on her slippers when Clay returned.

"Ready?"

He had donned a bottle green velvet jacket over a white shirt and tied on a cravat. The effect, together with his snug breeches and glistening black boots, was heart-stopping.

His mouth curved into a wicked smile as if he'd read her thoughts. "If you keep looking at me like that, we'll never get out of this room."

Her heart burst into frantic beats. "I-I wasn't looking at you. I was . . . admiring your coat."

His smile deepened, and he offered his arm. "What would you say if I told you my mistress gave it to me for Michaelmas?"

Amber sucked in a breath. "Clayton! How dare you speak to me about such."

"Why? Did you think I didn't have one?"

She lifted her chin. "I never gave it a thought one way or the other."

He chuckled as he led her through the door. "Liar."

Deciding to keep her mouth shut before she got in any deeper, she clamped her lips together and walked stiffly beside him.

The cobbled walkway was clean and smelled of rain. Apparently, the storm hadn't passed that first day. Fallen leaves from trees lining the thoroughfare gathered in clusters against the sides of brick and frame buildings spaced closely together. An overhead sign announcing Stephenson's Millinery creaked as it swayed in a breeze.

It was a pretty town, with its backdrop of rolling green hills dotted with oak and maple trees. In a way, it reminded her of the land surrounding Markland. "This is such beautiful country. I couldn't imagine living anywhere else."

Sadness shadowed Clay's eyes. "My mother felt the same way about England. She loved it more than anything, even the Captain."

"I don't—"

"Come on, let's get back." Taking her arm, he turned toward the inn.

She'd always been able to read Clay, and in that instant, she knew what was wrong with him. He was comparing her to his mother. He thought Amber was a social butterfly like Elaina had been.

Maybe it was for the best. Clay unnerved her, and the less time she spent with him, the better.

Still, later that night, as she lay in bed, Amber couldn't erase Clay's comment about a mistress. She envisioned him and a sultry woman with black hair wrapped in each other's arms, laughing and kissing, and . . . she wasn't sure what else, but it wasn't proper.

The next morning she was tired and cranky, and even the mounds of satin pillows Clay had placed in the carriage for her comfort didn't improve her disposition.

She snapped at him when he lifted her into the conveyance and grumbled while he inspected the wheels and axles—and the basket of food the cook had sent with them.

Clay noticed that Amber was unusually ill tempered during the journey. When she wasn't being short with him, she kept her gaze fixed on the scenery outside the window and her hands folded. Her attitude concerned him. It was so unlike her that he was afraid she might be feeling unwell. But the healthy glow had returned to her cheeks, and she didn't appear to be overly tired.

Baffled, he shifted his gaze to Georgina. She was sound asleep, her shoulders wedged into the corner of the seat, her bonnet-draped head slumped to the side. Poo was silent, too, as he meticulously cleaned his feathers.

His attention returned to Amber, and he felt a tiny surge of remembered fear. When he'd found her on the bedroom floor curled into a ball, he'd been frightened. But when she had stopped breathing, he had gone wild with panic.

He closed his eyes, remembering the feel of her mouth beneath his as he struggled to force air into her lungs. It was the second time their lips had touched.

Unbidden, his thoughts drifted to the first time—to the time he had thought to punish her by ravaging her youthful mouth, ruthlessly demonstrating the true consequences of arousing a man's lust. But she'd turned the tables on him. Her eager, innocent kiss had shaken him to the core, and it had taken every ounce of control he possessed to end it.

He raised his lashes and explored that soft, pink mouth. Her lips were full, temptingly moist, and in the shape of a perfect bow, but it was the unconscious way she held them that drew him. Her mouth begged for a man's possession.

"Am I chewing my lip again?"

He dragged his gaze upward. "No."

"Then what are you staring at?"

"I was remembering how your mouth felt against mine."

Her breath caught, and she brought a slim hand to her throat. "Don't you dare bring that up."

"Why? We can't deny what happened."

"I was fifteen years old!"

"How well I know. If you hadn't been, I couldn't have stopped."

Her lips drew into a line of disgust. "Don't patronize me. I remember exactly how repulsed you were."

"How *what?*"

"What is it?" Georgina lurched up. "Is something wrong?"

Clay was still staring at Amber. He couldn't believe what she'd said, but he certainly wasn't going to respond in front of her cousin. Repulsed, for God's sake. That was a laugh. "No, Georgina. Everything is fine."

"Quite," Amber seconded, then returned her attention to the passing scenery.

Clay settled deeper into his seat and crossed his arms. Of all the idiotic notions. *Repulsed.*

They reached Nottingham at dusk, and he found accommodations at the Robin's Inn. No one, including Albert, objected when he ordered adjoining rooms for him and Amber. Unfortunately, since the inn was small, there was only a single bed in their chambers, and Amber's cousin ended up in a room across the hall.

At supper Clay was the first to arrive, and he kept a close eye on their companions and other patrons of the inn as he waited for Amber. When she appeared in the doorway, he led her to a seat next to his. Albert gave him a cold stare, but he didn't say anything. No one did—not after what happened in Lutton.

There was an unusual, somber silence among Amber's friends as they ate, each sampling the taste of their food longer than normal. But, even at that, it only took them a short time to finish. Soon all had retired but Clay and Amber and a scattering of strangers.

Clay kept his voice low as he spoke to her. "We're going to leave the door between our rooms open tonight."

She glanced up from her plate. "Why?"

"I'm not letting you out of my sight again, so it's either that . . . or we share a bed."

"The door is fine." She tossed her napkin down and rose. "If you'll excuse me, I'd like to bathe and change *before* you open it."

"I'll allow you one hour."

"Of course." Her spine stiff, Amber marched from the room.

Smiling, Clay leaned back in his chair and envisioned her covered in soapsuds.


"Which gown do you want to wear tomorrow?" Georgina asked as she poured the last of the rinse water over Amber's hair.

Amber wiped the water out of her eyes. "The green taffeta."

"I'll take it down to have it pressed as soon as we're finished, then."

Picking up a cloth and soap, Amber nodded toward the door. "Might as well go now. I'll be awhile, yet."

Georgina set a towel on a stool beside the brass tub. "Would you like me to bring a cup of lemon tea when I return?"

Amber smiled, remembering how Georgina used to bring her lemon tea every night before she retired, and how Georgina would read to her from a book of pirate tales Amber loved so much. How wonderful those times had been when she was a child. How untroubled. "Yes. I'd like that."

Her cousin gathered the gown from a trunk. "I won't be long, love."

When the door closed, Amber glanced at the clock on the mantle, wishing she could remember what time she came upstairs. Clay said he'd give her one hour, but she'd been so flustered by his remark about sharing a bed, she hadn't even glanced at the clock. Still, it didn't matter. Clay would knock before entering. Satisfied, she began to wash.

Smelling like a bouquet of fresh lilacs, she rose and stepped from the tub and reached for a towel on the stool.

The door opened. "Amber, I brought you a . . ."

Startled, the towel slipped from her fingers . . . and she found herself facing Clay without a stitch on.

He froze midstride and slowly slid his gaze down her dripping body. Then, without a word, he tossed a book on the bed and walked out.

Amber sank back down into the water, wondering what it was she'd seen in his eyes. Desire? Or disgust?

Cold salt air blew through the broadleaf trees bordering the lane that led to Westshire. The carriage horses labored as they climbed an incline, winding their way up to a vast, level plateau above the cliffs.

Westshire sat like a giant gray pearl amid emerald

satin. Acres of manicured lawns and shrubbery encompassed the stately stone mansion with its long verandas and wide balconies. A high stone fence jutted out from either side, enclosing more of the spectacular grounds from view. It was imposing. It was impressive.

It was Clay's.

*"Awk.* Land ho! Land ho!"

Amber glanced at the lorikeet. "That's right, Poo. We're almost there."

"Thank heavens for that," Georgina grumbled. "Even with the pillows His Grace provided, I'm certain every inch of my flesh is bruised."

"So you've mentioned several times," Clay muttered as he crossed his arms and leaned his head back. He watched Amber for several seconds, then lowered his lashes.

Amber couldn't help staring at him across the expanse of the swaying carriage. His thick lashes fanned out on his tanned cheeks, and he was so attractive with that dark lock of hair dancing on his brow. She didn't even want to think about how those thick muscles in his arms stretched the linen material of his shirt. Or how his long legs were again encased in snug breeches that left little to the imagination. The evidence of his gender was clearly defined. Generously so.

Heat rushed to Amber's cheeks, and she jerked her gaze away, trying very hard not to remember how much of her Clay had seen last night. Although nothing had happened, the feelings churning inside troubled her. She couldn't allow herself to become ensnared in the same trap she had before.

She closed her eyes, knowing she had to put a stop to these growing feelings. She had to keep Clay at a distance. The image of his mother came to mind, and in that instant, she knew exactly how to keep the duke of Westshire at bay.

"*Awk.* Clay is a fool. Clay is a fool."

"Hush, now," Georgina scolded. "The duke is a good man."

Amber wasn't so generous. *No, Poo, he is a fool—and a blackguard of the first water.*

The coach lurched to a shuddering halt, and Amber gazed out the window to see imposing pillars guarding the veranda and double-doored entrance to West-shire. They reminded her of Clay. Strong. Looming.

When a footman opened the carriage door, Clay stepped out, then caught her by the waist and lifted her down. The warmth of his hands sent shivers through her middle, and the instant her feet touched the ground, she stepped away.

He watched her for a second, then turned to say something to his servant.

The Chatsworths' conveyance swayed to a stop behind theirs, and Albert leaped out. "Thank God," he groaned. "I didn't think we'd ever get here." He looped an arm around Amber's shoulder and walked with her toward the front veranda. "Well, at least now you're out of danger and the duke won't be so damned high-handed."

Amber smiled weakly. She wouldn't wager anything of value on that.

Clay motioned to an elderly servant who'd emerged from the house.

Dressed in a black waistcoat and breeches, he had stern features and a tightly drawn mouth. By the look of authority about him, she guessed him to be the butler.

"Bowling, have Lady Sinclair's trunks taken to the room that adjoins mine."

The older man's eyes widened just a fraction, but he simply motioned a second footman toward the baggage.

Albert swung on Clay. "You're not serious."

"Aren't I?"

"I must protest, Your Grace," Ellison proclaimed as he joined them. His wig had slipped to the side, and he straightened it. "On the journey, I know it was necessary. But here?" He swung a chubby hand. "I simply cannot allow it."

"Absolutely not," Katherine concurred as the footman helped her and her yards of skirts and petticoats from the carriage. "Why, the very idea . . ."

"Don't you think you're making too much of this?" All eyes turned on Georgina.

She blushed profusely and began to stutter. "I-I mean, William t-trusted the duke to p-protect her."

"It is not proper." Katherine drew herself up straight. "Why, the *ton* would—"

"I will not let this continue," Albert hissed.

Clay arched a brow. *"You* don't have anything to say in the matter."

Amber felt rising panic. With Clay that close, she knew without a doubt she'd end up making a fool of herself. "I'll share a room with my cousin."

Clay crossed his arms. "No."

"But there's no danger here."

"That's the end of it, Amber."

Anger shook her. "End, my foot. I'd rather sleep on the blasted beach!" Whirling around, she marched off toward a path that led down the cliffs to the sand.

"Amber, wait!" Albert started after her.

Clay stopped him. "If you plan on staying in my home, Chatsworth, you'd better have your things carried to a room right now. Otherwise . . ."

Amber didn't listen to any more. She lifted the hem of her skirt and hurried along the seashell path, her nerves stretched to the breaking point. Sweet Providence, why did Clay's mere presence turn her inside out?

Halfway down the hill, she sensed someone watching her. The muscles down her spine tightened, and she nervously glanced over her shoulder.

A field hand stood on the ledge above her, carefully scanning the beach below. He smiled and waved.

Some of the tenseness left her spine. He must be one of Clay's men. Robert said he'd ordered his field hands to guard Westshire.

When she reached the sand, she found a large smooth boulder in the shade of a rocky ledge and sat down. Her hands trembled as she folded them in her lap. A cool, salty breeze ruffled wisps of hair, and she gave a light shiver, wishing she'd had the foresight to grab her wrap.

Unfortunately, foresight was not one of her virtues. If it had been, that awful night would have never happened.

Unbidden, the memories wove their way into her thoughts.

*It was past midnight, and the Markland household had retired. Amber felt a shiver of excitement race through her as her gaze returned to the mirror. She studied her image critically, trying to see herself through Clay's eyes.*

*Even though she was only fifteen, her breasts had grown enough to fill out the bodice of her mother's gown. Her hips were still slim, but the cut of the gown made them appear shapely. Surely, Clay would see she was a woman and look at her in the same way he did Rachel Mather. Although Clay had never said as much, Amber knew Rachel was the woman he stayed with when he came to town.*

*Lifting her chin, she smiled at her reflection. Well, after tonight, he wouldn't want Rachel's companionship. He'd only want hers.*

*She knew what she planned to do was horribly scandalous, but it didn't matter. She loved him, and she knew his honor would demand that he marry her afterward.*

"Amber, stop sulking and come back to the house."

Startled, she glanced up to see Clay towering over

her, holding her cloak in one hand. She wanted to reach for it, but she didn't dare. "I'm not sulking."

"Yes you are."

She stood, pulling herself up to her full height—all five feet of it. "If I were sulking, I wouldn't speak to you."

He grinned and drew the cloak around her shoulders. "I stand corrected."

Warmth enveloped her, and her heart did a funny flip. He was so handsome when he smiled. Long-buried emotions rushed to the surface with such a force, she swayed from the impact.

He caught her by the shoulders to steady her.

They were too close. She could feel the heat radiating from his body. Smell his warm scent.

Their eyes met . . . and held. For a heartbeat, neither of them moved, then slowly, oh so slowly, he lowered his mouth to hers.

A rumble shook the ground.

Clay's head whipped up. "Bloody hell!" he bellowed, an instant before his body slammed into hers.

They hit the ground hard and rolled.

An avalanche of sand and rocks crashed over them. Clay covered Amber and buried her face in his neck, shielding her.

The horrible roaring sound deafened her. Sand stung her arms. Rock hit the ground near her ear. A scream tried to claw its way up her throat, and she bit her lip to silence it. Please, God, she prayed. *Make it stop.*

As if in divine answer, the roaring dwindled to small thuds as the last of the rocks struck the sand.

Amber went weak with relief. She took deep breaths to slow the pounding in her chest. Clay's scent filled her senses, and she became aware of him lying on top of her, of the warmth of his body, the taut contours. Her heart picked up speed again.

Clay's lips touched her ear, and his warm breath sent shivers along her flesh. "Are you all right?"

*No.* "I think so."

Using great care, he eased himself off her, and she regretted the loss.

Sand cascaded from his head and shoulders, and she quickly closed her eyes. When she felt him roll away, she berated herself for her foolish thoughts and peeked through her lashes to see him brushing off his clothes and hair.

Sunlight glinted off a silky strand that had come loose from the leather strip at the nape of his neck, and she had the strongest urge to touch it. Then she thought about how he'd almost kissed her, and she clenched her teeth. She was falling under his spell again.

When his clothes were dusted, he helped her to her feet, but he didn't offer to help her brush off her clothes. It was a good thing. If he'd touched her, she'd probably have fallen apart.

As Amber swiped at the sand, she noticed Clay studying the large pile of debris in front of them and the cliff overhead.

His eyes narrowed. "I'm praying that was caused by an act of nature and not by one of your companions."

"Don't be ridiculous. Besides, *your* man was the only one I saw up there."

He gripped her wrists. "What man?"

"A field hand, I think."

"What did he look like?"

"Gray-streaked beard, worn tricorne, dusty brown clothes."

Clay relaxed. "Jonathan."

"Who's he?"

"My, er, maid's brother." Taking her arm, he guided her toward the path, and when they reached the grassy top of the cliff, he inspected the ledge that had broken away. "I was hoping I could tell what happened from up here, but I can't. One thing did come out of this, though. Your sleeping arrangements have definitely been settled."

Clay's words were like a death knell. Without comment, Amber drew the edges of her cloak together and headed for the manor. But inwardly, she knew the man was truly going to be the death of her. One way or another.

## Chapter 7

Clay escorted Amber to the house through a rear gate in the stone fence, then upstairs to the second level, where a door led to a narrow staircase and the third story. At the top was a short hall with two doors on the right.

He opened the first one and ushered her inside.

Amber could only stare at the opulence of the room. The entire chamber was done in white and bronze, from the sheer bed drapings to the satin quilts, to the lacy curtains framing tall, square-paned glass doors. Even the washbasin, pitcher, armoire, desk, and plush throw rugs were of the same hues. The effect was stunning.

Her gaze drifted back to glass doors. "Where do those go?"

"I'll show you." He opened one and gestured for her to follow him.

Hesitantly, she did so, then gaped in awe. Beyond the doors was a rooftop balcony with delicate white wrought-iron furniture. The back side of the balcony overlooked the courtyard, the end, a magnificent garden behind the high stone fence, a long stretch of beach, and miles of blue, blue ocean. The view was breathtaking.

"I've never seen anything so lovely." There was no way she could keep the reverence from her voice.

Clay studied the view with fondness. "This was my grandmother's favorite place. I used to come up here and sit with her for hours, listening to her tales of grand parties, elite guests . . . and grizzly events."

"Grizzly?"

"Mmm. So she said. At least once a season, a guest would fall from the cliffs to their deaths." He smiled. "I doubt if the tales were true, though. I think she only told me that to keep me from venturing too close. It must have worked, because I don't recall ever playing near the edge."

Amber remembered the duchess of Westshire from her many visits to London. She was a tall, stately woman, but she didn't strike Amber as one to make up tales. "It was a good thing you didn't, with the way the sand breaks away from the cliff so easily."

"To my knowledge, that's never happened before."

Knowing he was again hinting at treachery, Amber lifted the edges of her skirt and turned away. "Then, apparently, the avalanche was long overdue."

"Possibly," he said in a thoughtful tone, then walked to the doors. "Why don't you stay here and enjoy the view while I see everyone settled, then I'll help you unpack."

"There's no need to inconvenience yourself, Georgina will help me."

"No."

"What?"

"No one is allowed on this floor except you and me, and occasionally one of the maids in my employ."

Panic struck swift and hard. "But—"

"No buts, Amber. That's how it's going to be."

"For heaven's sake, how will I dress?" she cried urgently. She'd have to start at midnight just to dress for breakfast by herself.

He gave her a slow smile. "I'll help."

When Clay saw everyone situated, he headed for the servants' quarters on the lower floor.

He wasn't sure which room he'd find Miranda in, but he'd wager it would be the biggest.

Approaching the door at the end of the hall, which he knew was the largest room, he knocked softly.

Miranda jerked open the door—and threw herself into his arms. "Oh, Clayton. I thought you'd never get here." She showered him with kisses. "I've missed you so much."

"Let go of me, imp, so I can get a look at you." He set her away from him and inspected her. Huge green eyes framed by long, thick black lashes stared up at him. Her glorious black hair was drawn into a bun at the nape of her neck, making her look older than her three and twenty years, but nothing could detract from her exquisite beauty. She was small, but her body had been created by the gods, strictly for a man's pleasure. "The servant's clothes become you," he teased.

"Very funny." She waved him inside her room and shut the door.

He could only stare at the room. A bed from a guest chamber was stationed against one wall. The silk wall drapings from another. A chest-on-chest from still another. The Roentgen desk from the library. The armoire from *his* room, and a gilded mirror from the parlor. "Good Lord. Is there anything left in the house?"

She plopped down into a settee that had been in the

gallery the last time he saw it. "If you expect me to pose as a maid, I might as well do it in comfort."

A tinge of heat moved up his neck. "I'm sorry I had to ask that of you, pet. But it's important." He quickly explained about Amber and the threat to her life and how he wanted Miranda to pose as a maid to keep an eye on the others and glean as much information about each of them as she could.

"I think all this subterfuge will be fun, but isn't Amber the same girl who had you in such an uproar a few years ago?"

For the first time, he wished he and Miranda weren't so close. "Yes."

"How old is she now, eighteen?"

"Almost nineteen."

Miranda smiled, showing an even row of small, pearly teeth. "Hmm. Not a child anymore, is she?"

"Don't start."

She chuckled. "I wouldn't dream of it. So. How do you want me to go about my spying? Use the secret passages? My charm? What?"

"Just stay in the background and listen. I don't know that her companions are in any way involved in this, but the more I know about them, the better I'll feel. And you can start by helping Lady Chatsworth and Mrs. Becker dress for supper."

"I've already tried my hand at getting acquainted with your guests, since I figured that's what this was all about. By the way, who's going to help Amber dress?"

"I am."

"I see."

Clay shook his head. "I don't doubt you do." Giving her a kiss on the cheek, he tugged her ear, then opened the door. "I'll be back tonight."

In his room, he pulled on a clean pair of breeches and a shirt, then stared at the closed doors that separated him from Amber. He didn't like her being that close, and the thought of his offer to help her dress made him sweat—a task he fortunately would avoid for the moment since she didn't plan to change for supper.

But he'd have to assist her sooner or later, whether he wanted to or not. It was ironic. Never had he objected to removing a lady's clothing before, but with Amber it was different. Every time he got close to her, he wanted to pull her into his arms and kiss her senseless. Hell, he almost had.

The mere thought made him shudder. She was the daughter of his friend. But worse, she was a part of London's elite set. Something he never wanted to be.

Still, he had no choice when it came to keeping her close. He didn't trust anyone. Until recently, he'd assumed the murderer was an outsider—and it still might be—but that was an assumption that could have cost Amber her life. He wouldn't make that mistake again. Even her cousin wasn't above suspicion any longer.

Amber would never believe his summation, though. She was convinced someone else was lurking in the shadows. Well, that was a possibility, so he'd taken precautions—just in case. He'd ordered his field hands to guard the only road to Westshire day and night. He'd also stationed men on the cliffs to watch the beach.

Unless the person was already in his house, no one would get to Amber.

But that didn't solve his problem. He desired a woman he'd sworn to protect . . . a social butterfly he could never have, and there wasn't a damn thing he could do about it.

When the meal was over, Amber and the others joined Clay for a sherry outside in a courtyard at the rear of the house. She was impressed by the magnificence of the grounds. To the left of the courtyard a gate led to five acres of tall hedges that were flanked by the eight-foot walls. Amber had heard that Clay's great-great-grandfather had commissioned the maze to entertain his never-ending multitude of guests.

She was awed by it and by a splendid rock waterfall in one corner of the patio that tumbled into a small pool at its base. Draped by thick green foliage, it reminded her of something out of a fairy tale.

Several polished benches sat near the foot of the waterfall, illuminated by hanging lanterns. Golden-leafed trees formed a canopy overhead, while shelled paths wound through the gate to the gardens on the right, their edges bordered by clusters of heather bursting with fall blooms.

She sat on a bench near the maze entrance, and Katherine and Ellison shared another. Georgina, claiming fatigue, had retired for the night, and Albert stood at the edge of the pool. Clay was on the other side with a foot braced on a rock. He swirled the sherry in his glass and took a drink. When he lowered the goblet, he glanced at Albert. "You know, Chatsworth, you've spoken often about the field of honor, I was just wondering if you still enjoy fencing?"

Albert tossed back his drink and smiled. "Very much."

"Then, perhaps tomorrow we can have a bout."

"Nothing would please me more."

"Albert, perhaps you should reconsider," Ellison suggested. "We've all heard tales of the duke's expertise with swords."

Clay chuckled. "No. You've heard about my pirate days and the way I handled a cutlass. It's not the same. By the way, I didn't see you after we arrived. Where were you?"

Ellison shifted uncomfortably. "In your stables. I'd heard about your thoroughbreds, and I was anxious to see them. Horse-breeding and racing have always held a particular fancy for me."

Amber was incensed by Clay's questions. He wanted to know if Ellison was near the cliffs when the avalanche occurred. How could he possibly suspect her godfather?

"What did you think of my beauties?"

"They were . . ." Ellison searched for words. "Absolutely flawless. I've never seen finer horses, especially the stallion."

"Thank you."

"I'd like to see them, too," Albert added. "The Westshire stud has been the talk of the racing enthusiasts for some time now."

Clay nodded. "I'll be happy to take you on a tour." He smiled. "After our bout."

He glanced at Katherine. "By the way, Lady Chatsworth, did you find your rooms adequate? My valet tells me you left the chamber right after we arrived."

Amber sighed. The man was impossible.

Katherine straightened the folds of her skirt. "Yes, I did. I was curious about what lay on the other side of these great walls"—she waved her hand, indicating the towering stone fence—"so I went to investigate."

Albert wasn't so easily fooled. "And before you ask, *Your Grace,* I was in my room for at least an hour. You may check with your maid, Miranda, if you like."

Clay arched a brow. "She was with you for an hour?"

Albert smiled. "She helped me unpack, and we enjoyed a pleasant conversation."

Amber felt her cheeks warm. An hour with a maid in his room? Albert's behavior could use improvement. Amber's gaze slid to the gate leading to the maze of hedges. From the stories she'd heard, she knew there was only one way in or out. If Clay remained at the entrance, she wondered if she'd be safe to explore on her own. "Do you mind if I go into the maze, Your Grace?"

Clay gave the matter thought, but before he agreed to her request, he glanced around at the others, taking stock of everyone's presence except Georgina's. "Go ahead. But if you're not out within half an hour, I'll have to come after you. More than one person has gotten lost in there." He raised his glass in salute. "But there is a prize if you manage to find the center."

"Are you sure it is safe?" Katherine voiced.

"Quite sure," Clay answered. "There's only one way into the maze, and I'm standing in front of it."

"It still might be wise for someone to go with her."

"No."

Katherine gave an audible sniff. "Come along, Ellison. Escort me to my chamber. Albert, you stay. Make certain Amber gets safely to her room *after she emerges.*"

"That won't be necessary," Clay countered.

"But, Your Grace . . ."

Amber didn't listen to any more as she followed the shell-covered path into the narrow rows of towering hedges. All this bickering over her well-being was beginning to make her ill. Breaking off a shiny leaf, she twirled it between her fingers, enjoying its pungent scent and smooth surface as she walked.

She allowed herself to relax as she went deeper into the maze, past narrow benches lining each path. Off to her right, several more openings cut through breaks in the hedges. She chose one near the center, enjoying the earthy scents of elm and maple and salt air as she turned this way and that—toward what she assumed was the middle.

Unfortunately, it didn't take her long to become thoroughly lost.

Clay pulled his timepiece from his pocket and shook his head. Amber had been in the maze for thirty-five minutes. He glanced around the vacant courtyard. Everyone had retired to their rooms—even Albert, after a little persuasion, well, maybe a lot, leaving only himself . . . and Amber. Smiling, he sauntered in after her. If she was like most of his adventurous guests, she should be in the northeast corner about now.

As he wove his way through the rows, he remembered the first time he'd explored the hedges. His grandfather, Emerson Wingate, the sixteenth duke of Westshire, had brought him here when Clay was five.

Clay had been Emerson Wingate's first male heir, and the old man had lavished all his wisdom and authority on the future duke. He had been enraged when Clay's mother married a pirate and had thought to curb any inherited traits before they arose. For four years, Clay stayed at Westshire, learning etiquette, table manners, studies, horsemanship, fencing, and the pecking order of the aristocracy.

His grandfather had ruled with a firm, sometimes cruel hand, and Clay often sought the security of the courtyard. The old duke had forbidden him to enter the maze, but that didn't stop a curious five-year-old. Of course, he became lost within minutes. The ordeal wouldn't have been so bad if his grandfather hadn't seen fit to teach Clay a lesson in obedience by leaving him in the maze for an entire day . . . and night.

His grandmother had nearly succumbed to vapors, but the old duke refused to relent.

Clay would never forget the absolute terror he felt. However, contrary to what his grandfather hoped to accomplish, Clay went into the maze again and again, determined to learn its secret. The consequences were many and frightening, but he refused to be bested by overgrown shrubs. When he was nine, he entered the maze and discovered the long-awaited prize.

Ever since that day, on every yearly visit, and whenever possible after he was grown, he would steal away to enjoy the maze's secret. But he'd never shown it to anyone, not even the score of guests he'd rescued from the winding depths. Only he and the previous dukes of Westshire knew what lay in the hedges—and it was said, only the true masters of Westshire could conquer the maze.

He found Amber sitting on a bench in the middle of a dead-end path with her arms folded.

She glanced up as he approached. "That was a deucedly long thirty minutes."

Trying to contain a grin, he helped her up. "Did you find the prize?"

"You know very well I didn't."

He slipped an arm around her small waist, liking the feel of her sweet curves against his palm as he guided her down a row. "Too bad. We could have enjoyed it together."

"Why don't you take me now?"

"The secret of the maze is only for those who discover it for themselves." He led her to the end of a hedge, and the intoxicating aroma of her perfume drifted around him. He inhaled quietly, yet deeply, savoring the delicious scent of lilac and Amber. His fingertips tingled where they touched her waist.

"Since you won't show me the secret, you'd better be prepared to rescue me often. You *know* I can't tolerate an unsolved mystery."

Clay laughed. Yes. He did know—and as long as the entrance was guarded, maybe it would keep her from getting too bored. "All right, sweetheart. I'll allow you the privacy of the hedges whenever you like."

"Tomorrow? After breakfast?"

He smiled. "Tomorrow." The second the words were out, an uneasiness swept over him. What if she found the secret, then what?

He let out a breath and urged her toward the house. Even if she did, she probably wouldn't discover *all* of it.

Amber was nervous about sharing a floor with Clay, especially after he locked the door at the head of the stairway and pocketed the key. They were completely alone.

Knowing she had nothing to fear but her own wayward emotions, she sternly refused Clay's offer to help her undress and closed the door between their rooms. She unearthed her white nightdress and shook it out. Still, as she fumbled with the laces down the back of her gown, she remembered the way Clay's hand had felt on her waist. The warmth. The strength. And his scent. He'd smelled so earthy, so wonderfully male, it had taken all her control not to lean into him and bury her nose in his broad chest.

After many thwarted attempts, she managed to free herself of the gown and undergarments and pull on her nightdress. Supremely satisfied, she crawled into bed and blew out the candle, then lay in the darkness.

For several minutes, she stared at the glow of moonlight slipping in through the glass panes, then her eyelids started growing heavier and heavier. . . .

*The door to her room burst open.*

*He stood in the opening, his black clothes blending with the night, his gold earring glinting in the moonlight.*

*"So, my pretty, you thought to escape me. Ha! Never. You belong to me." He pulled her to her feet, then hard against him, his smile a slash of brilliant white in the*

*darkness.* "*You belong to the Black Wind . . . and her captain.*"

He swooped her up and tossed her over his shoulder, then climbed out onto her balcony and swung down to the ground. He ran like the wind, twisting his way through the maze of hedges, then over the high stone wall, giving her barely a jolt as he raced to his longboat anchored near the beach.

Minutes later, the deck of the Black Wind exploded with cheers from his crew as he carried her aboard, then to an enormous cabin decorated in scarlet.

Amber was frightened and excited at the same time. What would he do to her? Did she care?

He lowered her to the bed, then fell on top of her, his mouth hot and hungry as it ravaged hers.

She hit his shoulders. "No! Oh, please, stop!"

He leaped from the bed, his big chest heaving. "What's this? You rouse a man's lust, then refuse his pleasure?"

"We aren't married," she burst out frantically. "I can't let you. . . ."

He laughed evilly. "You can't stop me. This ship and you are mine to command." He jerked her to her feet and kissed her hard, ruthlessly. Over and over again. Her senses spun. Her flesh tingled. Her breasts tightened. Then his lips brushed her ear. "Now take off your clothes, my pretty. Show me my long-awaited prize."

She bolted upright in bed. Her gaze flew frantically around the dark room, and relief washed over her when she realized she'd been dreaming.

Dreaming.

Giving herself a mental scolding for allowing Clay to slip beneath her guard *again*, she drew the covers up to her chin and stared into the darkness, listening to the night sounds.

She thought she heard the soft pad of footsteps, then a light scraping sound.

Of course, it had to be her imagination. Clay was in bed, and no one else could get to this floor without the key that was safely tucked in his pocket.

She snuggled deeper into the quilts, relaxing as she listened to the shrill of crickets and croak of a frog, the slap of waves against the shore. But the soothing sounds couldn't overshadow the sudden feeling that she was completely alone.

# Chapter 8

"Miranda, come to my room. I don't want to leave Amber alone," Clay said as he opened the door.

"I didn't expect you so late. Give me a minute to put something on, and I'll be right up."

"Use the passage," he instructed as he headed again for his chamber.

He stood on his balcony for what seemed like hours before Miranda finally showed—and when she did, she was wearing a silk robe that he recognized as his grandmother's, which was open to reveal a thin sheer night rail. He mentally shook his head. Miranda had never learned the virtue of modesty. "I see you've been raiding Grandmother's chest again."

Miranda shrugged a slender shoulder. "She has no use for the clothes. The old hag's been dead for ten years."

He couldn't argue that point. "What did you learn from Albert?"

"That he's a womanizer. The fool offered me a crown to spend the night with him."

"That much?"

"Very funny. Just for that, I've a good mind not to tell you what I found out."

He sobered instantly. "What?"

"Oh, nothing much," she taunted, playing with the ties on his shirt.

Clay ground his teeth. The woman loved dramatics. "Damn it, Miranda. . . ."

She gave him a cheeky grin. "Being snippy with me isn't going to get you anywhere. You should know that by now."

"All right. I'm sorry. Now, *please* tell me what he said."

She patted his cheek. "Much better." She sat down and straightened the folds of her night rail, then primly folded her hands. "Did you know that Albert was betrothed to an heiress his father had chosen *and* that the woman died in a mysterious accident?"

Clay felt something ugly move through his middle. "What kind of accident?"

"A fall down a staircase. Rather convenient, don't you think? Since he told me he had no intention of marrying her."

"Do you think he killed the woman?"

"Albert doesn't strike me as the sort, but you never know."

Clay crossed his arms and stared out over the maze, trying to imagine what Albert could possibly gain from Amber's death. Not one thing came to mind. Still . . . "Miranda, I hate to ask it of you, but could you spend more time with him? Find out everything you can?"

She rose and came up behind him. Her slender finger trailed down his spine. "It'll cost you."

He turned, smiling. "Name it, sweet. Everything I have is yours."

Her beautiful green eyes softened. "How about a hug to begin with?"

He drew her into his arms, loving her so much he ached. She had been shunned and shamed and abused all of her life, and if there was anyway he could make up for it, he would. Drawing her protectively closer, he placed a light kiss on her lips. "I wish—"

A quick intake of breath stopped his words. He whipped around to see Amber standing in the doorway.

"I-I heard voices, and I thought . . . I . . . Oh, God." She clamped a hand over her mouth and raced back inside.

"Amber, wait!" Clay started after her, but Miranda caught his arm. "Don't. She's too upset to listen right now. Give her time to get over the shock."

"She doesn't understand."

"I know. But for now, it's probably better that way. Besides, a little jealousy won't hurt her."

"You're a shrew."

She grinned. "I know. But you love me anyway."

Amber didn't sleep the rest of the night. She spent most of it on her balcony, crying, cursing Clayton Cordell—and herself for letting him get under her skin again.

But even now, with the morning sun brightening the walls of the manor, the image of him in that woman's arms cut into her like a razor.

She wished with all her heart that she could hate him. Desperately wanting to lose herself in a book as she always had in the mornings at home, she rubbed her temples.

Something rattled a thick wall of ivy clinging to the side of the house directly below her.

Startled, she raised her head, then leaned over the rail, trying to see what caused the movement.

Albert's head popped up through the foliage. "Hello, gorgeous. I brought you something." He was holding on to a ladder with one hand, but she couldn't see what was in the other.

"What are you doing? For heaven's sake, Albert, if Clay should see you—"

"He already has," Clay grated from behind her.

Amber stiffened.

Albert let out a soft groan. "Clay, you've got the wrong idea." He held up a book with a drawing of a pirate's chest on the cover. "Amber likes to read in the mornings, and I . . ."

Clay didn't look in the least convinced as he approached the rail. "You've got three seconds to start down the ladder."

Albert's eyes narrowed. "Damn it, Clay, you can't keep her a prisoner like this."

"Time's up." He placed a finger on the top of the ladder—and pushed.

"Don't!" Amber cried.

Albert leaped from the ladder just before it crashed into a lilac bush.

She bent over, trying to see if he was all right. "Albert? Can you hear me? Are you hurt?"

He stood, brushing off his clothes. "Only my pride." He glared up at Clay. "But I'm definitely looking forward to our fencing bout today."

"So am I," Clay returned.

With a mock salute, Albert straightened the lapels on his coat and stalked across the empty patio.

Clay lifted her away from the rail. "If I catch him sneaking around like that again, Amber, I'm going to lock him up."

She jerked away from him. "Don't touch me, you, you *blackguard*. Albert is—"

"Spare me his list of attributes."

"It's a good deal longer than yours," she spat. "And, considering the horrid way you treat him, I don't know why you don't just send him away."

He glanced again at where Albert had been. "I wish

I could, but I want him where I can keep an eye on him." He studied her for a moment. "What were you doing out here?"

"Cursing you."

The corner of his mouth quirked. "I see." Taking her arm, he led her to the small table. "I've ordered tea. It should arrive soon."

She pulled free of his hold. "I'm perfectly capable of walking by myself."

"Amber, about last ni—"

The door opened and the maid she'd seen him kissing on the balcony came strolling into the room, carrying a tray. She was wearing a drab gray woolen gown, but the buttons down the front were open to her bustline, revealing a great deal of flesh. She leaned low over the table to set the tray down, allowing Clay an unobstructed view of her dipping neckline.

He arched a brow and stared at jiggling breasts. "Thank you, Miranda."

The huskiness in his tone made Amber blush. Then the woman's name struck her. This was the maid who spent an hour with Albert having an innocent conversation? Ha!

"Should I pour, Your Grace?" Miranda asked in a throaty voice.

Clay dragged his gaze from her bosom. "No. That will be all . . . for now."

The maid gave him a sultry smile, then, completely ignoring Amber, she sauntered inside, her hips swaying seductively.

Amber wanted to rip her hair out. She took a sip of tea to stop any vicious words she might let slip. She would not let Clay know how much his relationship with the maid hurt. When she was sure she was composed enough to speak rationally, she set her cup down. "I'm tired of being closed up. I want to explore the house today."

"I'll give you a tour."

"I'd rather see it by myself."

"No."

"Fine. When can we go?"

"Whenever you like."

"Now?"

"We wouldn't get past the bedchamber with you dressed in your nightclothes."

The man's *mind* never got past the bedchamber, as far as she could tell. "I'll change."

"You'll need my help."

About as much as she needed the pox. "I'll manage on my own, but thank you, anyway."

He popped a piece of scone into his mouth and washed it down with tea, then glanced at his timepiece. "In that case, I'll send up your bath . . . and see you in a few hours." With a slight curve to his lips, he strolled into the house.

Wishing she were big enough to wipe that smirk off his face, and hoping she could maintain her composure in his presence today, Amber finished her own tea and went inside.

The amount of time she would need not only to bathe but with all the layers of petticoats, tabs, laces, corset, and stockings she had yet to place on her person was staggering at best.

Sighing, she opened her trunk.

After unearthing a clean chemise and corset, she sat on the bed and waited until the servants arrived with her bath water.

Clay's elderly maid, Isabel, a no-nonsense woman with a narrow mouth and stiff spine, had two young boys fill the tub, then all of them promptly left.

Wishing desperately for her own maid, or at least Georgina, Amber pulled off her nightclothes and sank into the steaming, lilac-scented water and mentally went over all she needed to do in order to dress properly. Curse Clayton Cordell, anyway. Why wouldn't he let Georgina help?

Amber had just finished washing and rinsing her hair when she heard someone in the room. Had Isabel taken pity on her? Or had Clay relented and allowed Georgina to help? Praying it was the latter, she turned.

Miranda stood in the doorway with her arms folded. "His Grace told me to help you."

Amber stared at the woman whose eyes she'd like to scratch out. "That won't be necessary."

"I'm afraid it is, your ladyship. I would never disobey the duke's command."

Amber wondered if Clay had "commanded" her to come to his room last night. The thought made the muscles in her stomach tighten. "I don't want your help. Now go."

"But—"

*"Go,"* Amber hissed.

"Very well, your ladyship." She opened the door, but just before she stepped out, Amber could have sworn she saw the woman smile.

Stepping from the tub, Amber furiously yanked a towel around her, then, her hands trembling with anger, she reached for her clothes.

An hour later, she had managed to get into most of her garments, but she hadn't been able to tie the laces at the back of her dark wine-colored gown. Wanting to stomp her foot in frustration, she tried again to reach the laces.

"Amber!" Clay's voice rumbled from the door. "Aren't you dressed yet?"

Knowing she'd never be able to fasten her gown on her own, and refusing to ask him to help, she snatched up her jacket and pulled it on over the gaping material.

She hurriedly ran a brush through her slightly damp hair, then approached the door. "I . . . I'm ready."

He swung the panel open and gave her a quick

inspection. "You would have been ready a helluva lot sooner if you'd let Miranda help you."

She jabbed her hands onto her hips. "As you can see, I managed quite well on my own."

"And wasted half the day," he mumbled, motioning her toward the hall.

Ignoring his remark, she followed him down the corridor.

When they reached the second level, he gestured with a wave of his hand. "There are twelve bedchambers on this floor. Your companions occupy four of them."

"Four?"

He nodded. "The Chatsworths wanted separate rooms. Apparently, they don't share a bedchamber."

For some reason, that saddened her. If she were married to a man she loved, she'd never want to be separated from him. For the first time, she wondered about Katherine and Ellison's marriage. Had it been a love match? Or, like so many other *ton* weddings, a merging of wealth and station? A business arrangement.

The thought made her uncomfortable. That was the type of marriage she had planned. She and Albert would have a very special, but platonic, relationship. It couldn't be any other way. She could never love another man the way she had once loved Clay.

Angry with herself for allowing the thought to slip in, she directed her attention to her surroundings, to the things she'd been too upset to notice when she arrived.

The entire second story sat in a square with a railed walkway leading to doors on every side. The center was open to overlook the massive stairway and entry below. It was an excellent arrangement for extended entertaining.

"Do you want to see inside the chambers?"

"Not right now."

They descended the wide stairs, and Amber admired the plush burgundy carpeting. It was an elegant contrast to the white walls and gleaming, brass-topped banisters.

Life-size brass figurines of Roman women in scant dress lined the marbled entry that had several doors and two halls leading off the main foyer.

Clay opened the first door on the right. "This is the library, and should you want to make use of it, I'll bring you down any time you like. There's quite a selection acquired by the Westshire dukes over several centuries. And, it's another of the few places you'll be safe."

She surveyed the room, wondering why he considered it safe. "Any volumes on pirates?" She could have bitten off her tongue. She hadn't meant to say that out loud.

He smiled. "I've contributed a few—which probably has my grandfather spinning in his grave about now." He closed the door. "Come on, I'll show you the study."

Amber was too embarrassed to look at him. Instead, she concentrated intently on the layout of the house. The door beside the library led to the study, the ones across went to an elegant dining room and parlor. At the end was the ballroom, and next to that a hall led to a large, airy cookhouse outside. Another corridor went to a chamber set aside for washing and mending clothing. But the best room was across from that. The gallery.

If it hadn't been for Clay's impatience, Amber could have spent the entire day in there, gazing at his magnificent ancestors. The Westshire males bore a striking resemblance to each other—especially their great height and muscular builds.

"Excuse me, Your Grace," a woman's voice purred from the doorway.

Amber swung around to see the sultry Miranda standing in the opening.

"What is it?" he asked.

"The guests. They've asked for tea in the courtyard and wanted you and her ladyship to join them."

Although her words were proper enough, Amber couldn't help but notice the message in Miranda's eyes—the one that said she wished they'd all disappear so she'd have Clay to herself.

"Tell them we'll be along shortly."

She curtsied low, causing her neckline to gape. "Yes, Your Grace."

His eyes grew bright with warmth as he smiled at her—the blackguard—and, when she left, he watched her walk down the hallway.

"I'm ready anytime you are," Amber said with only a hint of the peevishness she felt.

He arched a brow at her. "What? You mean you're actually going to tear yourself away from the likenesses of my illustrious relatives? The one's you've been gushing over for the last hour?"

She could have sworn she detected the smallest trace of jealousy in his tone—over paintings, for goodness' sakes. The thought made her smile. "For now. But tell me again about James Wingate."

As they walked toward the courtyard, Amber noticed a hard set to Clay's jaw. "What more do you want to hear? I've already told you my great-great-grandfather was responsible for at least two dozen bastard children, a score of mistresses, and he was suspected of murdering his first wife so he could marry a second, much wealthier one."

"Do you think it's true?"

"Which? That he was a murderer, a philanderer, or an opportunist?"

"A murderer."

He led her outside. "No. But that was his only redeeming quality."

"He had the maze constructed, didn't he?"

"Yes. In fact, family legend has it that most of his illicit affairs were carried on in the midst of those hedges. Supposedly, he'd entice a woman he wanted to bed to explore the maze, then, after a short span of time, go in to 'rescue' her."

"Much like you did for me."

"No. He seduced the women before he brought them out."

A flush rose to her cheeks, and she tried very hard not to imagine Clay and herself in those hedges.

"Amber, child. At last," Katherine called as they walked into the courtyard. "I feared we might never see you again the way the duke keeps you hidden." She gave Clay an irritated look, then hurried to embrace her.

Georgina, too, gave her a warm hug. "I've missed you, love."

Albert was behind Georgina, none the worse for wear from his earlier mishap. "Good morning again, gorgeous." He lifted her hand and kissed her fingers.

Ellison cleared his throat. "It's good to see you've fared well, Amber."

"His Grace has taken excellent care of me."

"Doggedly so," Albert mumbled as he slipped an arm around her waist.

"Come, come. Sit," Katherine instructed. "The maid is just about to serve tea." She wedged Albert out of the way and took Amber's arm. "Tell me about your room. There must be an incredible view from up there."

"It's magnificent," Amber admitted as she sat down, then she glanced around. "Where's Poo?"

"The butler put him in my room last night," Georgina said. "I'd planned to have him taken to yours today."

"Thank you. I miss his company."

Katherine fingered one of Amber's loose curls.

"Child, what has happened to your hair?" She directed a stern gaze at Clay. "Is there no one in your employ who you will allow to tend the child, Your Grace? Her appearance is appalling."

Georgina gasped.

Amber wanted to sink through the bench.

"Amber's hair is beautiful," Clay grated in a tight voice.

"When it is styled properly, yes."

"Always," Clay and Albert said in unison.

Ellison coughed lightly.

Albert scowled at his mother for several tense seconds, then turned to Clay. "I believe we were going to try our hand at fencing today." He gestured to the wide expanse of stone patio. "Shall we?"

Clay hadn't taken his eyes from Katherine. At last, he did so and nodded to Albert. "Ask Bowling to bring the swords."

While Albert was gone, an older maid set up a small table and placed trays of sweet rolls, scones, jams, biscuits, and various blends of tea on the linen covering.

Instantly, Amber's thoughts drifted to what happened at the inn, and she was suddenly afraid to eat or drink anything.

Clay poured her a cup of tea, and as he handed it to her, he said so only she could hear, "It's all right, sweetheart. The food's been well protected."

Relieved, she gave him a shaky smile, then, wanting to lighten the moment, she teased, "What? You're not going to sample it first?"

"Not this time." The corners of his eyes crinkled. "I don't care for lemon tea the way you do."

Surprise held her motionless. How on earth had he known that? She opened her mouth to voice the question, but Albert and Bowling returned at that moment with the fencing swords.

As Clay and Albert took their places for the match,

Amber couldn't help comparing them. Against Albert's fairness, Clay was a dark, smoldering presence with his snug black breeches and loose white shirt. His hair glinted like dark, polished cherrywood, and she wondered if those red highlights contributed to the volatile temper she'd seen him display over the years.

Unbidden, a childhood memory of her father came to her. Her father had viciously reprimanded her in front of Clay and the servants for riding so recklessly, then angrily sent her to her room. As she had climbed the stairs, she'd heard Clay's enraged voice, the crash of glass against a wall, and his impassioned threat to kidnap Amber if William ever publicly humiliated her again.

She recalled Clay's fury the day she and Albert were fencing, and Albert's sword slipped, drawing blood on her wrist. Before she was able to stop him, Clay had grabbed Albert by the shirt and slammed him against the wall. Only her grip on Clay's arm had saved Albert from a deadly blow. An odd thought hit her. Did Albert still take exception to that . . . even now?

Her gaze shifted to Albert as he raised his sword for the mock battle. He had taken off his coat, revealing a white shirt, similar to the style Clay wore. Until this moment, she'd never realized how muscular Albert was. His shoulders were broad, his arms well defined, his hips trim. Without her even realizing, he'd grown up. For the first time, she saw him as he truly was. A man.

The clank of metal startled her, and she focused on the swordplay.

Clay lunged.

Albert retreated, then pivoted to strike from the side.

The move was anticipated. Clay blocked, pirouetted, and lunged again. Clay appeared relaxed, while Albert was overly intent on the battle.

Clay whirled and blocked another jab.

Helplessly, Amber became entranced by the play of muscles in his strong legs, by the swiftness of his moves, and by the way his firm buttocks tightened when he dodged a thrust.

Suddenly the day turned very, very warm, and she averted her gaze, concerned by the overpowering feelings moving through her. She didn't want to feel anything for him.

Suddenly a scream split the air.

"Amber, look out!" Clay roared.

Amber jerked her head up—and saw the blade of a sword coming straight at her.

# Chapter 9

Something slammed into Amber's arm, knocking her to the side, just as the blade slashed through the air over her head.

"Amber! Oh, Jesus, Amber, are you all right?" Albert dropped to his knees beside her and pulled her into his arms. He was shaking so hard, it scared her more. "My God. The sword slipped out of my hand. I almost killed you."

Clay wedged him out of the way and hauled her to her feet. His long fingers remained curled around her upper arms as he quickly examined her from head to foot.

Amber trembled. The terror of moments ago caused her stomach to churn with nausea.

Satisfied that she was unharmed, Clay eased his hold. "She's not hurt."

Cradling her next to him, he turned to Katherine. "Lady Chatsworth, you are to be commended. If you hadn't pushed Amber out of the way when I dislodged the sword from Albert's hand, Amber could have been . . ."

Katherine trembled visibly as she clung to a sobbing Georgina, but she didn't speak. She didn't look as if she could.

Albert kicked his sword, sending the metal clanking across the stone patio. "I'll never lay hand to another blade. Never."

Amber's heart went out to him, but her voice was still too shaky to speak.

Ellison approached his son. "Had you a better grip on your sword, the accident might never have happened."

"That doesn't change the fact that I could have killed her," Albert grated.

Amber finally calmed enough to speak. "But you didn't." She reached down and took his hand. "It was an unfortunate mishap, but everyone is fine. Stop punishing yourself."

He kissed her fingers. "I'm so sorry."

"Don't be. Now, get up from there. You look silly sitting on the ground."

Albert came to his feet.

Another quiver shot through Amber, she took a breath to calm herself, then glanced at her cousin who was leaning heavily into Katherine. Georgina's face was so pale.

Her cousin was such a sensitive person. Moving out of Clay's hold, she put an unsteady arm around Georgina's narrow shoulders. "I'm fine, Georgina. Truly, I am."

The frail shoulders quivered. "I was so frightened. I-I don't think I could go on without you." Tears trickled down her cheeks.

Katherine took Georgina's arm. "Come with me, dear. I am sure a short repast would do us both good."

Georgina hesitated.

"Go on," Amber urged. "Get some rest. I'll see you at dinner." She touched Katherine's arm. "And thank you for what you did."

Her godmother simply acknowledged with a dip of her head.

When the women left, Ellison poured himself a cup of tea and sat down. "Your swordsmanship is outstanding, Your Grace. I'd often heard tales of your expertise, but, in truth, I thought they were fabricated."

Clay joined Ellison at the table. "The tales are exaggerated." He filled his own cup and sat, unable to hide the relief in his eyes as he glanced at Amber, then back to Ellison. "Even I couldn't fend off twenty men while cradling a woman in one arm."

Albert shoved his hands into his pockets. "I believe the story said there were twenty-one."

Ellison snorted. "Such nonsense."

Clay took a sip from his cup. "Oh, I don't know, Ellison. I've held my share of women. I just don't recall sword fighting while doing so."

"Your Grace, please," Ellison scolded. "Remember there is a lady present."

"Oh, for heaven's sake, Father," Albert countered. "Amber has heard these tales a hundred times. And I'm sure his true experiences went far beyond the minor incidents we've heard about."

Amber had the feeling that Albert would give most anything to know about those other experiences.

"Nonetheless," Ellison insisted. "A true gentleman would not speak of such in front of a lady."

Albert studied his father, but Amber couldn't tell if he was pleased or angry over the comment. Things were always so volatile between them, she never knew what to think.

Clay leaned forward and braced his arms on his knees, but he didn't say anything.

Still, Amber could see the anger brightening his

eyes. He didn't like being reminded of his lapses in decorum. He knew his station as the duke of West-shire and his extreme wealth were the only reasons he was tolerated by the *ton*.

But she knew, too, that he'd never want to change what he was. He had cherished his days aboard ship . . . and he'd never been able to hide his satisfaction at seeing the inflexible aristocracy forced to accept him.

Deep down, it gave her satisfaction, too. Not one member of the *ton* was as truthful or loyal or honorable as Clay.

Uncomfortable with the direction of her thoughts, Amber rose. "Your Grace? I believe I'd like to make another attempt at the maze."

"I'll go with you," Albert offered.

"No." The harsh tone of Clay's voice told them all there would be no discussion on the matter.

But Albert tried. "You can't hold her prisoner like some common criminal."

"I will if that's what it takes to keep her safe."

Albert clenched his hands. "This has gone far enough. . . ."

Amber didn't want to listen to any more. She touched Clay's arm. "Thirty minutes?"

He checked his timepiece. "Thirty minutes."

She strolled through the gate, and when she came to the row where several paths led in different directions, she took the farthest one. As she walked, her thoughts turned to what had just happened. Had it been an accident, in truth? Of course it had, she quickly admonished. Albert would never hurt her. Never. Forcing the unwelcome thoughts aside, and vowing to put the accident out of her thoughts, she concentrated on locating the center of the maze.

After a score of minutes, she came to a dead end. She stood there in frustration and thought about returning by the same route—if she could remember it. No, she decided. Clay would come for her before she even made it to the main row.

Besides, it would serve him right to have to look for her. He was the one being pigheaded about not showing her the maze's secret.

Gathering her skirts, she sat down on a narrow bench to wait, but a sudden prickling sensation tripped up her spine. It was as if she could feel someone close. Someone watching her.

Fear tightened her flesh, and she rose. She had to find a way out of here.

Footsteps sounded just ahead of her.

Her fear turned to panic. Oh, God.

Clay stepped out of the hedges, and she almost wept with relief.

But it was short lived. He was very upset.

"Damn it, Amber. Don't you ever do things the way normal people do?"

"What do you mean?" she said, trying to keep her voice steady. She didn't want him to know what a frightened mouse she'd been.

"I've been searching these wretched hedges for the last half hour. How the hell did you end up here?"

"I'm not sure."

"Well, you've made a complete circle. You're only twenty yards from the main entrance. Since I never imagined you'd be that close, I've been all over the maze."

"Even to the center?"

"Yes."

She was dying to know what was there. "Take me."

A dark brow arched. "I wonder how many of James Wingate's women said 'take me' to him in here."

Her tongue stuck to her teeth or her mouth would have fallen open. "Clayton Cordell. You know very well that's not what I meant."

"Do I? You were extremely fascinated by my way-ward ancestor and his amorous adventures."

"I was not. I was merely . . . intrigued."

"Were you?" He approached her slowly, then slid his hands around her waist. They were so close, she could feel his minty breath touch her cheek. "Or were you wondering what it would be like to make love in the depths of a maze?"

She blushed, remembering her earlier thoughts, then lied emphatically. "N-No."

"Sure you were." He sent her a lazy smile. "And I'm damned tempted to show you."

"Clay, I—" Oh, merciful heavens. She *wanted* him to.

Clay stared down at Amber, at her wide, wary eyes, and damned himself for baiting her again. This wasn't one of his mistresses he could play games with.

This was Amber Sinclair, the woman he'd vowed to protect.

He lowered his hands from her waist and stepped away. "Come on. Let's go."

The relief that softened her eyes only made him angrier at himself.

When they emerged from the hedges, Albert was the only one in the courtyard.

He stood in front of the waterfall with his arms crossed, his mouth set in a grim line, his eyes filled with suspicion as he stared at each of them in turn, then fixed on Clay. "The maze must be very complicated." He glanced at his timepiece. "Why else would it take you nearly an hour to find Amber and return?"

Anger hit Clay swift and hard. The strutting peacock, who the hell did he think he was making accusations like that? Clay determinedly controlled the urge to flatten Albert's nose and settled for taunting him instead. "It's not complicated at all, Chatsworth. In fact, it was a very"—he smiled down at Amber as if they shared an intimate secret—"a very pleasurable experience, and we were reluctant to end it."

Albert drew his hands into fists at his side, nearly crushing the watch he held. "Were it not for your station, *Your Grace,* I would give you the thrashing you deserve for such insolence."

"Don't let that stop you."

Amber pulled away from him and planted her hands on her hips, her eyes bright with anger as she faced her friend. "Then am I to assume, Albert, that I am without honor?" Her tone barely concealed her fury. "That I would mindlessly wilt beneath a man's amorous advances?"

That would be the day, Clay thought morosely.

Albert fumbled for words. "Amber, you don't understand. I meant . . . well, you were . . ."

She held up her hand. "I understand perfectly. Now, if you'll excuse me, I'd like to return to my room." Without another word, she marched toward the house.

Trying not to laugh at Albert's miserable expression, Clay kept his features blank as he went after Amber, but inwardly he was applauding.

By the time he caught up with her in the ballroom, she was in a temper. She swung on him, those eyes still flashing, her stance rigid. "Curse you, Clayton Cordell. How dare you make Albert think we had a rendezvous in the maze." She poked his chest. "That *anything* untoward happened."

She was adorable when she was like this. "Forgive me, sweetheart, but I just can't help goading him. He's so easy to anger."

"Well, I wish you wouldn't do it at my expense."

Trying to contain his humor, Clay took her arm and guided her toward the stairs. "I'll try, but you're almost as easy to anger as he is."

She sighed. "I know. But you don't have to take advantage of the fact."

"As I said, I'll try."

"Rogue."

He threw his head back and laughed. She was absolutely priceless.

They made a stop in the library before they went upstairs, then Amber settled herself on her balcony to read Fanny Burney's novel *Cecilia*.

Clay took a seat at his desk, where he could see her through the open doors and began Sheridan's farce *The Critic*.

They read silently for some time before he heard a distant knock on the door at the end of the hall.

Amber looked up and started to rise, but he waved her down and went to answer it.

Miranda stood on the other side, wearing a soft cotton blouse that molded her generous breasts to the point of indecency. She wasn't wearing petticoats beneath her skirt, and the fabric clung to the shape of her well-rounded hips.

Her green eyes twinkled when they met his, and she licked her full lower lip. "Cook sent me. Said to tell you dinner would be served in half an hour." Her gaze drifted down his front and up again. "And to see if you needed anything in the meantime."

The invitation couldn't have been clearer if she'd written it down. Clay mentally shook his head. The temptress. She was bent on causing trouble, and just when Amber was being civil to him again.

"I don't need anything at the moment." He gave her a warning look that promised retribution. "But, I *will* see you later."

Miranda smiled provocatively. "Anytime, Your Grace."

When he closed the door, he turned to see Amber standing in her doorway.

"A rendezvous, Your Grace? Whatever will you do with me while you're about it?" Her sarcasm was as clear as Miranda's invitation had been. She was jealous.

Ridiculously pleased by the notion, Clay couldn't

help taunting her. As if giving the matter great thought, he rubbed his chin. "I suppose you could stay on your balcony while we . . ." He was talking to thin air.

Amber had stalked away.

Amber was so furious with Clay by the time they reached the dining room, she could have broken horseshoes with her bare teeth.

"Amber, child. Come, sit by me." Katherine patted the seat of a chair between her and Albert.

Well, that suited her just fine. Ignoring the chair Clay had pulled out for her beside him, she skirted the table and took a seat.

Clay glared.

Knowing that whoever said revenge wasn't sweet had lied, she turned all her attention on Albert. "I miss London terribly, don't you?" she said just loud enough for Clay to hear. "We used to have such wonderful times going to balls and the theater."

Albert nearly choked on his wine. He quickly set his glass down and dabbed his mouth with a napkin. His puzzled gaze met hers. "We did? I mean, yes, we did."

Amber grinned and lowered her gaze to her plate. Out of the corner of her eye she saw Clay's hand tighten on his glass.

A noise caused her to glance up.

Miranda, decently clothed for once, approached carrying a platter of roasted pheasant. Instantly, Clay's manner changed. He took the tray, his fingers lingering on hers a moment more than necessary, then he gave her a sensual smile.

The maid beamed as she headed back toward the cookhouse.

Amber saw red, but fortunately, she was saved from making a scathing remark by the arrival of Georgina.

Georgina scanned the table, and her gaze came to

rest on Amber, then softened with the warmth of an adoring mother's. "You look well, love."

"Aside from a little boredom, I'm fine."

"Maybe a stroll would help," Albert suggested, then hardened his tone. "That is, if His Grace will permit it."

"No." Clay answered firmly.

Amber bristled. "There's not a blessed thing wrong with going for a walk within sight of your guards."

Their eyes held in a battle of will, then Clay stabbed a knife into the pheasant. "Fine."

"Am I late?" A harried Ellison asked as he finished tying his cravat and took a seat on the other side of Katherine.

"As far as I can tell," Clay muttered, "you're right on time." He carved off a slice of white meat.

Miranda and the pair of young boys who'd filled Amber's tub earlier came in carrying trays laden with fruit, cheese, bread, shellfish, and steaming potatoes.

Amber watched Miranda send Clay secret smiles as she set various bowls on the table.

Something ugly slithered through her, and she forced herself to lower her gaze.

Talk ceased as everyone began filling their plates.

Amber had no appetite. She placed tiny portions on the china in front of her, then only picked at those. She could feel Clay watching her, but she ignored him.

Katherine rambled on throughout the meal about a new Paris fashion book she'd received shortly before they left for Westshire, but Amber barely heard a word she said. She was too intent on considering all the ways she could inflict pain on the duke of Westshire.

Near the end of the meal, Clay summoned Miranda and whispered something in her ear. The maid licked her red lips and smiled. "Of course, Your Grace. Two hours."

Amber felt as if someone had plunged a knife into her heart. In two hours, Clay and Miranda would— She set her napkin aside and came to her feet. "How about that stroll, Albert?"

He glanced up, then down at his half-full plate. Shrugging, he rose. "Sure."

Clay stared as they walked arm in arm out the door.

"What's going on?" Albert asked as they emerged from the rear gate of the courtyard.

"Everything."

He chuckled. "Want to expound on that?"

"He's having an affair."

Albert nearly stumbled on the shell path. "Who?"

"Clay."

"*With* who?"

"Miranda."

Albert snorted. "I don't believe it."

"Why not?"

"He only sees you." He lifted her hand to help her around a rock jutting into the path. "He's been in love with you for as long as I can remember."

Something inside Amber's chest kicked. "Did he tell you that?"

"No. But I'm not blind. The way he looks at you says it all."

She wished she could believe him, but she couldn't. If Clay had been in love with her, he would have married her long ago.

"You're mistaken." A cool, salty breeze feathered a lock of hair against her cheek, and she shoved it over her shoulder. "Besides, if he was, he wouldn't have stayed away for four years."

"He still sent you presents."

Amber recalled the packages in her secret chest that she'd refused to open. "He's brought me presents since I was five years old. That doesn't mean he's in love with me, it just means he considers us friends.

Like you and I do." She lifted her skirt to avoid a clump of weeds. "I'm the one who saw more into our relationship all those years ago, not him."

Albert guided her across the sand to a flat boulder and sat down, then pulled her down beside him. "I think you're wrong, but I also think something about you frightens him."

She couldn't imagine Clay being afraid of anything, especially her. "Yes," she teased, "I'm such a fierce person, I can understand why he's scared."

Albert smiled. "He's not afraid of you in that way, imp. But I do think he's afraid of admitting to himself that he's in love with you."

"You're certainly defensive of him, considering how much you dislike him."

"I don't dislike him, but I'm not going to let him hurt you again, either."

She sent him a smile, marveling at how attractive he was, how kind. Her thoughts drifted to the problems awaiting her at Markland, and she decided that now was as good a time as any to approach Albert with her proposition. "Albert, will you marry me?"

His head whipped around. *"What?"* He lunged to his feet and moved several steps away from her, as if she had a contagious disease. "Have you lost your mind?"

She'd expected him to be surprised—not horrified. Feeling quite insulted, she rose. "Perhaps I didn't say that right." She explained about Markland and how she was afraid of Ellison taking charge and how she didn't want to live with his parents and that she knew Albert wanted to run one of his own.

Albert shoved his fingers through his tousled blond curls and walked away. He stood with his back to her for several seconds, then at last turned. "I can't marry you. I . . ." He searched for words. "I . . . I'm in love with someone else."

"Who?"

His eyes shifted from hers. "Ummm . . . you don't know her. I just met her a few weeks ago. Right before you returned from France. I . . . haven't had a chance to tell you about her yet."

"So tell me now."

"No. It's . . . too soon. We'll talk about it another time."

Albert wasn't a very good liar, and she knew this 'girl' didn't exist. "But what about Markland?"

"Just because I won't marry you doesn't mean I won't help. Somehow I'll convince Father to leave me in charge. Don't worry. You and Markland will be just fine."

"Unless I'm married, I can't live at Markland."

He shifted uneasily. "We'll figure out something."

She wasn't convinced. Something about his attitude really bothered her. "Albert, is there something offensive about me?"

He chuckled, a deep, vibrating sound. "How in heaven's name could you even think that? You're one of the kindest, most beautiful women I know."

Then why wouldn't he agree to marry her? She didn't believe for one second that there was another woman. He would have told her before now. Albert never kept important things from her.

Suddenly angry with all men, she headed toward the path. "I think I'd better get back." Leaving Albert standing by the surf, she marched toward the manor.

When she saw Clay waiting at the head of the path, she became even angrier. He had been watching them and was even now probably waiting to walk her back. She stopped in front of him. "There's no need to escort me, Your Grace." Whisking her skirts to one side, she sidestepped around him.

The soft thud of footsteps on the grass told her he was following.

She hurried ahead, desperate to escape. Desperate for a few second alone. She raced into her room and locked the door, then rushed to do the same to the connecting ones.

Strolling onto the balcony, she leaned on the rail and stared at the gardens below, trying to calm her volatile emotions.

A loud pounding thundered from inside. "Amber! Damn it, Amber. Open this door!"

She defiantly ignored him.

A horrendous crash exploded inside the chamber, and a second later, Clay stormed onto the balcony. He spun her around and gripped her shoulders hard. "Don't you *ever* do that again." He shook her. "Did it ever occur to you that someone might have sneaked up here while we were gone? That the murderer could have been waiting for you? They could have—" He jerked her against him. "Damn you."

His mouth came down on hers hard, ruthlessly.

Emotions Amber wasn't prepared for tumbled over her. How many times had she dreamed of kissing him again? Of being held in those strong arms? She felt herself wanting to melt against him.

Then thoughts of Miranda slipped in, and she jerked away. "Get away from me."

"What the hell's wrong with you?" He stared at her for several seconds, then a knowing light entered his eyes. "Miranda. Of course."

No matter how hard she tried, she couldn't stop the words. "Don't mention that woman's name. And you can rest assured, I won't interfere in your rendezvous *two hours from now*. However, I would ask that you take her elsewhere. Lock me in if you must, but I will not stay on the balcony and listen to you—"

He chuckled. "Oh, Amber. Miranda and I aren't having a clandestine meeting. She's bringing a tray of food."

"What?"

"When I saw how little you ate at dinner, I asked her to bring one up in a couple of hours."

"Then you're not . . . ?"

"No, sweetheart. I may be a lot of things, but I'm not insensitive enough to bed a woman in your presence."

"But I saw you kiss her, and you said—"

"The kiss was innocent, and I was baiting you earlier." He gave her a slanted smile. "I like to see the way your eyes flash when you're angry."

"Are they flashing now?"

"No."

"They should be," she said softly, then soundly kicked him.

His laughter rang out as she grabbed her book from the wrought-iron table and marched into the bed-chamber. Stepping over the pieces of broken wood that had splintered from the connecting doors, she flopped down at the desk and gripped the tome so hard her hands ached. She couldn't stop the tiny flood of pleasure that seeped in. Clay wasn't going to meet Miranda.

Not in two hours, anyway.

Clay strolled through the room and left for a short time, then returned to retrieve his book. With a smile still curving his lips, he went into his own room.

Amber tried to read, but she couldn't stay focused. Finally, she closed her eyes and leaned her head against the back of the chair. Soothing sounds surrounded her, the low twitter of birds, the distant crash of waves against shore, the rustle of paper as Clay turned the pages of his book. She felt herself drifting off. . . .

*"Which wench do ye claim for your own, Captain?"*

*The dark, wickedly handsome captain studied each of them, then held out his hand. But she couldn't tell if it was to her . . . or Miranda.*

A knock on the outer door jerked Amber to her senses.

Clay answered it, then returned a moment later, carrying Poo's cage. "I believe this belongs to you."

"*Awk.* Make for home, mate. Make for home."

Amber set the cage on the desk and glared at Clay over the top of the wires. "I'd love to go home, Poo. But the captain of the *Black Wind* is holding us prisoner."

"*Awk.* Run the blighter through. Run the blighter through."

"My sentiments exactly." She opened the cage door to let him climb on her finger.

"Amber, don't let him—"

Clay's voice was cut off by the excited flutter of wings.

Poo flew out the open glass doors.

"Poo!" she cried. "Oh, Poo. Come back." She hurried to the balcony—and got there just in time to see the parrot soar down into the gardens below.

"Bloody hell," Clay bellowed from behind her. "Stay here. I'll get him." He rushed inside, then a second later, she heard the outer door close and the lock click into place.

Anxiously, she leaned over the rail, keeping an eye on Poo and waiting for Clay to appear. When he finally emerged into the courtyard, she pointed frantically to where the bird had landed in a lilac bush.

Clay had just about reached him when Poo took flight again.

Amber watched to see where he landed, then yelled to Clay. "He's in the back, in the heather."

Clay sprinted toward the back of the garden. By the time he got there, Poo had flown up into a maple tree.

Undaunted, Clay grabbed a limb and swung himself up, disappearing into the thick, golden leaves. He emerged seconds later, holding Poo.

Gracefully dropping to the ground, he held up his

hand to show her the bird, then sent her a wink as he strolled back to the house.

Amber couldn't help smiling. It was so hard to stay angry with him. She leaned on the rail and braced her chin on her palms, enjoying the play of muscles as he walked. The lithe way he carried himself. The way the breeze ruffled his dark hair and molded the shirt to his powerful chest.

He was absolutely superb.

*What is the matter with you, Amber? Wasn't the last lesson painful enough?*

Angry with herself for mindlessly slipping under his spell again, she straightened abruptly. Not again. She would not let him—

A sudden prickle of fear darted through her, and she stiffened. She could hear someone breathing.

Right behind her.

# Chapter 10

When Clay reached the hall door and found it unlocked, the jolt that went through him caused every muscle in his body to tense.

Poo squawked in protest.

Easing his grip, Clay hurried to the balcony.

Amber stood with her spine to the rail, facing Miranda, her eyes wide, frightened.

"What the hell's going on?" he demanded.

Miranda whirled around. "Nothing, Your Grace. I just brought the food you wanted." She gestured to a tray. "I came out here to tell her ladyship, but I guess I startled her."

He swiftly explored Amber's pale face, the trembling hand at her throat. "Are you all right?"

She gave a jerky nod.

"Then take Poo inside. Miranda, you stay. I want to talk to you."

When Amber and Poo were out of earshot, Clay turned on Miranda. "Don't ever do that again."

She narrowed her eyes. "I didn't startle her intentionally, and I brought the damned tray up myself so I could pass some news on to you."

That cooled his anger. "What?"

"Bowling told me several articles around the house have come up missing since yesterday."

"What articles?"

"A setting from the silver service, a crystal snifter, and one of your marble chess pieces."

"Why would anyone take such inconsequential items?"

"I have no idea. But I thought you should be made aware of what was happening."

Feeling a twinge of guilt, he gazed down into her lovely face. "I'm sorry I jumped to conclusions."

She snorted. "It's not the first time."

"No, but I still apologize."

"Well, in that case"—she kissed his cheek— "you're forgiven." She started to turn. "Oh, by the way, what happened to the door in there?"

"I broke it."

She arched a wing-shaped brow. "I see. Well, I'll send someone up to repair it."

"I've already sent for a carpenter."

"Good." With a saucy tilt to her head, she sauntered inside. A moment later, he heard the outer door close.

Glancing through the glass doors, his gaze drifted to where Amber sat on the edge of the bed, staring at Poo in his cage. She looked angry and lost and frightened, all at the same time, and it made him want to strangle Miranda.

Rubbing the nape of his neck, he went inside. "I'm sorry that happened."

"How did she get in? I heard you lock the door."

"All my maids have a key, sweetheart. Since we don't have leprechauns who make the beds and gather soiled laundry, I thought it necessary. Besides, it's not anyone in my employ who's trying to harm you."

"Well, I don't like that woman having access to my chamber."

"That's going to be rather difficult, since I'm going to ask Miranda to be your personal maid." He'd been giving that a lot of thought, and he knew she'd protect Amber.

*"What?"*

Clay tried not to wince at the outrage in her voice. "It's either that or I'll have to do it."

"What about Isabel?"

"She runs the household. She doesn't have time."

"The other one, then. The one who served tea in the courtyard."

"Rebecca helps the cook, and she helps Miranda tend the other guests." He felt her frustration, but there wasn't anything he could do about it. At least with Miranda, Amber wouldn't be in danger from the murderer . . . or from him. Too, he'd been thinking about what Albert said, and as much as it galled him, he knew the youngster was right. Amber was being treated like a prisoner. She'd been cooped up and under constant supervision since she'd been here.

Well, that was something he could remedy. He gestured to the tray. "Now, why don't you eat something before a worker comes to repair the doors, and afterward, I'll take you riding."

Her head snapped up, and he could tell she was torn between irritation and excitement. Evidently excitement won. She smiled. "Truly?"

"Truly. Come on, eat. Then we'll choose a mount for you."

Amber tried, but she just didn't have an appetite. Finally, he relented and allowed her to leave her almost full plate.

On the way to the stables, Clay left her by the ballroom door and went to talk to Bowling in the servants' quarters. "I want you to keep an eye on the guests. Amber's cousin and Lady Chatsworth are stitching in the sitting room, and the gentlemen are in the parlor playing whist. Don't let any of them out of your sight."

Bowling puffed up his thin chest. "I'll have Isabel watch the ladies, and I'll make sure the gentlemen stay put."

Nodding at the servant who'd been at Westshire as long as he could remember, Clay returned to Amber and guided her through the gate at the rear of the courtyard, then to a long building behind the stone wall.

The scent of hay and manure drifted from inside the shaded stables as they entered. Sunlight poured in through the open door, illuminating the rows of stalls on either side of a wide, hay-strewn aisle.

Clay's stallion spotted him and whinnied excitedly.

"He's magnificent," Amber whispered in awe. "I've never seen a horse that color. What's his name?"

Clay ran a hand over the sleek coat and mane that glistened like liquid silver. "Mercury."

"A thoroughbred?"

"Yes. His bloodline's as royal as the king's, too. Mercury is a direct descendant of Byerly Turk, the first Arabian horse imported to England."

She approached him slowly and traced a finger down the stallion's narrow nose.

Instead of jerking back, as Clay had expected, the horse merely blew softly and nuzzled Amber's hand.

"May I ride him?"

"No. He was bred for extreme speed and stamina, but his temperament suffered in the process. He's unpredictable and spirited and . . . dangerous."

Amber didn't appear concerned as she slid a small hand down the underside of the horse's neck. "You ride him, don't you?"

"When I'm up to the battle."

"Do you race him, too?"

"Sometimes. For my own pleasure. But for the most part, I leave that up to my groom, Franklin. He trained him from birth."

"Do you have another one like him?"

"The mare I'm going to breed him to next week. She should be in season by then."

"You mean you were going to return to Westshire *before* my accident?"

"Yes, sweetheart, I was. I'd spent the last eight months on ships with Bragen Alexander and his wife, Nichole, and I wanted to feel solid earth beneath my feet for a while before I boarded a ship for the Colonies. But I needed to see Robert first . . . and William. Your father had expressed an interest in Mercury's first foal."

Her eyes misted, and she leaned her cheek against the horse's neck. "I wish he could have lived to see the colt."

The tightness in his throat made it hard to speak. "So do I."

Amber was silent for several seconds, then she straightened and wiped a tear from her cheek. "May I ride the mare?"

His better judgment shouted no. The mare, although not as unpredictable as Mercury, was a very spirited animal. But he couldn't deny that Amber was an excellent rider, and from years of experience, he knew that trying to get her to ride a docile animal would be like trying to maintain a straight course in a nor'easter. Warily, he realized, he just wasn't up to the fight. "I'll saddle her."

"Where's your groom?"

"He went to the village to pick up a special bridle I ordered for Mercury." He led Amber to the end stall.

"Oh," she exclaimed in surprise. "She's lovely."

Clay ran a hand down the mare's sleek neck. Taut muscles rippled beneath her pale, orange-gold coat. A mane of the exact same hue brushed the back of his hand. "Don't let her delicate appearance fool you. She's as cunning as she is beautiful."

Undaunted, Amber placed a hand on the mare's jaw.

As he swung his grandmother's old sidesaddle onto the horse's back, the animal pranced excitedly.

Amber talked softly to her, then, as if they came to some kind of understanding, the mare nickered and bobbed her head up and down.

Not really surprised at Amber's easy way with horses, he tightened the cinch and checked the single stirrup for length, then picked up his own saddle and headed for Mercury.

"What's her name?"

He glanced back over his shoulder at the mare whose color had always reminded him of a morning sunrise. "Sahara Dawn, and there's a mounting block near the door, if you don't want to wait for my assistance."

She grinned and immediately caught the mare's reins and led her to the block.

By the time Clay finished with Mercury, Amber had mounted and had her right leg securely fastened around the saddle horn. Wearing a dark burgundy gown that draped yards of satin over the mare's rear and side, she held the animal in tight control.

She was breathtaking to behold. Her long, wavy hair tumbled down her back like a waterfall of newly minted gold pieces, while her pale skin glowed like pearls. Long, thick lashes curled upward, away from slanted violet eyes that looked as if they could see right through him.

His gaze drifted to the curve of her breasts. Although the snug satin covered her completely, the generous evidence of her femininity couldn't be hidden. Her breasts were full, uplifted, and beautifully shaped. Need rushed through him, and he tightened his hold on the saddle.

"Are you ready?" Amber asked, watching Clay warily. The way he kept staring at her made her skin burn.

Turning away from her, he led Mercury from the stall and swung into the saddle, his movements so smooth and graceful, they were almost fluid. The animal danced in protest, but Clay expertly brought him under control. "Come on," he urged. "Let's take the path down to the beach, and I'll show you a part of Westshire my guests rarely see."

The saddle horn dug into the flesh behind her knee as the mare followed the stallion.

As they rode along the shelled pathway, Amber saw several men wave at Clay as they passed. By the way they were dressed, she knew they were the field hands Clay had summoned.

The reminder of what she could only call *her imprisonment* darkened her spirits.

Guiding the mare down the steep trail ahead, she tried to push the thought from her mind. Cool, crisp air lifted her skirts as they descended, and she recalled the carriage horse's struggle up the front trail yesterday. Yesterday? Good heavens, had she only been here a day? It felt like weeks.

"Come on, Amber. I know you're a better rider than that."

Startled, she glanced up to see Clay waiting several yards ahead of her, his dark head tilted to one side, his hands folded on the saddle horn. Wind played with a lock of hair on his brow and molded his shirtsleeve to his arm, defining a wealth of hard muscles. With a shiver, Amber remembered how good those muscles had felt against her.

The stallion shifted uneasily beneath him, and he tightened his thighs, giving her a remarkable demonstration of the power in those limbs. The kiss they'd shared earlier came to mind, and she felt a flush warm her cheeks. Disgusted with herself, she nudged the mare into a trot. "Sorry. I guess I was daydreaming again."

His green eyes crinkled with humor. "About pirates?"

"Not this time."

He reined his horse around. "Too bad."

They rode across the sand in silence for several minutes, and Amber enjoyed the wind tousling her hair, the mare's spirited gait, and, to her, the animal's easy manageability. Clay's mount, however, was more disagreeable, but he was an excellent horseman, so he had little difficulty managing the stallion.

When they reached an opening in the cliff, Clay turned his horse into the recess. The mare followed but became spooked by the shadows. A less experienced rider may have lost her seat, but Amber quickly brought the skittish mare under control.

Clay, too, had to calm Mercury. "Neither one of them cares for shadows or storms."

"I don't blame them."

The air was cooler in the shade, and she wished she'd had the foresight to bring a shawl. But no more had a chill set in when they broke out of the rocks into a clearing where sunshine poured over a sparkling white cove that was surrounded on three sides by towering boulders.

Amber drew Sahara Dawn to a halt and stared at the cove for several seconds, unable to speak. It was lovely. And so very private.

Clay dismounted and helped her down. "Come on, I want to show you something." He took her hand and pulled her toward a solid rock wall.

He stopped in front of it and glanced upward for several seconds, then he stood on tiptoe and stretched the full length of his body and arm upward. His fingertips touched a spot the average man could never reach, and part of the rock wall moved inward.

Amber gasped. "A secret cave?"

Clay let his arm drop to her shoulder. "Compliments of James Wingate. Or did I forget to mention that he was a smuggler, too?"

"You most certainly did." Cautiously, she peeked inside the opening.

"Wait. Let me see if there's a candle." He disappeared into the darkness. A few seconds passed before she heard the scrape of a flint and saw a small flickering glow appear from inside.

"Come on in."

"What about the horses?"

"They won't wander far."

Feeling a thread of excitement, Amber slipped into the cavern. For several moments, she surveyed the cave. Rotting crates and barrels were stacked against the shale walls of a room as big as the ballroom in the main house. A circle of rocks that had once contained a fire centered the sandy floor, while a crumbling stack of wood was mounded next to the opening.

Amber gave a light shiver. It was cold in the cave.

Either seeing or sensing her discomfort, Clay gathered several pieces of the wood and tossed them into the circle of rocks. He set the candle flame to the crumbling pieces, and within moments, the fire took hold, sending clouds of smoke out the opening and waves of warmth over her.

Removing a threadbare blanket from a weathered trunk, he spread it out and motioned for her to sit.

As she did so, her gaze drifted to a narrow passageway at the rear of the cave. "Where does that go?"

"To the house." He tossed another piece of wood into the flames. "When the exchequer, England's superior court, suspended cash payments in 1672 for a year, James Wingate turned to piracy and smuggling. Goods were brought into the manor through the caves and sold as part of Westshire's assets for gold. That's how our family survived then and during the war with the Dutch that followed."

"So, your piratical traits weren't inherited solely from the Captain."

"Apparently not."

"Why are you going to the Colonies?"

"I plan to live there and raise thoroughbreds."

Amber wasn't sure how to respond to that. He was going away. Forever. Disturbed by the thought, she shifted. "Do you think you'll be happy away from the sea?"

"I don't know, but I'm thirty years old, and it's time I started thinking about settling down, about getting married and raising children. No matter how much I love the sea, I can't do that if I'm never home."

In all her dreams, Amber had never imagined Clay getting married—to another woman—and raising a family. The numbness that settled over her made it hard to breathe. "You could if you married a woman who loves the sea, too." Like her. Sweet Providence. She couldn't bear this.

"True. But, believe me, sweetheart, the sea is no place to raise a child. Children need a home and family and friends."

For the first time, she wondered if she'd been wrong about Clay loving the freedom of a seaman's life. Then another thought ocurred to her, and she knew, no matter how much it hurt, she had to know the answer. "Do you have someone in mind for the future duchess of Westshire?"

"No." He took her hand and pulled her to her feet. "Come on. Let's explore the passage."

The heat of his palm, and the thought of his final departure from England and inevitable marriage, made her tremble as he led her into the dark corridor.

Suddenly she missed her father terribly. Her life as

she'd always known it was falling apart. Her father was gone, and soon Clay would be, too. Even though she'd avoided him during the last years, she'd always looked forward to his yearly visits, always waited breathlessly for her father to tell her the latest news about Clay after he was gone. Again.

A weakness trembled in her knees, and she grabbed a boulder for support. Nothing was ever going to be the same.

Clay pulled her into his arms and just held her in the darkness. "Try not to think too much about your father right now. Give yourself time to heal first."

It amazed her the way he could read her thoughts. She leaned into him, absorbing his strength. He always made her feel secure. "I miss him so much."

He rubbed his cheek against her temple. "I know you do. I miss him, too. But I know he wouldn't want you to grieve for him. He loved life too much for that."

It was true. Her father did love life and laughter and a warm fire on a chilly day. She glanced down the passageway to the fire pit in the other room, needing desperately to feel its warmth. "Could we . . . ?"

Firelight caught the way his eyes softened with understanding, then he lowered his head and brushed his lips lightly over her brow. "We can explore the cave another day."

When the golden flames danced warmly over her once again, Clay sat beside her and draped his arm around her shoulder. "Remember the first time you tried to light a fire in the gazebo in your garden? You nearly burned it down."

"I was only ten."

"And too stubborn to allow a mere male to give you instructions."

"I'm just glad you reacted quickly," she admitted, "and put it out before the fire did damage."

He leaned back against a crate, taking her with him.

"At least you consented to let me teach you properly. Otherwise, heaven only knows what might have happened once I left on the *Black Wind* again."

She rubbed her cheek against his shoulder. "I used to hate to see you leave, and I couldn't wait for you to return so I could hear about your exciting escapades. I only wished I could have been in the room with you and watched your face when you talked, instead of having to sneak around. But you refused to tell me about your voyages. You only talked to my father."

"If I'd known you were eavesdropping, I wouldn't have done even that. You were too young to hear about such things."

She studied him in the firelight. "Clay?"

"Hmm?"

"Did you truly 'ravage' women?"

He smiled. "Only the willing ones."

She wasn't sure if that's what she wanted to hear, but at least he hadn't forced himself on a woman. Sighing, she closed her eyes and listened to the crackle of the fire. "What did you do after you dry-docked the *Black Wind?*"

"Bought some freighters and began my own shipping line. But the war with the Colonies broke out shortly afterward, and I began smuggling goods for a friend."

"It's a wonder you weren't caught and hanged."

"I almost was. My friend Derrick Fleming asked me to take a load of gunpowder to a man named Carl Malderon in the Colonies, but off the coast of Virginia we were boarded by a customs official who discovered the smuggled cargo. I was arrested and sentenced to hang. Fortunately, my crew rescued me before that happened."

"Did you do any more smuggling after that?"

He gave her a quirky grin. "Yes."

They fell silent for a span of time, each enjoying the comforting crackle of the fire, the warmth, the gentle slap of waves, and the relaxing peace they'd had so little of during the last days.

"Do you still get those 'feelings' you used to?" she asked.

"Yes." He looked away.

Her heart went out to him. How awful it must be to know someone was going to die and not be able to prevent it. She was sure she couldn't bear it.

Clay was a remarkable man.

For the first time in four years, she allowed herself to enjoy being close to him, to inhale his musky ocean scent, to absorb his heat. But she couldn't allow it to last. She had too many questions. "How did stories of your madness start?"

He shifted and drew her a bit closer. "I took a strap to a nobleman for beating a servant. A young girl." He sent her a sideways glance. "Why? Did you think they were true?"

"Hardly. You're many, many things, but insane isn't one of them."

A pleased smile curved his lips, and he leaned his head against the crates behind them and lowered his lashes. He was quiet for several seconds, then he spoke without opening his eyes. "We should hear from your father's solicitors soon. The day before we left, they told me they had a report almost ready."

Wishing he hadn't reminded her of her situation, she sat up. "Do you think they've learned anything?"

"Possibly."

"Well, I hope so. Maybe then you'll stop suspecting my friends."

"I suspect everyone, Amber. Not just them." He stretched out his long legs and crossed them at the ankles. "But tell me about them. Make me understand why you're so sure of them."

"Will it do any good?"

"Maybe."

She rose and walked to the opening of the cave and rested her shoulder on the wall. "Where do I start?"

"Wherever you want."

How could she explain how she felt? How she was so sure of them? Her inability to put her thoughts into words frustrated her. "You want to know about my friends? All right, I'll tell you. Let me tell you about Georgina and how she tended my scraped knees while my mother was on a social whirl across Europe. How she would bring me lemon tea every night and read stories to me. How when I became bored with those tales, she'd make up new ones.

"Or perhaps you want to know about Katherine and how she was always there for me when my mother's engagements kept her away for weeks, how Katherine taught me embroidery and to play the pianoforte, or how she instructed me on grace and social mannerisms, or the way she would fuss over me and praise my accomplishments."

She went on, desperate for him to understand. "Of course, there's still Ellison, isn't there? But you have no way of knowing that he almost shot his prize horse because it threw me, or that he patiently gave me lessons in numbers when everyone else thought my desire to learn was foolish. After all, women have no use for such knowledge." Irritation overwhelmed her, and she jammed her hands on her hips. "He's just one of the people you think are trying to murder me!"

He studied her for several seconds, then met her eyes. "There's still Albert."

She knew he was wondering if the fencing accident that afternoon really *was* an accident. Not that she had any doubts. She most certainly didn't. "Ah, yes. Albert. Well, let's see . . . he was born six months before me, and our parents were great friends. That's why the Chatsworths are my godparents. Since only a short distance separated our parents, Albert and I spent most of our childhood together."

"Any arguments?"

"Several—not that I recall any of them. They were petty disagreements. Certainly no reason for him to want me dead."

"I hear he imbibes a great deal and spends a lot of time at the clubs."

Amber sighed. Was there anyone in all of England who hadn't heard of Albert's failings? "Do you believe all the gossip you hear?"

"No. But in this case, I've seen him myself. Several times."

"So you spend a lot of time in the clubs, too."

He chuckled. *"Touché."*

She folded her arms and stared out across an expanse of white-capped ocean. "My father used to call him a wastrel who'd never amount to anything, but I don't think he really knew Albert. Father thought he was too pampered, too spoiled, never giving thought to responsibility. He didn't see the same side of Albert I did. He never knew the side that begged his father for some responsibility on the estate, only to be refused again and again, or the man who resorted to fisticuffs because a gentleman was discussing my virtue, or the one that carried me over a mile when I fell and sprained my ankle, or the one that buried my puppy, said a prayer over its grave, then held me while I cried." She sent him a sour glance. "And you never saw the man who sobbed openly because he'd cut my wrist in a fencing accident."

"You love him, don't you?" Clay's voice was strangely defeated.

"Yes, I do. Not as a woman loves a man but as a friend. I love him very much."

"Maybe his feelings are stronger."

"If they were, he wouldn't have refused my proposal."

Clay went deathly still.

Warily, she watched him battle an emotion she couldn't identify, then slowly, he rose. He moved in front of her and closed his hands around her upper arms. His eyes burned like green fire, and when he spoke, his voice was low and thick and frightening. "You asked him to *marry* you?"

# *Chapter* 11

Clay could feel the tremors running through him as he gripped Amber's arms, but he was too angry to care. Just friends, huh? Sure. Everyone asked their "friends" to marry them. "You lied to me when you said you didn't love him."

"No, I didn't." She tried to jerk free, but he held on to her. "I asked him to marry me because I need him. I can't run Markland alone."

Her words took some of the steam out of him, and he eased his hold. "Since according to you, his sole desire is to run his own estate, why did he turn you down?"

She pulled free and rubbed her upper arms. "I don't know. He gave me some feeble excuse about being in love with someone else, but I don't believe him. He would have told me about her before now."

As close as they were, Clay figured that was true. So why had Chatsworth backed off? Any man, friend or not, would give his fortune to marry a woman like Amber. Something wasn't right.

The rumble of hoofbeats jarred into his thoughts.

He whipped around and ran outside, then through the short canyon that led to the main beach.

Two men sat on horseback, looking around in confusion. It only took a second for him to recognize them. "Well, I'll be damned."

Amber huffed up behind him, then stood on tiptoe, trying to see over his shoulder. "Who is it?"

"Robert and Morgan." He gathered the horses' reins. "Come on."

When they reached the beach, Morgan had dismounted and was walking toward the edge of the water.

"Morgan," Clay called. "Wait up."

His brother turned, and Clay was struck again by the power that surrounded Morgan like a low-hanging cloud. Maybe it was the way he carried himself or the calm, direct way of looking at people that made other men warily step aside. Although Clay—and Robert— were tall men, at six and a half feet, Morgan dwarfed them both.

No one could deny Morgan was handsome. With that head full of thick, curly black hair, that deeply tanned skin, and those startling cornflower blue eyes, he'd turned more than one lady's head for sure.

Very few people would think they were brothers if they didn't know them. The only resemblance Clay could detect was in the shape of their mouths and the square angle of their jaws. But the eyes were as different as trees and rocks. Morgan's eyes appeared hard and impenetrable, completely at odds with the gentle giant Clay knew him to be.

Morgan sprinted toward him with a grace that, for such a big man, surprised most. But he went right past Clay and pulled Amber into his arms. "I'm sorry to hear about your father, honey. Is there anything I can do?"

Amber shook her head and wrapped her arms around Morgan's waist. She hugged him warmly. "It's good to see you."

He kissed her forehead, then turned to greet Clay. "Well, big brother, I see you've taken good care of her so far."

"It hasn't been easy." Clay smiled as they shook hands. "How'd the sale go?"

"Fine. The funds for your ships are being transferred as we speak."

Robert hurried to them and put an arm around Amber's shoulders. "Is that bear I call a son the only one who gets a hug around here?"

Amber peered up into Robert's clear blue eyes, just a shade darker than Morgan's. With a sad smile, she embraced him and kissed his cheek. "How is Sara doing?"

"I wish I could tell you, but I don't know. She left the same day you did."

"What?" Sara was in such a fragile state, Amber was worried about her mental welfare. "Left for where?"

"She told her maid she was going to her aunt's place in Heathrow."

That eased some of Amber's fears. At least there, Sara would have someone to take care of her.

Clay appeared disturbed. "What time did she leave?"

"I'm not sure, son. When I went to check on her in the afternoon, her maid said she'd left earlier that day." He appeared mildly disappointed. "She didn't tell anyone she was leaving."

Amber knew what Clay was thinking. He was wondering if Sara had followed them. Of course, Amber knew it wasn't so. Sara was her dearest friend. "I'll post a letter to her today." She glanced pointedly at Clay. "Just to make certain she arrived safely."

"That reminds me," Morgan spoke up. "William's investigators asked me to give you this." He handed Clay a sealed envelope.

Amber felt a thread of excitement. Had the investigators learned who murdered her father? Was the answer to all her problems in that envelope? She was dying to know, but apparently Clay wasn't. He merely stuffed the missive in his pocket and motioned his father and brother toward the house. "I imagine you could use something to drink after your long journey."

Morgan grinned, showing straight white teeth and engaging dimples in his cheeks that made him look a good deal younger than his twenty-seven years. "Got any brandy?"

"I'd prefer sherry," Robert mumbled as he led his horse up the shelled path behind his son.

Clay was smiling as he grabbed their mount's reins and started for the stable.

Amber wanted to scream. What about the letter? But she held her tongue and followed them.

Once inside the manor, Clay ushered everyone toward the parlor.

"Lord Frazier. Morgan. How good to see you," Amber heard Katherine say as she emerged from the sitting room. She stood in front of the two big men, smiling in welcome. Georgina was right behind her, cradling a basket of yarn.

Apparently hearing the commotion, Albert and Ellison came out of the parlor.

For several minutes Amber watched her friends greet each other. Ellison, she noticed, seemed in awe of Morgan. He kept a healthy distance from him— just as he did Clay.

Albert shook Morgan's big hand, not in the least intimidated. He'd known Morgan too long.

Her gaze drifted past her companions to the maid,

Isabel, and the butler, Bowling, hovering nearby. She had the strangest feeling they were policing her friends, which, knowing Clay, was probably true.

The cook appeared and nodded to the butler, who announced that supper would be served in an hour.

"Isabel, see that my father and brother's luggage is taken to a room."

The maid curtsied.

"Well," Katherine said. "Since supper will be in such a short time, I believe I shall retire to my room." She gave Amber a warm smile. "You know how dreadfully long it takes to change. Why do you not come along, too, child. I will walk you to your room."

"Thank you, anyway, Lady Chatsworth," Clay countered. "But I'll escort Amber." He spoke to the maid. "Isabel, show Robert and Morgan to the parlor and see to their thirst."

Katherine whirled around in a huff.

Amber could only sigh as Clay led her upstairs behind her stiff-backed godmother. Well, she consoled, at least now she'd find out what the investigators had to say.

When they reached the third floor, he checked both rooms and the balconies before he was satisfied that no one was lurking in the shadows.

"Was that really necessary?"

"Yes."

Amber knew he had to be the most frustrating male she'd ever known. She was concerned, too, but not obsessively so.

*"Awk.* Show him the cat 'o nine. Show him the cat 'o nine."

Amber smiled at Poo prancing back and forth across his perch, bobbing his head up and down. "That's not a bad idea."

"Just for that," Clay taunted, "I'm not going to show you the solicitor's letter until after I've read it."

*"Clay."*

He pulled the missive from his pocket and leaned against the desk.

Every time she tried to get a peek, he'd turn so she couldn't.

"Curse it all. What does it say? Did they find out who killed my father?" she demanded.

His grin turned into a deep frown as his gaze quickly skimmed the pages. Finally, he folded the papers and put them back in his pocket. "We'll talk about it after supper."

"We are going to talk about it right now—"

Miranda swept into the room, followed by two boys carrying buckets of steaming water and stacks of clean towels. "I'm supposed to help you dress."

Clay pushed away from the desk. "I hope there's enough water for my bath, too." Without waiting for an answer, he strode into his room and closed the door.

Amber wanted to stomp her foot. The man was impossible. She wanted to know what was in that letter. Resigned to the fact that she wouldn't learn a thing until after supper, she waited for the boys to fill both tubs and leave, then grudgingly allowed Miranda to help her out of her gown. It was a wholly unpleasant experience. The maid tore off several laces and buttons while trying to undo them. Of course, she mumbled apologies, but Amber wondered at her lack of experience. With the old duchess dead for years, Miranda probably hadn't had much experience tending a lady's toilet.

Finally, Amber was able to step into the tub. In her agitated state, she sloshed water over the edge.

*"Awk.* Nor'easter's coming. Nor'easter's coming."

"Oh, Poo. Hush." She glanced at the maid. "Cover his cage, will you?"

Miranda draped a piece of linen over the wire, then

picked up Amber's clothes and tossed them on the bed. Seemingly at a loss as to what to do next, she sat down.

"I thought you were going to assist me?" Amber reminded.

She cocked an eyebrow. "Do you want me to wash you?"

"I most certainly do not."

She leaned back on her elbows. "Then there's nothing for me to do until you're finished."

Amber gritted her teeth. "You could lay out my clothes."

Miranda shrugged and shook her hair away from her face. It slid off her shoulders like a waterfall of black satin, and her breasts swayed beneath her thin white cotton blouse. "Can't. Rebecca's pressing them."

Amber wished she'd go away. Grabbing a cloth, she began to scrub vigorously.

Miranda stared out the glass doors the whole time Amber bathed.

Finally, Amber rose and snatched a towel from the pile on the floor. "See what's keeping Rebecca."

The waspish tone of her voice caused Miranda to look at her sharply.

Amber felt embarrassed by her own tongue. Miranda hadn't done anything to deserve that.

The maid shrugged. "Yes, your ladyship." She eased off the bed and sauntered out the door.

"Where did Miranda go?" Clay asked, walking into the room. He had on his breeches and boots, but wore no shirt. Droplets of water wove their way through the forest of silky hairs on his chest and down across his flat stomach. A scar on his side peeked from his waistband, and Amber guiltily recalled her damaging wish about his appearance.

Her gaze drifted to his hands tying a leather strip

around his hair. The intimacy of him going about his ablutions only half dressed left her speechless—not to mention *her* state of undress.

When she didn't answer his question, Clay glanced at her. For a heartbeat, he stared, then his gaze drifted down to her bare legs and feet, then up again, over the damp towel to her naked shoulders. He lowered his hands to his sides, then wordlessly turned around and walked out.

Barely able to breathe for the wild pounding in her chest, she numbly pulled on her undergarments, wishing she'd never seen him like that. Wishing she wasn't again feeling the emotions that had caused her so much pain four years ago.

Clay stood on his balcony, gripping the rail, and fighting the waves of desire that threatened to consume him. No matter how hard he tried to deny the feeling, he knew he couldn't. He wanted to make love to Amber Sinclair.

And once he did, he knew he could never leave England.

Damn her. Why did she have to be so beautiful? So desirable? The image of her in the bath at the inn rose, and now, with her only wearing a towel. His whole body tightened at the visions.

The door opened, and he turned to see Miranda walk in carrying Amber's gown. Not daring to venture into the room again, he leaned on the rail and gazed out over the maze, determinedly turning his thoughts away from his body's urges.

He recalled the letter from William's investigators. Amber was going to be devastated when she learned what it contained, but there was no way to spare her. After supper he was going to have to tell her everything.

The only good thing that had come out of the day

was the arrival of his brother and father. At least, now he'd have help watching the others, and Amber would have more freedom. Although she hadn't complained much, he knew the confinement was starting to wear on her. It had to be. It was wearing on *him*.

He heard Miranda leave and assumed Amber was finished dressing, but he didn't want to go in just yet—not until he was sure she was clothed, and not until he was in better control of himself.

Another rush of desire swept him, and he clenched his teeth. If he didn't get hold of himself soon, he was going to spend the night clinging to the rail.

"Clay? I'm ready."

Amber's voice plunged into him like a knife. Not now, damn it.

"Clay?"

He took a deep, composing breath and forced himself to face her.

Late afternoon sunlight glinted off her molten hair that had been pulled back with a bow, then fell down her back in a tumble of glistening curls. The deep blue satin dress she wore, though high-necked and long-sleeved, clung to her shapely curves like wet silk before falling to the floor in a cascade of ruffles. She wore a trace of lip rouge that made her mouth look moist and full.

The urge to taste that mouth staggered him.

Hanging on to what little control he had left, he motioned her out, then reluctantly followed her.

They had almost reached the closed door to the second landing when he heard voices.

"Wait," he whispered, catching her arm and drawing her to a stop. Cautiously, he pushed the door open a crack.

Amber drew in a stunned breath.

He could only stare.

Albert had Miranda pressed to the wall two doors

down, his lower body against hers, a hand encircling her waist. "Come back," he murmured, "when you can stay longer."

Miranda eased away from him. "We wouldn't have had even these few minutes if her high-and-mighty ladyship hadn't decided to do her hair by herself. His Grace thinks I'm with her, or he'd have me off doing some other dirty chore."

Clay arched a brow. He'd get her for that one.

"You don't like him much, do you?" Albert murmured.

"Oh, I like him well enough, but after all the years I've been here, he still hasn't shown me what he's got under them tight breeches."

Albert nuzzled his lips against her neck. "I'll be more than happy to show you what's under mine."

Miranda gave him a sensual pout and gently shoved him away. "Later, love."

"I'll look forward to it." Running his hand over her shapely hip, he gave her a slow, lingering kiss. When he pulled away, he sauntered downstairs, whistling as he walked.

Miranda smiled as she made for the servants' stairs.

Clay was afraid to move. Every inch of his body had started to burn. An ache settled low in his body, and he struggled to hold on to his composure. Every part of him cried out to kiss Amber the way Albert had Miranda.

Then Amber's ragged breathing reached his ears, and he turned to look at her.

She was leaning against the wall with her eyes closed, her hand at her throat.

"Amber?"

Slowly, her lashes raised, and her eyes met his. They were a deep, deep violet, darkened by the weight of desire. She'd been as affected by Albert and Miranda's display as he had.

The knowledge sent heat racing through him. He

tried to speak, to bring some sense into what was happening. "Amber?" It was more of a broken whisper than a word.

Her eyes darkened even more, and her lips parted.

The last of his control slipped. "Oh, Jesus," he groaned, then lowered his mouth to hers.

"Ellison, do hurry. It is not my desire to make the entire household wait supper for us."

Clay jerked away from Amber just in time to see Katherine sail by, with a harried Ellison right behind, awkwardly trying to tie his cravat.

Clay let out a harsh breath and moved away from Amber, damning himself for his loss of command of his own body. When he was sure the second level was unoccupied, he opened the door and drew Amber out into the hallway.

She stepped away from him the moment she could. "Clay, I . . . *you* are going to have to stop . . . trying to kiss me. We—there is nothing between us. And there isn't going to be. Please keep your hands to yourself." Without waiting for his response, she rushed down the stairs.

He glared at her retreating back. Hell. The way she acted, you'd think he was the *only* one who'd instigated that 'almost' kiss.

Women. They had damn funny ways of thinking.

In the dining room he found Amber seated between Morgan and Albert. As he walked to the table, he noticed Amber's cheeks were unusually bright as she darted peeks at Albert. She was probably embarrassed by what they'd seen in the hall.

After the meal of pheasant, boiled potatoes, fruit, cheese, and sweet yams was served, Clay filled his plate and ate silently, listening to Morgan bantering with Amber.

"Isn't your birthday the day after tomorrow?" Morgan asked her.

Clay's fork stopped halfway to his mouth. Morgan

had a memory like a bull elephant. Clay purposefully hadn't mentioned the date, hoping Amber would think he forgot. He had purchased her present six months ago and had it well hidden in the stables. He'd recently decided on another, too, but there was one more he still wanted to get. An important one.

Amber smiled warmly at his brother. "It most certainly is. I'll be nineteen."

"Such a tender age," Albert taunted, being only six months older. "I think we should have a party."

Amber still couldn't look at him without blushing.

"No," Katherine announced. "It is not proper for Amber to partake in such frivolities with her father so recently laid to rest."

"Who would know?" Albert asked. "Only those of us here would attend."

"It is not proper."

"Oh, for bloody sake, Katherine," Ellison hissed. "Stop being such a prude."

"I don't see any harm in a few decorations and a bit of music," Robert said softly.

Katherine clamped her lips tightly together.

"Perhaps I shouldn't . . . ." Amber let the words trail off.

Georgina dabbed her mouth with a napkin. "Of course, you should, love. Your father would demand you enjoy your special day."

Amber's eyes misted.

Morgan took her hand. "Then it's all settled. I'll go to Middlesbrough tomorrow and round up some minstrels."

"I'd like to accompany you, if I may," Georgina said.

Morgan nodded and started to say something, but at that moment, Miranda walked in, wearing a coarse woolen gown and white apron. Morgan's eyes widened.

So did Robert's.

Before they could give the game away, Clay stood. "If you'll excuse me, I need to speak to my . . . maid." He motioned Miranda out. "In my study."

Robert arched a gray brow but kept his mouth shut. Morgan continued to look dumbfounded.

"When did they get here?" Miranda asked as Clay closed the study door.

"About an hour ago. I thought you knew."

She shook her dark head. "No. I was helping Amber, then I went to see the cook about the supper menu."

*"After* you met with Albert."

"How did you—*you saw us?"*

"Was that remark about what was in my breeches really necessary?"

She had the good manners to flush. "Well, yes. I wanted Albert to think I was experienced. Men have such loose tongues when they think they're going to get a woman into bed."

"How would you know that?"

"I was raised here, Clay. I saw more than one of the old duke's maids obtain information for him from 'special' guests."

"You're going to get yourself in trouble."

She grinned. "If I do, I know you'll be close by to rescue me."

"Perhaps I should see to it that you do some 'dirty chores' to keep you occupied so that doesn't happen."

"Clayton, you're getting snippy again."

"And you're getting in over that lovely head of yours. I have enough to worry about with Amber. Don't make extra work for me—and stop taunting her. She has enough trouble right now."

"I'll do my best." She drew a finger along the edge of his grandfather's cherrywood desk. "But I do think I should explain to Morgan."

"Fine. But wait until he gets to his room, and use the secret passage."

Chuckling, she started for the door. "Those old halls haven't been used this much in centuries."

"One more thing. I want you and Robert to keep an eye on Amber for me tomorrow. I'm going to Middlesbrough with Morgan to get Amber another present for her birthday."

"Another? What's the first?"

Knowing that if a servant overheard, word would spread through the manor like billowing smoke and Amber would know before the night was out, he wrote down all three presents he intended to give her, although he knew it was the first two that would catch Miranda's eye.

She stared at the parchment he handed her, then looked up. "That's a little extravagant, isn't it?"

"Yes, it is," he answered quietly, "but she's worth it."

# Chapter 12

Amber was as edgy as a cornered mouse as she waited for Clay. She had penned and sent her letter on its way to Sara, she had straightened her dressing table, her trunk full of slippers, and her writing table. For goodness' sake, she'd even rearranged the items in her secret chest. But nothing made the time pass quicker. She was absolutely dying to know what was in that message from the investigators, but Clay insisted she wait while he went to see his trainer in the stables. Apparently, his new bridle was more important than Amber.

Drawing her shawl closer to ward off the chill, she studied the dusky sky from her balcony. It was growing dark and becoming overcast, and she could feel dampness in the air. On the horizon she could detect a thick bank of fog rolling toward shore.

She hated the fog. It was so cold, so frightening. It reminded her of death.

Deciding to wait inside, she opened the glass

doors—and a rush of warm air hit her. Clay had built a fire before he left. Grateful, she moved toward the corner hearth, stretching her cold hands toward the heat.

A door opened and closed on the second level, then she heard the soft tread of footsteps in the outer hall. A moment later, a light knock sounded on her door.

"Come in," she responded instantly, knowing it was Clay and anxious to learn what the investigators said.

But it wasn't Clay.

It was Robert.

"My son wanted me to let you know he'd be late. He's giving Mercury a run with his new bridle."

"How late?"

"He didn't say, but he told me to tell you not to wait up for him."

Amber wanted to stomp her foot in frustration. Instead, she thanked Robert and watched him close the door before she gave the hearth a firm kick. Curse Clayton Cordell to the bottom of the ocean and back.

Struggling out of her clothes, she pulled on her nightgown and sat cross-legged in the middle of the bed, drumming her fingers on her knees. Within minutes, the position became uncomfortable, and she braced her elbows on her knees, then cupped her chin with her palms.

She tried to concentrate on what she'd do once she returned to Markland, *if* she was allowed to return. Ellison and Katherine might not let her—and certainly not to stay by herself—but no matter where she went, her first objective would be to find a suitable husband. The livelihood of Markland's people depended on its master.

All the plans and thoughts in the world wouldn't make the time go faster. Finally, in desperation, she lay down, hoping she could fall asleep.

Flames from the fireplace danced on the ceiling, entrancing her, luring her, but she couldn't rest. Her mind refused to do so until she knew what was in that message.

A clock somewhere in the manor chimed the midnight hour before she finally heard Clay stirring in his room.

Surprised that she'd been so deep into her thoughts that she hadn't heard his footsteps in the hall, Amber tossed back the covers and marched toward the connecting doors. Without knocking, she swung them open.

Clay started and whirled around.

Amber froze in place.

He was completely naked.

"Get out of here."

She couldn't move. She'd never seen so much of him. So much golden skin, so many muscles. Her gaze drifted over a small scar on his left thigh, then the long one from his waist to his hip. Even with the imperfections, he was a beautiful man. Something warm tightened her lower belly.

*"Amber.* Get the hell out of here."

Her palms growing moist, she dragged her gaze to his face. "Have you always looked like that?"

She could have sworn his neck turned red.

He snatched his shirt from the bed and covered his lower body. "If you're not out of this room in ten seconds, I'm going to throw you out."

"But, the letter . . ."

*"Get out!"*

She spun around and dashed into her room, firmly closing the doors behind her. "You've got thirty seconds to get dressed before I come back in," she warned haughtily, but her insides were trembling. He was magnificent.

In less time than she'd expected, he stalked into the

room. He wore only his breeches and a shirt open down the front. "If you could have held your patience in check for just a few minutes, I would have come in here. Mercury gave me some trouble when I tried the new bridle and tossed me in the sand. I was going to change and—Amber, stop staring at me like that."

She blinked and forced her attention upward. "Did you know that you're the only man I've ever seen without his clothes?"

He went deathly still.

The air in the room began to pulse. Heat from the fire moved across her flesh in waves. The oxygen in her lungs forced its way in and out.

Clay's eyes traveled down her length and grew bright. His nostrils flared, and a muscle at the side of his throat started throbbing. "Amber, put on some clothes."

"What?" Then it hit her. She was wearing only her thin nightgown—and she was standing directly in front of the fire. She darted to the foot of the bed and threw on her robe. More composed now, she faced him. "The letter?"

He looked like a man who'd just escaped from the gallows. The muscles in his shoulders relaxed, and he withdrew an envelope from his shirt pocket.

"Did they found out who killed Father? Can I go home now?"

"No to both questions." He unfolded several pages of parchment. "But they did learn a lot about your companions."

"What do they have to do with anything?"

"Maybe nothing." He shrugged. "Then, again, maybe everything."

"You're talking in riddles. Curse it all, Clayton, let me see the letter."

"No. I'd rather take one issue at a time." He scanned the first page. "What do you know about Ellison?"

She didn't have to give it much thought. "He's a kind man. Gentle. Sensitive. Why?"

"Were you aware that he and your father once had a duel?"

"That's absurd. Why would they do such a thing?"

Clay moved to the writing table and sat down, looking decidedly uncomfortable. "Ellison challenged your father because he'd learned that William and Katherine had an affair."

Amber went numb. "What are you saying?"

"I'm not saying anything, sweetheart. The investigators are."

Her knees folded, and she sank down on the bed. "My father and Katherine?" She felt sick to her stomach. Father couldn't have done such a thing. He just couldn't have. He wouldn't have done that to her mother. She stared into the fireplace. "They're mistaken. I never once saw father behave in a suspicious manner."

"From what the letter says, the affair happened before you were born. Just a few months after your parents married. It seems theirs was a marriage of convenience, and neither was particularly fond of the other. Shortly after the wedding, your mother moved into William's London townhouse, while he stayed at Markland. Apparently, during the time he was secretly seeing Katherine. Ellison learned about what had transpired, and he challenged your father to a duel. Only by the grace of God was neither badly hurt, and Ellison's—and Katherine's—honor was avenged."

"If that's true, then why did they remain friends?"

He glanced at the page. "The matter between them was private. No one knew. But after the duel, the gossipmongers went wild, making up tales. Because Katherine was so distraught over her ruined reputation, Ellison told everyone that his and William's dispute was over their property boundaries and all was settled. For the benefit of the *ton,* and Katherine, they kept up their mock friendship from then on."

It was hard to believe that her father and Ellison hadn't truly been friends. Everything Clay said was hard to believe. "Is that all that's in the letter?"

"No." He shifted uncomfortably. "There's some information about Georgina Becker."

Amber felt her stomach tighten. "What?"

"Are you sure you want to know?"

*No.* "Yes."

He glanced at a page. "It seems that your father threw her out of his home shortly before your tenth birthday. She lived with your cook's daughter, Hilary Sawyer for a few weeks, then your father mysteriously allowed her to return."

"Why would he throw her out?"

"The investigators apparently don't know, or they would have said." He glanced down at the next page. "But they do know about Albert."

*There was more?* "What about him?"

Clay scanned the pages, then turned one over. He read silently for a few seconds, then looked up. "Several men have threatened his life because of overdue gambling debts."

Amber massaged her temples with the tips of her fingers, wishing she could get her father's perfidy out of her mind. "At least that's something I can correct. I'll have my solicitor advance him the funds."

"Will you continue to do that the rest of his life?"

"Of course not."

"Then why do it now? He'll just go into debt again."

"I'll have a talk with him. I'll make him promise not to go to the clubs."

"You're daydreaming again, sweetheart. Albert won't stop until the root of his problem is corrected."

"What is the root?"

"I wish I knew."

Her gaze lowered to the letter in his hands. "Is there anything else?" *Please say no.*

"Nothing I wasn't already aware of."

"Meaning?"

"I'd already learned about the questionable accident Albert's betrothed had."

"Questionable? There was no question to it. Lady Bonet was killed when she fell down a flight of stairs, and Albert was devastated. I was there, Clay. I saw how grief-stricken he was. He didn't love her, but he did care."

Clay snorted. "Yes. He cared so much, he waited almost a whole day before heading for the clubs."

Amber knew he was right, but he just didn't understand how sensitive Albert was. She was sure he had gone to the clubs to drown his pain in spirits. "What has any of this to do with my father's murder?"

"I don't know, Amber. Nor do I know what it has to do with the attempts on your life, but I'm going to find out."

"How?"

"I'm going to have a private talk with each of your companions."

Knowing how brutal Clay could be sometimes, and not wanting to subject her friends to his ruthless side, she made a firm resolve to act as a buffer. "When you do, I insist on being there, too."

He lifted a broad shoulder in a shrug. "Whenever possible, you're welcome to join me." He walked to the adjoining doors. "Now, if all of your questions have been answered for tonight, I'm going to bed."

"There's one more thing I'd like to know," she said, cursing herself for even giving it thought.

"What?"

"Do you still have the clothes you wore aboard the *Black Wind?*"

A dark brow arched upward. "The black ones?"

"Yes."

He looked at her curiously. "They're in the trunk at the foot of my bed. Why?"

How could she say she'd like to see him in them again? "I, um, was just wondering if you ever wore them."

He gave her a slow smile. "Sometimes."

Clay decided to talk to Georgina first, since she was going to Middlesbrough with him and Morgan. He and his brother had spoken at length about the investigators' message last night, and Clay had voiced his intent to question Georgina, so he knew Morgan wouldn't be surprised when he did so.

Amber, however, wasn't going to like it. He was going against her wishes, but he couldn't allow her to come along on the trip, and there was no way his questions would wait until they returned home.

After making sure Robert and Miranda and the household staff looked after Amber, Clay donned his cape against the chilly fog that shrouded the roads and joined Georgina and Morgan in the Westshire coach.

Georgina, seated next to Morgan, adjusted the rug on her lap and pulled her heavy cloak tighter around her slim shoulders.

For several minutes, Clay watched her. She reminded him of Amber's mother with her sandy hair and hazel eyes. Even their builds were the same—both small and slight. Both very near the same age—or at least the age Victoria would have been if she hadn't died of influenza.

But the similarities ended there. Victoria had been a whirlwind of activity, where Georgina had always appeared reclusive. Victoria had been talkative, bright, and witty, while Georgina rarely had anything to say—witty or otherwise.

"Well, are we going to sit here all day and stare at each other?" Morgan asked impatiently as he opened the window curtain wider. "Or are we going to get this over with?"

Clay had forgotten how impatient and blunt his brother could be. Yet he knew, too, that Morgan's momentary impatience stemmed from being cooped up in the carriage. Morgan hated small spaces.

"Get what over with?" Georgina asked, shifting her gaze between the two of them.

Clay cleared his throat. "Mrs. Becker, I received a letter from William's investigators yesterday, and they mentioned some disturbing facts about you that I would like to have clarified."

She clutched the collar of her cloak together. "What investigators? What facts?"

"William hired investigators after Amber's second 'accident.' They reported that at one time William"—there was no gentle way to say it—"asked you to leave his home."

Her pale skin took on a grayish hue.

"What I want to know is why—and why he allowed you to return."

Her gaze darted around the carriage like a frightened rabbit cornered by a coyote. Nervously, she clenched her hands together in her lap. The lap rug quivered slightly with her tremors. "I-Is this necessary?"

"I'm afraid so."

Georgina fixed her gaze on her folded hands. "William told me to leave because Victoria's silver brooch was stolen, and he thought I took it."

"Did you?"

She didn't lift her head. "Yes. I was living in sufferance on William's charity after my parents disowned me, and I had little money of my own, so I stole the trinket, and I traded it for a bolt of fabric to make Amber a new dress for her birthday."

"Is that why William relented? He found out why you had taken the brooch?"

She hesitated, then shook her head. "He relented because I knew something he didn't want me to repeat to Victoria."

Morgan and Clay glanced at each other, then Clay nodded. "You knew about William's affair."

Georgina's head whipped up. "How did you find out?"

"The investigators."

Georgina appeared anxious. "Please don't tell Amber. She wouldn't understand. In her eyes William was a saint. She would be devastated to learn about his . . . activities."

Clay wished he'd talked to her yesterday. "Amber already knows. We discussed it last night. William's affair might somehow be related to the threat to her, and I felt she had a right to know. Besides, she plans to be there when I talk to the others. There's no telling what else we're going to learn."

Georgina was stricken. "Don't let her. There are things Amber shouldn't know. . . . Things that will hurt her."

"What things?"

"It's not my place to say, but truly, Your Grace, heed my warning."

"Tell her she can't be present," Morgan said.

Clay eyed his brother. "Have you ever tried to tell Amber no?"

"Not that I recall."

"Well, I have. It's like talking to a fence post."

Morgan shrugged. "So, lock her in her room, have your conversation, and report to her afterward, leaving out any details you don't want her to know."

"Shall I report before or after she crowns me with a chair?"

Morgan shook his head. "I don't believe this. My big brother, *the pirate,* and you still don't know how to handle women."

Clay bit his tongue to keep from mentioning Morgan's lack of control when a woman he thought he was in love with turned his life upside down and left him in a large heap at her feet. Two, in fact. "Amber needs to know the truth . . . even if it's painful. She deserves that much."

Georgina leaned back and closed her eyes. "What she may learn will go far beyond painful."

Amber threw her hand of whist down and glowered at her opponents. "I think you cheated."

Robert chuckled. "Amber, how on earth would one cheat at whist?"

"No one could cheat without all of us seeing," Albert, her partner, pointed out. "We're just going to have to admit that the *old ones* are better whist players."

"Here now," Ellison huffed. "I resent that remark."

"Old ones, indeed, you young dandy," Robert scoffed. "I played whist—and won—when I was even younger than you."

Albert looked affronted. "I'm not *that* young."

"And I'm not *that* old," Robert countered.

Ellison chuckled.

"Perhaps you weren't motivated enough," Robert chided. "Maybe a little wager would—"

"No!" Amber blurted, then blushed wildly. Surely, Robert was aware of Albert's debts. "I mean, you take the fun out of games when you gamble on them."

"Quite the contrary," Ellison countered. "I think a small wager might give us all a spark of inspiration."

Refusing to contribute to Albert's failings, she rose. "Then I'll leave the game to you gentlemen. I believe I'll retire to the library."

Without waiting for a response, she strolled out of the parlor. She could have kicked Robert for his innocent remark.

Miranda was in the foyer, staring out the window, a bottle of lemon wax and a cloth in one hand. She turned as Amber closed the parlor door.

"Did you want something?"

"No." Amber crossed the gold-and-white tiled floor and went into the library. As she did, she could have sworn she saw a flash of concern on Miranda's face. But, of course, that was ridiculous.

She lit a candle, then found a volume by William Falconer, an old one called *The Shipwreck,* and sat down at the long table to lose herself for a while in the adventurous tale.

A sound caught her attention, and she glanced around the room. No one was there, and nothing appeared out of place, but she could feel a presence, as if someone was standing right next to her.

Clay opened the carriage door and leaped down before the vehicle had come to a complete stop. With his gift for Amber tucked safely in his pocket, he left Morgan to help Georgina down and sprinted indoors. They'd been gone only a few hours, but it felt like days since he'd seen Amber, since he'd heard her voice.

Robert and the Chatsworth males were in the parlor playing cards, and he found Katherine in the sitting room reading.

"Have you seen Amber?"

Katherine glanced up. "No, Your Grace. Not since she went to the parlor to play whist, shortly after you left this morning."

Recalling Georgina's warning about Amber hearing things that might hurt her, Clay was tempted to question Katherine. Instead, he merely nodded and closed the door. Anything the woman had to say would affect Amber, and she had a right to know. Since Amber was no longer in the parlor, he figured she was in her room.

But she wasn't.

When he finally did locate her in the library, he was near the point of panic. "Damn it, Amber. Why didn't you tell anyone where you were going?"

She looked at him as if he'd lost his senses. "I told *everyone* where I was going."

"Not one servant knew."

"Miranda did."

Miranda? Clay hadn't been able to find her, either. He felt some of the tension leave him. If she told Miranda, then he knew exactly where the imp was.

His gaze shifted to a row of books on the back wall. One book was missing. The one with a peephole in the wall panel behind it.

Clay smiled. Miranda had been watching Amber the whole time.

"What are you smiling about?"

"Nothing. Listen, I saw Katherine in the sitting room a few minutes ago. I figured now is as good a time as any to talk to her about the investigators' letter."

Amber appeared uncertain.

Remembering Georgina's warning, he pounced on Amber's doubt. "If you're not up to it, sweetheart, I'll talk to her alone."

"No. I want to be there."

*Of course.* Hoping he wasn't making a mistake, he turned for the door. "Let's go."

# Chapter 13

Amber's stomach was in knots as they walked into the sitting room to confront her godmother.

Katherine glanced up when Clay opened the door. "Well, Your Grace, I see you found her."

Motioning Amber to a chair near the window, he closed the door. "Yes, I did. But Amber wasn't the only thing I found, Lady Chatsworth."

"Whatever do you mean?"

"We know about—"

"Clay, please," Amber interrupted, gripping the back of the chair she had yet to sit in. "Let me tell her."

Her godmother was puzzled. "Tell me what?"

Amber joined her on the settee and took her hand. Clay was so insensitive. He didn't realize how Katherine would react to her indiscretion becoming public knowledge. "We . . ."

"What is it, child?"

"We recently learned about . . . what happened many years ago . . . between my father . . . and you."

176

Katherine gasped and brought a hand to her throat. She stared, wide-eyed, horrified. For a few awful seconds, Amber was afraid she would swoon.

Katherine's chin began to quiver. "Have you told Albert? Does he know?"

"No. No one knows but the three of us . . . and Father's investigators, who sent the information."

Katherine darted a glance from one to the other. "What are you going to do?"

"Nothing," Clay told her gently. "We just want to talk to you about what happened."

"Why?"

"Because hatred is a damned strong motive for wanting someone dead. And, correct me if I'm wrong, but Ellison didn't have the best of feelings toward William. What I want to know is did he hate him enough to kill him?"

Katherine rose and crossed her arms over her middle as she turned her back to them. She held her posture correct from so many years of practice. "Of course, he did. How would you react if you learned the son you worshipped was sired by another man?"

Clay went still.

Amber would have fallen if she hadn't been sitting down. Dear God in heaven, what was Katherine saying? She forced the question past her numb lips. "My father sired Albert?"

Katherine whirled around, her expression as stunned as Amber's voice. "You said you knew."

"About the affair." Amber could only manage a whisper. Dear God. Albert was her brother.

Katherine closed her eyes and arched her head back. "Oh, child. I never meant for you to find out this way. I am so sorry." Tears slid down her cheeks. "So very sorry."

Barely able to stand on her trembling legs, Amber rose. "I—" She couldn't talk. Her throat was so tight, she thought it would cut off her breath. Fighting her own tears, she whirled around and ran out the door.

Clay wanted to go after her, but he knew she needed a few minutes to compose herself. Hell, he was almost as shaken himself. *The man Amber had asked to marry her was her brother.*

Taking a breath, he returned his attention to Katherine. "Lady Chatsworth, I'd like to know what happened."

Katherine opened her misty eyes and stared at him as if he'd grown a pointed tail. "Your Grace, it is impossible for you to convince me that you do not know how children are conceived."

He managed to check a smile. Barely. "That wasn't what I was referring to. I wanted to know if Albert's birth was what Ellison and William dueled about."

"Yes." She lowered her gaze to the flowered carpet. "William had married Victoria out of obligation, but they cared nothing for each other. They lived separate lives entirely. I had been in love with William since I was a mere child. He was desperately unhappy in his marriage, and when Victoria went to reside in London, I spent a great deal of time with him, trying to make things easier for him. Unfortunately, our close association got out of hand. William was on the verge of petitioning the king for a divorce so he and I could marry when Victoria had a riding accident."

Katherine's mouth thinned. "She was severely injured, and it was William's duty to go to her. But when he returned after a fortnight, he had changed. The time he had spent with Victoria had brought them closer, and he wanted to give his marriage an honest try."

She massaged her wrists. "I did not tell William I was already carrying his child. It would have only served to complicate matters. Instead, I accepted the first marriage proposal—Ellison's—and gave myself to him the same night, faking my purity, and hoping he would think the child was his and simply born prematurely."

"But he didn't believe it?"

"Oh, he did for the first few years, but I made the mistake of telling William about Albert shortly after Amber was born. William insisted he include Albert in his will. I did not disagree, but when William gave me a copy of the document, I should have destroyed it. I did not, and Ellison found it when Albert was three years old. *That* was what they dueled about."

Clay studied the proud woman standing before him. She must have been beside herself when that happened. A tainted reputation would destroy a woman like her. "Albert doesn't know?"

She shook her head of dark curls. "It would crush him to learn that Ellison was not his true father."

Clay understood that as perhaps no other could. He had been devastated when he found out about Robert and the Captain. "If it's at all possible, Lady Chatsworth, we won't mention this to him."

Her stiffly held shoulders slumped in relief. "I do not know the words to tell you the depth of my gratitude, Your Grace."

Feeling a twinge of sympathy, he gave her a gentle smile. "No words are necessary."

When Clay left the sitting room, he found Miranda outside the door.

"Where is she?" he asked, knowing Miranda knew exactly who he was referring to.

"On the beach."

He started toward the rear of the manor.

"Clay? Whatever happened in there hurt her terribly." She met his eyes. "I'm hoping it wasn't something you said. After all these years, I'd hate to have been wrong about you."

He smiled, loving her more than he ever had. "You weren't wrong, imp." His smile faded. "It was Katherine's words that caused her pain, and I'm going to do my best to help her." He gave her a quick kiss on the cheek, then hurried toward the beach.

Clay didn't see Amber when he reached the shoreline, but one of the guards on the bluff motioned him toward the caves.

She was in the cove, sitting on the sand, staring out at the water. Her legs were drawn up to her chest, her arms wrapping them protectively, her chin resting on her knees. The dying sunlight glinted off the tears staining her cheeks.

Clay wanted to hold her, protect her from further anguish, but nothing he could say would make her feel any better. Only time and acceptance of the situation could do that.

As he turned Katherine's words over in his thoughts, he wondered about Albert. Katherine had said he didn't know the truth about his birth, but Clay had his doubts, and it made perfect sense why Albert had refused Amber's proposal. He couldn't marry his own sister.

Clay studied Amber and decided he wouldn't mention his suspicions right now. Amber had been through enough upset today. "Amber, I'm sorry you had to find—"

She whirled to face him, then surged to her feet, her eyes sparkling with anger. "Get away from me."

"Sweetheart—"

*"Don't call me that."* She stalked up to him. "All of this is your fault." She hit his chest with her small fist. "Why couldn't you have left well enough alone?" She hit him again. "Why do you have to keep prying and prying until you destroy the lives of everyone around you? Curse you, Clayton Cordell." She hit him again. And again.

He pulled her into his arms. "Amber, don't . . ."

She gripped the front of his shirt and began to cry—deep wrenching sobs that nearly cut him in two. "Oh, Clay. He's my brother. *My brother.*"

He kneaded her spine. "I know, sweetheart. And I'm damned sorry you had to find out this way. If I'd had any indication at all, I could have spared you the hurt."

"Spared me?" She jerked out of his arms and moved several feet away. "Oh that's rich—coming from a man who did his best to destroy me."

He knew she was referring to what happened four years ago. Until this moment, he never realized the crushing depth of the pain he'd inflicted on her. He thought of all the things he might say to her, but none of them seemed right.

Only the truth.

He peered into her eyes, glistening with tears. "I never meant to hurt you. You have to know that. But I had to stop the madness. In your innocence that night, you had no idea what you were doing to me— and if things had progressed any further, I couldn't have stopped myself from taking you. No one could have stopped me, and the result would have been hatred—yours and mine. I would have hated you for forcing me into marriage when I wasn't ready. And you would have hated me because I would have left you to go back to the sea."

"Curse you, Clayton. Don't lie to me." She turned away from him. "I know exactly why you threw me out. You were repulsed by me and my behavior."

"That's the second time you've uttered that ridiculous statement. I was never repulsed by you. Damn it, woman. I *wanted* you. Don't you understand that?" He spun her around to face him. "I wanted to make love to you more than anything I'd ever wanted, but you were a child. I couldn't do that to you. I tried to show you what you were getting into when you kissed me, but your innocent passion brought me within a thread of losing control. If I hadn't ended the kiss right that second and gotten you out of there, I wouldn't have been able to stop. I know I said some cruel things—things I've regretted—but damn it, it was the only way."

He lowered his hands. "I almost rode my horse to death that night, trying to rid myself of the guilt and get you out of my head."

She was gazing up at him with disbelief and confusion. "I—" She massaged her temples with her fingertips. "I don't want to talk about this." Whirling around, she hurried toward the manor.

Clay felt as if someone had parked a wagon on his chest. She didn't believe him.

Amber sat numbly in the tub, her thoughts whirling crazily. Clay had wanted her. He'd really wanted her.

All these years . . . She couldn't believe it. But she did. Clay had never lied to her. Except perhaps in that one moment of desperation, he never said things he didn't mean. That's why she'd so readily believed him that night when he told her he liked 'real' women—with experience, not simpering virgins. When he told her to come back after she'd grown up.

She should have been elated by the thought. She *was* grown. But too much had happened today for her to feel anything but numb.

Grateful that she hadn't seen Miranda on her way in, she sank deeper into the steaming water and closed her eyes. It was rare these days that she had any time to herself at all.

She heard a movement in the room behind her, and she sighed. Miranda had located her, after all. So much for privacy. Opening her eyes, she turned to face the maid.

A blur of hands shot toward her. They clamped down on her head and shoved her face beneath the water.

Water surged into her nose and open mouth.

Terror exploded. She clawed wildly at the gloved hands holding her down. She kicked and fought with everything she had. Her lungs screamed for air. Her senses spun.

She grabbed the sides of the tub, but she couldn't raise her face out of the water. She bucked and twisted wildly. Pain burned through her lungs. Her mind whirled with panic. *Oh God, help me.* The fire in her chest was unbearable. She could feel herself slipping into a black void. Distantly, through a buzzing tunnel, she thought she heard pounding.

The hands jerked away.

With the last of her strength, she pushed herself up out of the water. Air rushed into her chest, and she began gasping and choking, drawing in huge gulps. An eternity passed before her senses cleared. She frantically darted a glance around the room. Whoever had been there was gone. She began to shake so hard her teeth chattered.

"Damn it, Amber. Did you hear me?" Clay's voice penetrated the hall door, followed by a loud knock. "I said Miranda had your gown pressed and asked me to bring it to you. Are you decent? I'm coming in." Clay shoved the door open.

Tears blurred her vision as she stared up at him. "S-Someone tried to d-drown me."

"What? *Who?*"

"I d-don't know."

"Son of a bitch." He bolted for the balcony door and threw it open. Through the buzzing in her head she heard his footsteps pound across the floor, then to his room and down the steps to the second level. Then his bellow nearly shook the rafters. "Miranda! Morgan! Get up here!"

Within seconds, she heard his muffled curses as he spoke to Morgan and Miranda. "Damn it. Why didn't I see them? How did they . . ." His voice lowered, and she couldn't hear the rest of his words.

A moment later the door burst open and Miranda rushed in. There was no mistaking the concern in her eyes. "Are you all right?" She grabbed a towel. "Come on, get out of there."

Too shaken to be concerned with her nakedness, she rose and allowed Miranda to dry her and pull on her dressing robe. Then the maid stalked to the door and shouted down the stairway. "Isabel! Brew a pot of tea for Amber."

After locking the door, she pulled a chair near the fireplace, then guided Amber to it. "Come on. Let me brush your hair. It'll help soothe you."

Oddly, Amber thought Miranda was acting more like the mistress of the house than a maid. Still, she didn't argue. She was too shaken by the knowledge that someone had tried to kill her—*someone in this house.*

"I'd like to apologize for my earlier behavior," Miranda said as she drew the bristles down the length of Amber's hair. "I haven't been very nice to you since you came here, but in my defense, I'm usually not very nice to a person who's hurt someone I love. You hurt Clay, and I wasn't ready to forgive you for that."

She set the brush aside and drew Amber's hair upward. "Clay knows I love subterfuge and games, that's why I was so willing to preten—I mean, keep an eye on you, even though I didn't want to like you, but this isn't a game anymore. Someone really is trying to kill you. And since you've been here, I've realized there was more to what happened four years ago than what Clay said."

Amber felt heat flood her cheeks. "He told you what happened?"

"Not all of it, I'm sure. In fact, I doubt if he'd have said anything at all if he hadn't been so upset. But he was so busy berating himself for 'nearly ruining an innocent' that I was only able to piece together what I thought happened. I gathered that you had put him in an awkward position. That *you* had caused him considerable grief. For that I wasn't going to forgive you."

Amber folded her still trembling hands in her lap, trying to forget the awful moments in her bath and wondering why Clay would confide in a maid—if that's what she was. Amber was tempted to ask, but she was afraid of the answer. "But you're ready to forgive me now?"

The brush stilled. "Well, not exactly, but I am willing to listen to your side."

Amber wasn't sure she wanted to tell her. And she was very unsure about Clay and Miranda's relationship.

Miranda was aware of her reluctance. "If you don't want to tell me what happened, I'll understand."

Amber stared at the woman through her nervous shivers, wondering who Miranda really was. Amber knew she wasn't a maid, but there was something disarming and comforting about Miranda. Something Clay apparently saw in her, too. "It was my fault. I was the one who put Clay in such an awkward position."

"What happened?"

Amber didn't know where to begin. "I made a complete fool of myself—at Clay's expense." She straightened the folds of her dressing robe and glanced at the dancing flames in the fireplace. Heat drifted around her. The scent of wood smoke filled the lilac-scented air. It was hard to believe that only moments ago she'd been near death. She drew in a breath and decided that talking might take her mind off what happened. "I was in love with Clay for as long as I can remember. Every year, when it came time for his visit home, I'd be such a mass of nerves, I couldn't eat for days." She smiled with fond memories. "He was so dashing in his black clothes and wearing that gold earring. I used to lie awake at night and imagine him coming to my room, throwing me over his shoulder, and whisking me away to the *Black Wind*. He was my dashing—if a little unsavory—knight." She smiled. "And, of course, we'd live happily ever after."

"So what caused the problem?"

Amber sighed. There was just no easy way to say it. "My impatience. When I was fifteen, I knew I wanted to marry him more than anything I'd ever wanted, and I knew, too, because of his friendship with my father—and his honor—if he compromised me, he would." A pin scraped her scalp, and she winced. "So I decided during his visit that I'd waited long enough. I sneaked out of my house in the middle of the night and went to Clay's."

"He let you in?"

"No. He wasn't there. But I knew he'd come home sooner or later, so I crawled in a window and went to his room to wait for him."

"What did he say when he saw you?"

"He was speechless. I was waiting for him in his bed."

"Good God."

"Anyway, he tried to get me to leave—without going near the bed, but I was certain I knew what I was doing. I got up and walked toward him. He kept moving, but I finally managed to corner him. I came right out and told him I wanted him to make love to me."

"What did he say?"

"He became angry—and I became desperate. I threw my arms around him and kissed him. He was stiff at first, then his mouth softened, and I thought for a moment everything was going to be all right. But it wasn't. He shoved me away from him so hard I almost fell, then he started yelling and shoving me toward the door. He said he wanted a real woman, an experienced one, not some simpering virgin—and for me to come back when I was grown. Then he bodily threw me out."

Miranda gathered Amber's nearly dry hair and drew it up on top of her head, fastening it with combs. "You were a brash little thing."

"Apparently."

"But you're all grown up now, aren't you?"

Amber glanced over her shoulder to see Miranda smiling.

"I mean," the maid—or whatever—went on, "that he might be more receptive now that you're not a child anymore."

"If Clay wanted to marry me, no one would have to force him to do it."

"True. But, it wouldn't hurt to give him a little nudge."

"No," Amber countered. "Clay and I just weren't meant for each other. I've finally accepted that."

Miranda stared at her thoughtfully.

"Amber!" Clay's voice roared down the hallway.

Miranda sighed and set the brush aside. "I guess I'd better let him in before he breaks down another door."

# Chapter 14

As much as Amber wanted to, she couldn't stop thinking about what Clay had said—or about almost being drowned. Shuddering lightly, she recalled her horrible nightmares that had ended with her father rescuing her one time, then Clay another.

She glanced across the table where Clay sat talking to Morgan. No one had mentioned the attempt on her life to her friends. Her friends. What a jest that was. One of them had tried to *kill* her.

Clay blamed himself for what happened. He said his questioning was making the killer nervous, and he wasn't going to talk to anyone else. Amber wondered if that meant one of the women was responsible, since they were the only ones he'd talked to, but Clay said no. Either woman could have mentioned their 'talk' to the men.

She shoved her food around on her plate with a fork, her stomach too upset to eat. One of the people she loved and trusted wanted her dead.

Surreptitiously, she glanced around the table at

each of her friends in turn. Her gaze came to rest first on Albert. Her brother. An ugly thought slipped in. With her father dead, if she were to die, too, the Markland estates and fortune would go to him.

No, she quickly admonished. Katherine said he didn't know about his parentage.

She shifted her gaze to her godmother, then Georgina. Neither of them would gain from her demise. In fact, just the opposite in Georgina's case. She would be without a home. And Katherine wouldn't benefit in the least.

Her gaze drifted to Ellison. There was no advantage to him for her death, either. So who did that leave?

No one.

She even considered Clay. Briefly. But he, like all the others, had absolutely no reason to hurt her. Besides, it he'd wanted to murder her, he could have done it a hundred times over in the last few days and blamed it on someone else.

No, Clay wasn't the one. Nor Morgan. He'd been out of town when the accident happened—and when she'd been poisoned at the inn.

"Any chance of another game of whist this evening?" Albert asked.

Amber glanced at him. Her brother. She still couldn't believe it. Oh, she'd always had a warm spot for him, but she'd never imagined they carried the same blood in their veins. "No. Thank you. I don't care for card games the way you gentlemen do," she lied. The truth was, she was still too skittish to be around any of them.

"I haven't played a good game in months," Morgan said lazily. "I'll have a go."

Robert too, agreed, while Clay and Ellison declined. Ellison wanted to read the periodical Morgan had purchased in Middlesbrough, and Clay said his mare had come in season that afternoon, and he wanted to oversee the animal's breeding when supper was over.

"Why don't you join Lady Chatsworth and me in the sitting room?" Georgina asked Amber. "She's instructing me on Italian hemstitching."

Amber noticed a scratch on Georgina's wrist and felt dread squeeze her chest. She had clawed desperately at the killer's gloved hand when they were trying to drown her. She could have scratched her wrist. No, she cried inwardly. It couldn't be.

"Amber's going to the stables with me," Clay answered for her.

Amber bit her lip and pulled her gaze from Georgina's wrist, grateful for Clay's comment. He understood her nervousness and was trying to help. The mare wasn't due to come in season for another week.

When the meal was over, Clay pulled a cloak around her shoulders, then took her by the arm and led her in the direction of the stables.

"Clayton," she said as they emerged into the courtyard. "You can stop the pretense now. We're out of sight of the others."

He glanced down at her as they walked. "What pretense?"

"About the horses. I know you made up the tale to keep me away from the others—for which I'm grateful. I know now that one of them is responsible for what happened." She tightened her hand on his arm, wondering if she should mention the scratch on Georgina's wrist. No. Georgina would never hurt her. Never.

He opened the rear gate. "I'm sorry you had to discover that for yourself, sweetheart, but I didn't lie about the mare. According to Franklin, Sahara Dawn came in season shortly before I returned from Middlesbrough."

"Then we're really going to watch them . . . ?"

"Yes."

A blush stole up her face. "Oh."

"She's ready, Your Grace," Franklin said as they entered the stables. "Edgar's been waitin' for you to come before he brought Mercury 'round. The stallion's been chompin' at the bit, he has. Knows his lady's ready for him." The slight, wiry man darted a look at Amber. "Er . . . beg your pardon, your ladyship. I meant no offense."

Amber nodded, hoping neither of them noticed her flaming cheeks.

Franklin bowed several times as he edged toward the rear door.

"If you don't want to watch," Clay said from behind her, "you can wait in another room." He gestured to a door that led to a second set of stalls.

The deep timbre of his voice sent tingles over her, and it made her angry that the sound could affect her so, not to mention the fact that the man was *still* treating her like a child. "Watching horses breed is not that traumatic, Clay. I'll be fine."

He arched a brow but didn't comment.

A moment later, Franklin and who she assumed was Edgar, a jolly man with muttonchop sideburns, brought the anxiously prancing stallion inside. The animal's eyes were bright and excited, its nostrils flared. He strained toward the mare, quivering visibly.

"Put them in the largest stall." Clay motioned toward an enormous railed pen near the far door.

Sahara Dawn was led in first, her golden coat glistening in the lantern light. She reared her head and swished her tail, her manner as anxious as the stallion's.

As Franklin and Edgar led Mercury in, then moved outside the stall, their attention fixed on the horses. Clay stood behind Amber and placed his hands on her shoulders. "They're going to make a magnificent foal," he whispered.

Amber could feel the heat of his palms all the way to her toes. She took a breath and tried to concentrate on the animals.

Mercury tested the scent of the air.

Amber waited.

Sahara Dawn nickered softly.

Clay stepped closer to Amber. Their bodies touched.

Amber knew she should move away. She didn't want Clay touching her—not when his hands made her body react in unspeakable ways. But the will to move escaped her. She loved the feel of Clay's hands.

Mercury reared up on his hind legs, then powerful hooves came down on the mare's back as the stallion thrust.

Clay tightened his fingers on her shoulders.

Amber swallowed.

The stallion labored for breath, his thick muscles bunching and straining under his sleek coat.

The mare whinnied.

Clay's hands moved down her arms and up again, his breath heavy as it touched her ear.

She could feel the tension in his body, the hardening muscles, and her own responded with a rush of heat. Dizziness assailed her, and she leaned her head back against his shoulder.

His hands slid around her waist beneath the cloak, and she could feel the heat radiating from him, the slight tremors that moved through his body.

Amber tried to tear her eyes away from the mating horses but she couldn't. There was such beauty, such power in their movements. Her breathing grew unsteady.

Clay shifted and drew her closer against him. "It's almost over, sweetheart."

His thumb brushed the underside of her breast beneath her cloak, and sweet tingles raced through her. *Shove him away,* her better judgment fairly screamed, but she couldn't. The other part of her, the woman part, wanted Clay's touch more than anything she'd ever wanted.

She sent a peek at the stable hands. Fortunately, their attention was directed at the horses and not at her and Clay.

Relieved, she tried to focus on the animals instead of Clay's hand.

Clay's thumb moved slightly higher, and a flash of heat burst through her lower region. She inhaled sharply.

Clay drew in a hissing breath and moved his hand higher still, until his fingers touched the very tip of her breast.

Pleasure darted through her, and her nipple grew hard and achy. Every inch of her body came alive, attuned to the slightest movement and sound. Her gaze fixed on the deep, labored thrusts of the stallion. On the erotic movement of Clay's fingers.

Suddenly, the stallion reared its head back and plunged a final time, then lathered and winded, he released the mare.

At the same instant, Clay released her, and she closed her eyes in relief. Or was it regret?

"Oughta get a fine youngin' outta that dance," Franklin crowed as he turned toward them, his weathered face alight with triumph.

"Yes," Clay agreed, but his voice sounded thick.

"Come on, Edgar," Franklin ordered, "let's get this boy back to his paddock before he has time to recover."

As the men led the horse out, Amber realized that Clay hadn't moved. He was still behind her. Still close. Feeling just a little anxious, she turned to face him.

He was staring at her with such an intense look, she

shivered. His eyes were emerald bright, yet weighted with desire. His nostrils flared, much like the stallion's had.

"Clay?"

His arm snaked around her waist and pulled her against him. He cupped her bottom and pressed her lower body to his, letting her feel his arousal.

Her heart nearly exploded. Her senses spun.

He bent his head to take her lips.

"Our boy gave quite a performance, didn't he, Edgar?" Franklin's voice carried through the door as he and the other man approached.

Clay pulled back, then quickly moved across the aisle.

Amber could only clutch her cloak tightly around her and struggle for composure.

"Sure did, Frank," Edgar agreed. "But the truth'll be in the puddin' eleven months from now."

"I hope it's a stallion. His Grace'll need another stud if he plans to breed them beauties in the Colonies."

"What's he goin' to do with Westshire when he goes?"

Franklin coughed. "Don't know for sure, but the way he feels about Miss Miranda, I figure he'll give it to her."

Amber clutched her throat against the pain, then another wave of dizziness swept her. She swayed and grabbed a stall rail for support.

Clay was beside her in an instant, supporting her weight against him. "What is it? What's wrong?"

She wanted to slap his hands away, but she was too weak. "I . . . want to lie down."

Without a word, Clay swung her up into his arms and strode toward the house.

The feel of his arms and the warm scent of his body made her even dizzier, and she was extremely grateful when he laid her on her bed.

Clay stayed bent over her for several moments, studying her lovely face. She was too pale. Her cheekbones were too prominent. Her eyes too shadowed. He straightened. "When's the last time you ate an entire meal?"

She brought a slim, shaky hand to her forehead. "I ate supper. You were there. You saw me."

"I saw you pick at your food, but I haven't once seen you eat a complete meal."

"I haven't had much of an appetite." She met his eyes. "Just like you didn't when the Captian died."

He took her hand and ran a thumb over the blue veins on her wrist. "But I had a little guardian angel who looked after me. She forced me to eat. If I recall rightly, she threatened to set my ship adrift if I refused."

A small smile curved her lips. "It worked, didn't it?"

"Yes. And it's time to repay the favor." He brushed the hair out of her eyes. "Which do you prefer, lamb or pheasant?"

"Neither."

He arched a brow.

"Oh, very well. Pheasant."

He kissed her forehead. "So be it."

After leaving Miranda at Amber's side, Clay found the cook and ordered a tray for Amber. While he was waiting for it, he sought out his brother.

Morgan was alone in the courtyard, staring at the dark liquid in the glass he held.

"How did the search go?" Clay asked. After the attempt on Amber's life, he'd asked Morgan to search the guests' rooms for clues.

Morgan glanced up. "It didn't. I had the servants go through every room—while the guests were at supper, as you ordered—but they found nothing to incriminate anyone." He tossed back his drink. "I did notice that Georgina had a scratch on her wrist, and I asked her about it."

"What did she say?"

"That she got it when she bumped into Katherine's hand when she was holding a needle."

"Did you talk to Katherine?"

"Yes. She told the same story."

Clay rubbed the back of his neck. "Anything else?"

"Ellison had dust on his shoes. I thought at first it might have come from the garden, but knowing how he likes to visit your thoroughbreds, I figured he got it in the stables."

Clay glanced at his little brother. "Garden?"

"Yes. Peterson found the gloves the bastard used. They were the ones he'd left in the garden. Whoever it was tossed them into one of the rosebushes after they tried to kill Amber. The damn things were still damp."

Clay shoved his fingers through his hair. "Morgan, what am I going to do? Whoever is trying to kill Amber might succeed next time."

"Take her away from here."

"I've thought of that, but it wouldn't serve any purpose. Sooner or later she'd have to return, and the threat would still be there."

"You could always marry her, then she'd never have to return."

Clay wanted to shake his brother, not because it was such an idiotic notion but because Clay had thought of it, too, and discarded the idea immediately. Hell, he was still kicking himself for touching her in the stables. Besides, to marry Amber would mean giving up his plans for the future. Amber was devoted to the *ton,* and he knew if he took her away from the social scene, she'd end up hating him—just as his mother had the Captain. "You'll have to think of a better solution than that."

"Such as?"

"I don't know, Morgan. Maybe we should try to set a trap for the killer."

Morgan's love of games caused his whole demeanor to brighten. "What did you have in mind?"

Clay thought for a few seconds. "Tomorrow's her birthday. Maybe we should give the killer access to her—with one of us watching, of course."

"Do you truly think they'd try something with everyone about?"

"Possibly. They've been pretty bold, so far."

"I don't know how we could arrange it."

"I have an idea that might work."

"Your Grace?"

Clay whirled around to see Bowling standing in the doorway holding a tray. "Cook said you wanted this for her ladyship."

He glanced at Morgan and nodded. "We'll talk more this evening, after everyone retires." Taking the tray, he headed upstairs.

Amber was sitting on the balcony, wrapped in a cloak, her gaze fixed on emptiness.

Clay motioned Miranda out, then carried the tray to Amber. She looked so alone. So unhappy. "Here, sweetheart. I want you to eat something."

She barely glanced at the tray. "I'm still not hungry."

"Hungry or not, you're going to eat if I have to feed you myself."

"Go away, Clayton."

Wondering what she was so angry about now, he set the tray on the small table. "What's wrong?"

"Nothing."

He approached her cautiously. She was in a temper, and he had no idea why. "You're acting like a child."

She surged to her feet. "A *child?*" She threw off her cloak, revealing a thin nightdress that molded her very generous curves. "There's nothing childish about me," she hissed. "Nor am I stupid."

"What are you talking about?"

She jammed her hands on her hips. "Just answer me this. Do you plan to give Westshire to Miranda?"

"Yes, I do." What did that have to do with anything?

"Why?"

"Because she deserves it."

Amber's chin quivered, but she held it up. "If you love her that much, then why don't you marry her?"

Warmth filled him, and he couldn't stop the smile that crept to the corners of his mouth. Amber was jealous, pure and simple. He moved closer, aching to pull her into his arms. "I can't."

"Why not?"

"Miranda is my aunt."

# Chapter 15

"Miranda is your *what?*" Amber was stunned. His *aunt!* A flood of pleasure shot through her. She wasn't his mistress.

"*Awk.* Clay is a fool. Clay is a fool."

Clay smiled at Poo, then brushed a lock of dark hair out of his eyes and returned his attention to her. "Miranda's the result of an affair between my grandfather and one of the kitchen maids." He tightened his mouth. "My grandfather graciously allowed her to live here with her mother after she was born, but her life was hell. My grandmother hated her and her mother. Whenever my grandfather was away—which was often—she made it a daily ritual to have Miranda beaten for some imagined wrong, mainly to punish her mother."

He shoved his fingers into his hair. "I was too young to do anything, so I could only stand by helplessly and watch her suffering. It doesn't show in her smile or stance, but Miranda's back is as scarred as a sailor who's had a taste of the cat 'o nine."

He leaned against the table and stared out over the ocean. "Miranda would have run away if she'd had any place to go, or any money, but she didn't. After my grandparents died and I inherited Westshire, I've tried my damnedest to make up to her for all the pain. You have no idea the hell she went through. And yes, as small recompense, I do plan to give Westshire to her. It's the very least she deserves."

Amber's heart swelled with love for him. His depth of caring for others was beyond measure. "I feel terrible for the way I've been short with her, but I thought she was your miss—er, maid, and was confused by her behavior."

"That was her doing. She was deliberately taunting you because of me. But you've got other things to worry about right now, instead of my impish aunt. First, you've got to eat, then we need to make plans to catch the killer during your birthday party."

"What plans?"

*"Awk.* Hang the blighter. Hang the blighter."

Clay glanced at Poo. "That's not a bad idea, but we have to catch them first. That's why I want to set a trap."

A tingle of fear slipped through her. "How?"

"I've come up with a plan I think might work. I want Morgan to fake illness after the festivities and retire, then you and I are going to have a very vocal argument. I want you to leave me and rush out to the courtyard. I'll pretend to be so angry at you that I refuse to follow you. You'll be alone, as far as everyone knows, but in truth, Morgan will be there, watching over you."

A tremor wiggled up Amber's spine. What if Morgan wasn't quick enough? What if the killer had a pistol and could fire from a distance? "There's a lot that can go wrong with that plan."

"Not if I can help it."

"But what if you can't?"

His eyes softened. "Sweetheart, I'm not going to let anything happen to you."

"What if there's no attempt? How long do I stay in the courtyard?"

"Until I come for you."

Amber had visions of standing in the cold half the night. "I don't think I like your plan, but I'll go along with it simply because I want this over with. I want the one responsible for my father's murder caught, and I want to go home."

Disappointment touched Clay's features. "Don't worry, Amber. There isn't much happening in London this time of year. You'll be home in plenty of time for the social season."

Social season? Why would he think she cared one whit about that? Then she remembered her remark to Albert about missing the social scene. But in truth, she'd rarely attended those boring functions, and then only to avoid Clay these last years. As far as she was concerned, her mother had done enough *socializing* for both of them. But Amber did want to go home. She had to find a husband as quickly as possible. "I just hope your plans work. The sooner I get back to London, the better."

He picked up a plate of food from the tray, his mouth in a grim line as he set it in front of her. "You'll get your wish if it's within my power to grant it. Now eat."

"I told you I'm not hungry."

"Eat on your own or I'll feed you."

The man just couldn't stop treating her like a child. "Fine. Hand me the plate."

When she'd eaten every bite she could force down, Clay finally relented and took the tray away.

Amber's belly ached, and the moment he left the room, she crawled into bed. She felt as if she'd eaten an entire cartload of melon and pheasant and scones and sweetmeats and . . . Oh mercy, her belly felt huge.

Yawning, she heard Clay moving about in his room and closed her eyes. Unbidden, the image of her and Clay in the stables rose. Even now, she could smell his oceany scent, feel again the gentleness of his hands.

Tingles caused gooseflesh to raise on her arms, and she pulled the covers up to her shoulders. But she couldn't help wondering if she shouldn't take Miranda's advice and *give him a little nudge.*

The morning of her birthday was shrouded with fog. A cold chill swept through her room, and even the fire Clay had lighted wasn't sufficient to ward off the dampness.

Sitting on the edge of the bed, Amber wrapped the bedcovers around her shoulders and stared into the dancing flames. Tonight she would risk her life to catch the person responsible for her father's death.

Sadness claimed her. How she missed him. How she would give anything she possessed to see him one last time, hear his gruff voice, watch his beloved face brighten with a smile.

Tears stung her eyes, and she rose from the bed. Dragging the quilt with her, she searched the armoire for something to wear. She selected a gray silk, then knelt to unearth her slippers from the bottom. Her hand brushed a small chest, and she glanced at it. A moment of trepidation held her motionless, her hand poised over the chest, then she slowly withdrew. She didn't want to look inside again. She knew what was there—the gifts Clay had given her over the years. Sweet memorabilia that made her ache.

Clutching the gray dress, she knocked on Clay's door. Since she wasn't allowed to leave her room, he would have to take her gown down and have it pressed.

Several seconds passed, and Clay didn't answer.

She knocked again.

Still nothing.

Gingerly, she turned the latch and opened his door, then peeked inside.

He wasn't there.

Curious, and feeling just a twinge of guilt, she walked into the room and glanced around. She'd passed through his chamber once, the night she'd seen Clay on his balcony with Miranda, but she'd never really seen it, and she was surprised to see his clothes draped over pegs on the wall rather than hung in an armoire.

Of course, since there was no armoire, that was understandable.

Something on the bureau caught her eye, and she moved toward the long, narrow package tied with ribbon. A small note was attached to the bow. Gingerly, she unfolded the square and read Clay's boldly written words.

This is to keep you safe tonight and always.

C.

Dying of curiosity, she reached for the package.

"You could at least wait for me to be here before you opened it."

Guiltily, Amber pulled her hand back. "I didn't mean to . . . I knocked but you didn't answer, and my dress needed pressing," she babbled with embarrassment. "I didn't mean to snoop. I-I found it by accident, and I was just going to lift it." She flushed. "Perhaps shake it a little."

His mouth curved into a beautiful smile. "Why don't you just open it?"

"Now? But tonight—"

"There's another gift for tonight. I planned to give you this one when you woke up, but I was summoned by the cook." His smile deepened. "She wanted to know what flavor cake and frosting you liked."

Amber arched a brow. "What did you tell her?"

"Lemon."

"How did you know— My father, of course. He told you."

"No, sweetheart. If you'll remember, I was there at three of your birthday celebrations. Your seventh, ninth, and twelfth. I saw the way you savored every bite of your lemon cake. In fact, all three times you went back for a second helping."

Her cheeks burned from the realization that he'd watched her make a pig of herself. "I was only a child."

"Yes," he said in a gruff voice. "I know." He picked up the package from the bureau and handed it to her. "Open it."

The way his manner changed every time she mentioned her childhood made her wonder as she carefully untied the satin bow and peeled back the white linen cloth to reveal a lovely gold dagger with emeralds, diamonds, and rubies winking from their mountings in the handle. "Oh, Clay. It's beautiful. Thank you."

He smiled down at her. "You're welcome. And I want you to keep it on you at all times. Day and night. I'll feel better knowing you have some means to protect yourself."

She doubted she could use it on another person, but it did give her some measure of relief. "I think I feel better, too."

After returning to her room, Amber studied the deadly dagger, then set it on the bureau and went about gathering her undergarments.

When Clay knocked a few minutes later and handed her the dress, he offered to help her change. She declined. She'd chosen the gray silk because it laced down the front, and the lack of a corset wasn't terribly noticeable.

The day passed in a flurry of activity—the cook preparing a feast, Morgan and Albert decorating the ballroom and refusing to let her enter until that evening.

Katherine, even though she was opposed to the party, acted as mistress of the manor by instructing the housekeeper and servants to their duties—even to polishing the silver goblets, tea service, and eating utensils.

Clay and Robert oversaw the building of a platform for the minstrels while Miranda shadowed Amber.

Georgina remained in her room, only to emerge shortly before it was time for Amber to dress for the celebration.

"Amber, love. There you are. I was just coming to find you." Sheepishly, she held up a lovely gown. "I made this for you."

"Oh, Georgina. It's beautiful." Amber was stunned to realize that Georgina had stitched the exquisite emerald green gown. She fingered the snow white lace dripping from elbow to wrist and from the back of the waist to the floor like a waterfall. She lovingly traced the bodice that dipped low and square, framed by tiny clusters of seed pearls, as was the shimmering satin skirt that draped in layers to a hem trimmed in lacy pearl loops. Amber had never seen anything so elegant.

But where had she gotten the money? Uneasily, she wondered if anything had come up missing at Westshire. Georgina was a wonderful person, but she did have a tiny flaw.

Stealing.

Clay watched Amber rush up the stairs and glanced at Miranda, who should have been following her.

Instead, she was talking to Katherine. Setting his hammer aside, Clay approached the women. "Miranda, aren't you supposed to help Amber dress?"

"I hope you do not mind, Your Grace. But I have asked your maid to assist me." Katherine cocked her dark head to one side, tipping the top of her towering hairpiece precariously. "I am certain you can find someone to tend my goddaughter."

"I'm sure I can."

Miranda glanced at him and smiled cheekily, but she didn't say anything.

Clay headed upstairs, making a decision he knew he was going to regret. He wasn't going to risk another mishap in the bath. He was going to assist Amber.

Amber was standing on the balcony, waiting for the water to arrive when he walked out the glass doors. "I'm going to be your ladies' maid tonight," he said without preamble. "So, after your bath, get into a chemise, and I'll help you with the rest." At least that way she'd be decently covered. *He hoped.*

"But—"

"There are no buts, sweetheart. I'm not taking any chances."

"But—"

"I'll be right outside your door. Call me when you've finished your bath." Without giving her a chance to argue, he strode out. With each step, he told himself his decision was made for Amber's safety, not because he ached to put his hands on that beautiful body.

After the boys filled Amber's tub and left, Clay paced back and forth between the hall door to her room and the one adjoining his. It seemed as if he'd walked fifty miles before he finally heard her voice.

"All right, Your Grace. You may assist me now."

He smiled at her formality and opened the door. For a score of seconds, he had to fight to keep from laughing. She was standing in the center of the room in her chemise with a corset pressed to her middle, the satiny laces dangling at her sides, and she had a quilt clutched over that, shielding her front.

Clay cleared a chuckle from his throat. "You don't need the corset."

"Bite your tongue. Katherine and Georgina would collapse in fits of vapors if I were to show myself at a party without proper undergarments. Now, please, no more remarks. Just lace me."

He mentally shook his head over the senselessness of wearing something he was sure had to hurt. "All right, sweetheart. Turn around."

When she complied, he tried not to notice how the soft batiste molded her shapely spine as he gathered the two bottom laces and looped them together.

"Tighter."

He undid them and tried again, more snugly this time.

"It's still not tight enough."

"Well, it'll have to do. I'm not going to break your ribs and squeeze the breath out of you just so you can have an eighteen-inch waist."

"Sixteen."

He rolled his eyes and tied the streamers to his own satisfaction, all the while listening to her mumbles about his inability to perform the simplest task. When he finished, he glanced around the room. "Where's your petticoat?"

"In the trunk."

He inspected the enormous mounds of lace and satin. "Which one?"

"All of them."

He stared in horror. "There must be twenty of them."

"Twelve."

Snatching a white one with several layers attached

to the waistband, he approached her. "This is all you need, and you're going to have to let go of the blanket before you can step into it."

"Clay it isn't prop—"

He glared.

"Oh, all right." She tossed the quilt on the bed and faced him, hands on hips.

Desire shot through him like a wildly dispersed arrow. The corset had pushed her breasts up so far, he could see the darker circles around her nipples peeking over the lacy edge of the chemise. The exquisite mounds of white flesh quivered with each breath she took, and he knew the slightest movement would reveal all.

He held his breath in anticipation.

"Do you expect me to step into the petticoat with you holding it to your chest?"

He dragged his gaze up. "What? I mean, no. Of course not." He knelt in front of her and extended the opening of the undergarment, but his eyes had returned to her chest.

She bent forward to gather the bottom of her chemise before stepping into the center of the frothy lace.

The chemise gaped. A nipple peeked out.

Clay sucked in a sharp breath.

She reached down to take the waistband from his stiff fingers, and the other nub escaped.

His shaft throbbed, then expanded, straining against the front of his breeches. His hands trembled. Damning his loss of control, he forced himself to look away.

"Clay? Did you hear me? I said you're going to have to lift my dress over my head."

His gaze drifted to the open armoire, to the green satin dress hung so carefully on a wooden hanger. He was going to have to cross the room to get it—and face her in that skimpy chemise again.

Well, he consoled himself, at least she won't have to bend over.

He gathered the gown and cautiously approached her.

With a wan smile, she turned her back to him and raised her arms for him to pull it over her head.

For a score of seconds, he explored the corset hugging her delicate ribs, the tiny waist he knew he could span with his hands. Then his gaze drifted over her shoulder . . . and down. With her arms up, the front of her chemise bowed outward, and he could clearly see both breasts, their pale pink centers stiff and thrusting.

A film of moisture beaded on his brow. No matter how hard he tried, he couldn't look away. Couldn't stop thoughts of closing his mouth around one of those beautiful peaks.

"Clay, will you hurry? My arms are getting tired."

Snapping to his senses—what was left of them—he quickly tossed the gown over her head and laced it. "I think you can manage the rest from here." Hurrying past her, he stalked to the open balcony doors and took several deep breaths, trying to calm the ache pulsing through his lower body and slow the pounding in his chest.

The woman unbalanced him as no other ever had. He wanted her, yet the unholy desire went against every moral fiber in his body. Her father had trusted him. She was an innocent.

And she belonged in London . . . the one place he would never live.

# Chapter 16

"Clay?" Amber called from her room. "Do you know anything about styling hair?"

He glanced across the balcony and glared at the glass doors. That's all he needed. The second his fingers slid into those silky locks, it would be all over. He couldn't do it. Not and keep his sanity, anyway. "No. But I'll see if I can find someone who does."

Marching into the room, he avoided looking at Amber as he crossed to the outer door. "I'll send someone back in a few minutes."

He locked all the doors and went in search of Rebecca.

When Rebecca returned an hour later, he headed upstairs to bathe and dress.

Slipping into his dark green velvet breeches and coat, he tied on a frilly white cravat that matched his shirt, then shoved his feet into buckled shoes. He curled his lip in distaste, and kicked them aside, settling for his Hessian boots instead.

After running a brush through his hair and tying it

back, he crossed to the double doors and knocked softly. "It's time to go, sweetheart."

"All right." There was a breathless quality to her voice that made his flesh tighten.

Cautiously, he opened the door and stepped inside.

Amber stood across the room from him, holding a diamond and amber necklace. "Would you fasten this for me?" she asked, lifting her hand to show him the piece of jewelry.

Clay was too dumbstruck to move. He'd always known Amber was a beautiful woman, but the creature standing before him was so lovely, he couldn't put his thoughts into words. The dress hugged her body like a coat of shimmering green paint. The pearly edges of the low bodice barely hid the peaks of her breasts, while the dripping lace on her sleeves covered her hands completely. The smooth tips of her well-shaped fingernails were all he could see.

His gaze lowered to the necklace in her hand, and he recognized it. He'd sent her the necklace for her thirteenth birthday. Still, he dreaded putting it on her. He would have to touch her—brush his fingers across the back of her neck.

"Clay? Is something wrong?"

His gaze darted to hers, then slipped away. He took a deep breath before he spoke. "No. I was just spellbound. You're breathtaking."

Her cheeks flushed, and she avoided his eyes. "It is a lovely dress, isn't it?" She smiled, showing her small, even white teeth. "Georgina made it for me." At her words, a sudden dawning entered her eyes, and she hesitated. "Um, Clay? Is there . . . I mean, has anything come up missing at Westshire recently?"

"Some minor items."

Amber tightened her fingers on the necklace. "I feared as much. And I'm afraid Georgina is at fault. She never has much money, and when she wants to give me a gift, which is too often, she will acquire the funds by any means possible—usually by taking small articles that don't belong to her and selling them to the nearest merchant." She gave him a weak smile. "I'll reimburse you for the items, and I'm sure you'll find them somewhere in Middlesbrough."

He smiled inwardly at Georgina's perfidy. A chess piece, for bloody sake. "Amber, I couldn't care less about those trinkets. Seeing you in that dress is worth that and a great deal more." The second the words were out, he cursed himself. *Again* his thoughts were headed down paths he'd tried to avoid. He took the necklace and stepped behind her.

Her warm lilac scent drifted upward, and he inhaled the tempting fragrance. With hands that weren't as steady as he'd like, he looped the necklace around her throat and rested his fingers against her nape to fasten it.

The silky warmth of her skin sent a streak of desire straight to his loins.

Quickly hooking the clasp, he snatched his hands away. "Ready?"

She settled the amber necklace in the valley between her breasts and nodded.

Determined to keep his gaze from that spot, he fixed on the tiny scar on her temple and offered his arm.

As Amber descended the stairs holding on to Clay's arm, she felt like a queen. Her gown was absolutely lovely, and her hair, piled at the crown with glossy curls, sparkled with scores of tiny diamond and emerald pins.

She smiled when she recalled the way his hands trembled when he'd helped her dress and how he'd finally decided to send Rebecca to her. It was a clear indication that he wasn't as immune to her as she suspected he was. The thought warmed her.

She sent him a sideways glance, and a tingling thrill ran through her. He was absolutely stunning in dark green. She knew his shoulders had never looked so broad or his waist so slim. His hair so dark. His eyes so very, very green.

"Have I told you how breathtaking you look?" Clay murmured as they reached the foyer.

"Yes, Your Grace. Five times now, if I'm not mistaken."

"So few?"

She laughed lightly, feeling happy for the first time in days.

The ballroom was alight with the glow from hundreds of candles, from the enormous chandelier in the center of the ceiling to the gold wall sconces lining creamy brocade-covered walls.

Green and gold streamers looped from the edges of the ceiling toward the chandelier. Matching bows adorned the minstrels' stage, beige curtains, and the corners of linen-draped tables—one filled with cheese, grapes, biscuits, apples, and meat pies, the other piled high with brightly wrapped gifts.

The scent of cinnamon and orange wafted from an enormous glowing fireplace at the far end of the room, and her gaze slid to Georgina, who was talking to one of the minstrels. Amber knew her cousin was responsible for the delicious fragrance. She couldn't count the times she'd seen Georgina toss cinnamon sticks and orange peel into the fireplace before a special occasion, claiming the welcoming aromas put everyone in cheerful spirits.

Well, it certainly worked on Amber. She felt as if she were floating.

"Happy birthday, beautiful. You look absolutely ravishing," Morgan said sincerely as he took her hand and kissed her fingers.

He was extremely handsome dressed in deep blue satin.

"So ravishing," he continued, "that I feel the constraints of bachelorhood melting away."

"Perhaps you should cool off then," Clay teased, "before you end up in a puddle at her feet."

Morgan chuckled and gave his brother a mock salute. "Aye, Captain."

Genuine fondness brightened Clay's eyes as he watched Morgan stroll toward the table piled with food, then he leaned toward her. "Morgan is going to make it appear to the others that he's overindulged in food, so when he retires early because he's feeling ill, no one will doubt him."

"Well, I hope it wor—"

"Amber, child. You look lovely," Katherine called out as she and the others descended on them.

Katherine was stunning in her deep blue velvet gown trimmed with pale blue lace. The front skirt parted to show layer upon layer of matching satin ruffles. Her hair had been styled in a high crown of curls and heavily powdered. At her gloved wrist hung the ever-present head scratcher.

Amber squeezed her godmother's hand in greeting.

Well wishes and hugs were given by each of her friends, and Amber had a difficult time believing that any one of them could want to harm her. Still, the knot of apprehension in her chest wouldn't ease.

The next hours passed in a gay atmosphere of clinking glasses, sparkling conversation, and the soft strains of violin music. Amber had danced with every male in the room . . . except Clay. And she'd had to bite her lip several times to keep from laughing at the way Morgan continually stuffed himself. If he didn't stop soon, he really was going to be sick.

As the musicians began another slow tune, Clay walked toward her. He had just held out his hand in an invitation to dance when Morgan lifted his glass and bellowed, "It's time for Amber to open her presents." He popped a handful of grapes into his mouth.

A flicker of regret touched Clay's eyes before he guided her toward the table filled with presents. As they walked, he spoke in a soft tone. "After you open your gifts, we'll dance. But near the end of the set, we'll have an argument."

"About what?"

"I don't know." Clay gave her a lopsided grin. "But I'm sure we can think of *something* to disagree about."

At any other time she might have agreed, but tonight she felt too happy to quarrel about anything.

"Amber, over here!" Albert called. He was standing by the table, motioning to a chair he'd placed near one end. His burgundy satin coat parted with the movement. "Sit here while you open your presents."

Ellison stood beside Katherine and Georgina, smiling broadly. Robert stood with a drink in hand, his foot braced on the fireplace hearth, watching the festivities.

Feeling a little giddy, Amber primly sat down and straightened the folds of her lovely gown.

Morgan stood at the opposite end of the table, and when he saw she had finally settled, he lifted a wrapped parcel, then pitched it high in the air toward Albert.

Her brother caught it with ease and handed it to her. Her brother. She still couldn't get used to that.

Trembling from excitement and a little trepidation over what might transpire later, she opened a piece of parchment that had been tucked beneath the ribbon. "Something beautiful for a beautiful woman. Love, Morgan."

She smiled at the big, attractive man, and he winked boldly in response.

Inside the package lay a magnificent diamond and emerald brooch in the shape of a rose with a leafy stem. "Oh, Morgan. It's lovely." Blinking back tears, she carefully pinned the brooch to the material of her gown near her shoulder. The jewels winked like stars in the dancing candlelight.

"Open mine next," Albert instructed, handing her another package.

He had given her a riding crop with her name intricately stitched into the leather handle.

Robert gave her hair combs made of iridescent abalone shells.

Katherine's gift was an ivory fan with gold tassels and tiny Chinese figurines etched on each thin panel.

Ellison had bought her a stunning gray riding hat with a white ostrich feather.

As if the exquisite gown hadn't been enough, Georgina also gave her a lacy white shawl twinkling with small amber beads.

Amber was so pleased, she was certain she was going to cry. Such lovely gifts, yet one of them . . .

Clay took her hand and pulled her up out of the chair. "My gift is too cumbersome to bring inside. We'll have to take you to it."

Her free hand automatically slipped to the gold dagger in her pocket, and she stared at him in confusion. "But—"

"Shh. Come on, sweetheart, don't spoil my surprise."

Realizing that he didn't want anyone to know about the dagger, she quietly followed him to the stables.

The others almost beat them there in their anticipation to see what Clay had given her.

If she lived to be a hundred years old, she knew she'd never get over the shock of seeing Sahara Dawn standing in the middle of the aisle wearing a stunning saddle painstakingly stitched with white leather—*and a giant bow dangling from her golden mane.*

Amber's gaze flew to Clay.

Tenderness darkened his emerald eyes. "Happy birthday, sweetheart. She's all yours."

Several gasps echoed through the stables.

Amber's eyes stung. "But what about your plans—"

"I'll take the foal when it's born, and I'll get another mare."

This time there was no way she could stop the tears. They slid down her cheeks as she buried her fingers in the horse's soft mane. Clay's generosity and understanding knew no bounds.

"Come on," Morgan grated, his voice thick with emotion. "I'm ready for a piece of your birthday cake."

The cake was superb, the wine intoxicating, and when the minstrels began to play, Morgan finally claimed illness and excused himself.

Clay watched his brother go, then swung Amber into his arms and swept her to the center of the ballroom floor.

Breathlessly, she tried to free herself from his arms. "What are you doing? We can't dance like this."

He smiled down at her and drew her closer until they touched from chest to knee. "Yes we can. It's a new dance called the waltz. I'm sure it'll be all the rage during the coming season in London."

"I never heard of it—and I certainly don't know how to *do it.*"

"Just follow me." He swirled her around the floor, his taut muscles flexing against hers as they swayed to the haunting strains.

Amber feared she would swoon. Never in her life had she felt a man's body move so erotically against her own. It was positively indecent. It was positively . . . marvelous.

She rested her head on his shoulder and let the music and Clay take her away.

"Don't get too comfortable, sweetheart. Remember, this is when we have our fight."

"Later," she murmured into the folds of his shirt.

Chuckling, he nuzzled her ear with his lips. "After this is over, we'll waltz all night if you want, but right now we have to put the plan into motion. Morgan's waiting."

With a sigh, she lifted her head. "Fine. Go ahead and start."

He studied her for several seconds, then said the one thing he knew would ignite her anger. "You look beautiful in that dress . . . for a child."

*"What?"* She wanted to kick him.

"You've filled it out quite nicely, but—"

"How dare you!"

He raised his voice for the others to hear. "Stop acting like such an adolescent, Amber. I was trying to compliment you."

"If that's a compliment, I'd rather be insulted!"

"You want an insult? Fine. Instead of looking like a woman, why don't you try *acting* like one?"

Getting into the game, Amber shoved away from him and jammed her hands on her hips. "You wretched cur. You have no right to speak to me like that."

"Your father gave me the right."

The rush of pain staggered her, and she clamped a hand over her mouth.

Instantly, he reached for her. "Amber, I didn't mean—"

"Get away from me. And *stay* away." Whirling around, she rushed out to the courtyard. Her heart was pounding so hard, she had to fight for breath. She knew Clay had tried to make their argument appear real, but the remark about her father had caught her off guard.

She knew he hadn't meant to hurt her, but sweet Providence, he had. Drawing in a settling breath, she wrapped her arms around her middle and walked to the center of the patio. Well, she consoled, if nothing else, they accomplished what they set out to do. Now all she had to do was wait to see who followed her.

Glancing around, she wondered where Morgan was hidden.

The ballroom door opened, and Amber felt a jolt of panic as she swung around.

Albert walked toward her.

*Oh, please, Lord. Not him.* Instinctively, her hand went to her pocket. She wrapped her fingers around the hilt of the dagger. It felt warm to her clammy hands.

He stopped a few feet from her. "Are you all right?"

"I will be when I calm down."

He gave her a boyish grin. "Want me to avenge your honor and call him out?"

He looked so adorable standing there in the lantern light like her avenging angel, she knew he couldn't possibly be the one. She eased her hand out of her pocket and massaged her opposite wrist. "No." She inflicted a note of anger into her voice. "I just wish Clay would open his eyes and stop seeing me as a child."

"What do you want him to see you as?"

That stopped her for a heartbeat, then the answer came on the wings of truth. "As a woman."

Albert rested his hip on the back of a bench and folded his arms. "If you ask me, I think that's the problem. He *does* see you as a woman, and he's not sure how to handle it."

"What makes you think that?"

"Just the way he looks at you when you're not watching. The way his eyes follow you around a room. The way he finds reasons to touch you."

Did Clay really do that? "What made you so observant?"

"I'm not particularly observant, but I'd have to be blind not to see what's going on between you two."

"There's nothing going on." That was the truth.

"If there isn't, I'm sure it's not by Clay's choice." Albert straightened. "Are you sure you're going to be all right?"

"Yes."

"Then I'll say good night."

That gave her a jolt of surprise. Albert never retired early. "You're going to bed?"

He looked disconcerted for a second, then gave a brisk nod. "Er . . . like Morgan, I think I overindulged."

He was lying. She'd known him all her life, and she knew when he wasn't telling the truth. Wondering at his true plan, she forced a smile. "Thank you again for the riding crop."

"You're welcome." Looking decidedly sheepish, he turned and ambled back inside.

"One down." Morgan's voice whispered out of the hedges behind her.

She opened her mouth to respond when the door opened again and Katherine stepped out. Her gaze darted around the courtyard and came to rest on Amber. "There you are, child. I was beginning to worry about you. Why do you not come back inside before you catch a chill."

Amber studied her godmother. She was the epitome of protocol and etiquette, obsessively so, but Amber knew she harbored a deep sense of compassion and caring for others. "Is Clayton still in there?"

"Yes, dear, he is."

"Then I'll wait a few minutes."

"If that is your wish, then I will—"

The hedge rustled.

Katherine's gaze fearfully swept the courtyard. "What was that?"

"Probably a rabbit."

Her godmother didn't appear convinced. "Are you certain it is safe for you to be out here?"

220

"There are guards posted everywhere. No one can get into the courtyard without being seen. I'll be fine."

Katherine still looked concerned. "If you are certain?"

"I am."

"Very well, child, but do not stay out too late." She started to turn but stopped. "I am glad Ellison insisted you have your party. Even though I was opposed for propriety's sake, it has put us all in better spirits." She gave a rare smile. "Happy birthday, dear."

Warmth infused Amber. She adored Katherine.

As the ballroom door closed behind her, Morgan grumbled from the hedge. "Sorry, Amber. I didn't mean to move, but a spider crawled down my collar."

"Did you get it out?"

"You can wager Westshire on that. Its hairy little corpse is lying at my feet."

"Amber?"

She stiffened, then turned toward Georgina's voice. Her cousin was leaning out the door, looking around. When she spotted Amber, she smiled. "There you are, love. Come along, now. It's much too chilly for you to remain outdoors. Besides, everyone has retired but us, and I'm looking quite forward to my soft bed."

"Everyone?"

Georgina tucked a strand of hair back into her bonnet. "Yes, love." She gave Amber a knowing look. "Even His Grace."

"I see. Very well, you go on up. I'll be along in a minute."

"Don't take too long. I'm not up to nursing you through a bout of the ague." Eyes twinkling, she closed the door.

Amber smiled fondly. Georgina had been more of a mother to her than her own had ever been. "You know, Morgan. I think we're wrong about all my friends."

"Morgan's not here."

Amber sucked in a breath at the sound of Clay's voice.

He was standing outside the gate of the maze, his head tilted to one side, lantern light playing over the silken strands of his dark hair. The cravat at his throat had been pulled loose, revealing the deep tan of his throat. The pulse throbbed steadily at its base.

Amber's heart picked up speed. He was so handsome, just looking at him made her shiver. "Where is he?"

"I sent him inside."

"Did he tell you we were wrong about my friends?"

"No. But he did say he'd given his presence away— and not everyone came out here."

"Only Ellison, and after Katherine and Albert were here, I'm sure he saw no need."

"Possibly." He moved toward her, his eyes on hers, his movements slow and graceful.

A sudden stillness pulsed through the night air. She could hear the beat of her heart. The rasp of her breath.

He stopped in front of her, so close she could smell the musky scent of his cologne, then he held out his hand.

Unsure, she stared at him.

His gaze sank into hers, and his mouth drew into a beautiful smile. "I believe this is our dance."

"Here?"

"No." He slid his fingers between hers and closed his hand. "In the center of the maze."

# Chapter 17

Clay felt Amber tremble as he guided her through the maze. For some reason, he had the awful feeling that she was afraid rather than excited about learning the maze's secret. Of course, that was ridiculous. She had nothing to fear from the hedges.

Still, for someone who was supposedly enthusiastic about searching for the secret, she hadn't once asked to go into the maze since he rescued her and they had the confrontation with Albert.

Was that the cause? Was she afraid of Albert's disapproval?

"Oh," Amber breathed. "It's beautiful."

Clay glanced up. He'd been so deep into his thoughts that he hadn't realized they'd reached the center.

He smiled, surveying the half-acre clearing surrounded by towering foliage. The thick lawn, as always, was immaculately groomed. Steam rose into the crisp fall air from the hot spring pool he'd enjoyed so much over the years. He loved the feel of the soft sandy bottom and the glossy red tiles rimming the edge. James Wingate had ordered them specially made from Italy, and Miranda took great care to see that the tiles gleamed like polished jewels.

"Is that steam rising from the water?" Amber's soft voice was filled with awe.

He smiled down at her. "Yes. There's a hot spring that feeds the pool. Though it was found quite by accident. When James Wingate had the pool dug, his original intention had been to tile it and fill it with fresh water, but the workers unexpectedly struck the spring. Of course, my illustrious ancestor never admitted that it was an accident. He took full credit for locating one of the few hot springs in eastern England."

Her gaze drifted to the covered gazebo with its cushioned benches, then to the small building to the right of it. "What's that?"

"It's used as a changing room and towel storage." It had another use, too, but he wasn't going to tell Amber about that. Not yet, anyway.

He drew her close to him. "I believe this is our dance, milady."

She chuckled warmly. "There's no music."

"We'll make our own." He molded her sweet curves to his own harder ones and inhaled her sultry lilac scent. That particular flower had suddenly become one of his favorites.

Amber hesitated briefly, then placed her slim hand on his shoulder as they began to move in a mock dance.

The whole evening he had watched her in that damnable dress. He'd watched the way her hips swayed when she walked and how the hem of her skirt would lift to reveal a trim ankle, the way the silk clung to her small waist and midriff and lovingly cradled the weight of her breasts.

He couldn't count the times he'd caught himself, and every other male in the room, staring at the low cut of her gown. The square neckline revealed enough of her soft flesh to make him nervous. He'd spent half the night expecting her breasts to pop out of the lacy bodice.

When they'd had their fake argument, he'd actually been relieved when she'd stormed out. He could breathe again. And think.

But he hadn't meant to hurt her. "Amber, about our argument—"

She placed a finger on his lips. "I know you didn't mean to upset me. There's no need to apologize."

It was all he could do not to kiss her finger.

She withdrew her hand and nuzzled into the crook of his neck. "Let's not talk anymore. Just dance." She began to hum a sweet lullaby he'd heard Georgina sing to her as a child.

A child. Amber wasn't a child anymore.

He brushed his cheek against her hair and swayed to the slow rhythm of her song. The tips of her breasts teased his chest through his silk shirt, and desire curled around his manhood. He breathed deep, trying to control the erratic beat of his heart and slow the blood rushing through his veins. It didn't help. The air was filled with Amber's scent. His sex began to pulse.

"Clay?"

The sound of her voice was like a caress. "Yes?"

"There's something I want for my birthday, and I was wondering if you'd give it to me."

He'd give her the moon if he could reach it. "What's that?"

She paused, then whispered softly, "A kiss."

"You've been kissed before."

"Only by you, and only when you were angry."

His heart kicked into uneven beats. She'd never let

anyone else kiss her. The thought was staggering. Easing her away from him, he looked into her eyes. "Are you sure this is what you want?"

"Yes."

He wanted it, too. Bad. Praying he could stop before things got out of hand, he slowly lowered his head. Very gently, he brushed his lips across hers and felt a jolt of pleasure when she inhaled sharply. He returned to sample more of her incredibly soft lips. They were warm and pliable, and erotically moist.

The moistness drew him, and he parted her lips. Slowly, so as not to frighten her, he touched her tongue with his.

A tremor ran through her, and she gripped his arms.

He deepened the kiss, savoring her taste, her softness. His hands took on a life of their own, learning the contours of her firm hips, the delicate curve of her waist, the tautness of her flat stomach.

A small moan trembled beneath his mouth, and he knew she needed more—not as much as *he* needed but more. He slipped a hand behind her head and brought her mouth closer while his other eased over her breast.

A quiver ran through her, and he closed his fingers around the firm mound. She filled his hand as if she were made just for him. He plunged deep into her mouth, mating with her tongue, while his hand drew pleasure from her woman's curves. Through the material he felt her nipple bead against his palm, and another burst of desire rushed to his shaft.

He pulled her closer, pressing her lower body to his. Hungry for her woman's heat, he manuevered closer still, kissing ear and neck, the beckoning swells of her breasts.

"Oh, Clay," she whispered, arching back, exposing more of her long smooth throat.

He slid his lips over the throbbing pulse at the base, then drew the tender skin at the side of her neck into his mouth. He nibbled gently, tasting and feasting, but he wanted more.

His mouth returned to hers as his fingers worked to free her laces and ease the top of the gown down her shoulders, then lower, until her breasts sprang free. He wanted to look at her, but he wanted to touch her more. His palms covered her naked flesh.

She was so smooth and firm, so beautifully shaped. He brushed his thumbs over her pearly nipples, marveling at the way they came to life for him.

She clutched his hair, her fingers trembling as she clung to him. "What are you doing to me?"

Clay froze. *Yes, Cordell. Just what are you doing?* Guilt swarmed him, and he released her. With unsteady hands, he righted her clothes and brushed the hair that had come loose out of her eyes. "I was kissing you the way a man does a woman." Swinging her up into his arms, he gave her another slow, lingering kiss. When he felt himself losing the battle again, he raised his head and started walking. "It's late, sweetheart. You need to be in bed."

"With you?"

His step faltered, but he quickly righted himself. "No. You wanted to be kissed for your birthday, and I've granted your wish. That's as far as it goes."

"Why?"

*"Why?"* He stood her on her feet and gripped her by the shoulders. "Tell me, Amber. If I asked you to marry me and leave London, right now, today, and never come back, would you do it?"

Her eyes brightened, and his hopes soared, then slowly the shine began to fade into a shadow. "I can't."

With superhuman effort, he controlled the swift stab of pain in his chest. He stepped back. "That's why we won't share a bed." Gripping her arm, he hauled her upstairs and all but shoved her into her room.

After securing the doors, he went out onto his balcony to breathe in the cool salt air, hoping to clear his foggy senses. Bloody hell. He'd never wanted to possess a woman so bad in his life. Thoughts of making love to Amber were clouding his brain. He had to look at the situation rationally.

He had two choices. He could make love to her and give up his dream, or he could leave her the hell alone. There was no thought to making love to her and taking her with him to fulfill his dream. Amber was like his mother. If Clay took her away from London, his beautiful lilac would wither and die.

He wasn't going to battle the *ton* for Amber's love the way the Captain had his mother. She had given up society and married the Captain—for all the good it did. Unless Clay gave up the idea of returning to the Colonies and spent the rest of his life in London, going to balls and the theater and the opera and the endless round of parties, listening to foppish men and feather-headed women gush and coo insincerely over his impressive title, he and Amber could never be together.

He cared for Amber. Hell, he *loved* her, but he could never be happy here, and in the end, he'd only make her unhappy. Damn it. He wouldn't do that to either of them.

He would not make love to Amber Sinclair.

Firm in his resolve, he headed for bed, vowing he wasn't going to dream about her, either.

But he did, over and over, until he finally got up to smoke a cheroot. Dragging on his breeches and lighting a candle, he crossed to the bureau and reached for a carved wood box. His fingers had just touched the clasp when he smelled the familiar odor of burning wood.

\* \* \*

"Amber, get up!"

"*Awk.* Fire on the bridge! Fire on the bridge!" Poo squawked wildly.

Clay's bellow and Poo's screech jarred her from a very pleasant dream, and she opened her eyes to see Clay standing over her, gripping her shoulders. "Damn it, wake up. The house is on fire!" He hauled her to her feet and shoved Poo's cage into her hands. "Go to my balcony. I'm going to wake the others."

"*Awk.* Gangway. Gangway."

Clay darted out the door and down the hall. A second later, she heard him swear. "Son of a bitch!"

She rushed into the hall with a flapping, squawking Poo. "What is it? What's wrong?"

"The fire's on the other side of this door." He slammed his fist against the panel leading to the stairs, causing the muscles in his bare shoulders to bunch in anger. "I can't open it."

Panic skipped through her. They were trapped. No! They couldn't be. She thought wildly for a way out. Clutching the cage to her chest, her gaze darted toward her room. "Clay, quickly. We can climb down the ivy."

He grabbed her by the arm as he raced back into his room. "No. For all I know, the whole damned manor may be on fire. We've got to help the others." As he spoke, he picked up a burning candle, then reached up and touched a lever above the fireplace. The whole wall, hearth and all, moved outward.

The familiar scraping sound jolted her. How many times had she heard that noise in the night, then moments later felt completely alone? He'd left her without even telling her.

Lifting the candle high, he took her hand and drew her into a dark winding staircase. Poo clung to the bars with his beak and beat his wings as they all but ran down the steps. They reached a small square landing that led to a door on the left and more stairs straight ahead.

"Hold this." Clay shoved the candle into her free hand. Cautiously, he approached the door, feeling its surface for heat with his palm. Apparently satisfied that a fire wasn't scorching the other side, he carefully turned the knob and opened it.

They were on the second level where the guest chambers were, and nothing, not even smoke, could be detected.

Clay rushed into the hall and glanced around.

Everything was as it should be.

He hurried to the closed door leading up to their rooms and touched the surface, then drew his hand back sharply. "Damn it! Amber, tear off a piece of your nightdress. I need to use it to open the door. Then get the servants and tell them to bring water."

*"Awk.* Man the boats. Man the boats."

She ignored the lorikeet and stared at Clay. A part of her nightgown? She glanced down at the thin material. From where? Setting the cage down, she grabbed the hem and tried not to wince as she ripped off a section clear to her knee and handed it to him. As he twisted it around his hand and reached for the hot doorknob, she grabbed the cage and bolted down the stairs after the servants.

She had just reached the foyer when she heard Clay's bellow. "Morgan! Get out here!"

The house erupted with activity as the servants rushed up and down stairs with buckets of water; Morgan shouted orders; Poo squawked; Clay roared obscenities; and her friends came rushing down in a variety of sleeping clothes, looking frightened and nervous, but whether from the fire or Clay's anger, she wasn't sure.

Poo pranced nervously on his perch while Georgina

clung to her arm, and Katherine wedged herself safely between her husband and son. No one said a word. They just stared at the staircase.

The chaos on the second level continued for several minutes, then all at once everything grew quiet, and she knew the fire was out at last.

Amber freed herself from Georgina's grasp and anxiously approached the foot of the stairs, looking upward, waiting.

Clay's voice exploded like a cannon blast. "I'll kill the bloody bastard!"

Morgan came rushing down.

"What is it?" she asked urgently.

"The fire was set deliberately." Morgan only spared her a glance before he turned on her friends. "All of you, in the parlor. *Now!*" His eyes were bright with rage when he swung back to her. "You stay here."

"What happened?"

"We found charred kindling, pieces of wax, and a broken lantern on the stairs."

Amber's hand flew to her throat. "Oh, dear God. Who did it?"

"I don't know, beautiful, but by the temper Clay's in, I wouldn't want to be in the bastard's shoes." Giving her a last look, he ushered the others into the parlor.

Amber stood in silence, hugging Poo's cage and watching for Clay. She knew how ruthless Clay could be when really angered.

Tingles of nervousness skittered over her flesh as she waited . . . and worried.

Several long minutes had passed before she heard his footsteps on the stairs.

She glanced up and saw him coming down. Her breath caught. He'd changed into the clothes he'd worn aboard the *Black Wind*. Why? Then she knew. He was going to do something scandalous, something reckless.

Her gaze lowered to the tight black breeches that hugged his hard thighs and buttocks and defined the abundant evidence of his gender with breathless accuracy. Knee boots encased his steely calves, and a billowing black shirt stretched across his wide shoulders.

Amber bit her lip as she perused the red sash tied around his trim waist, the dagger tucked into the band. A tingle of apprehension wiggled through her, and she lifted her gaze.

He had released his hair from its leather tie, and the gleaming dark locks hung loose, brushing his shoulders, framing his granite face. The rich color contrasted sharply with a gold earring glinting in his left ear. A deadly jewel-handled cutlass dangled at his side.

Her throat closed, trapping the air in her lungs. He was absolutely magnificent.

*And so very, very angry.*

# Chapter 18

Clay saw the shocked look on Amber's face, but he was too angry to speak. The attempts on her life had to stop. And they would—as of right now.

"Stay here," he ordered as he strode toward the parlor.

"Clay, wait!"

He pinned her with a glare. *"Not now."* His gaze shot to Miranda. "Take her to the library." Spinning on his heel, he threw open the parlor door and slammed it behind him.

Katherine spun from where she'd been facing the fireplace. "Your Grace, what is the meaning of . . . ?" Her eyes grew wide at the sight of his clothes, and her bejeweled hand went to her throat.

Smiling evilly, Clay withdrew the cutlass from his sash and pointed it in her direction. "Aye, wench. You have a right to be frightened."

Ellison's muttonchopped jaws started wobbling. "H-How d-dare you!"

With a swiftness he'd learned in battle, Clay sliced the blade through the air and stopped with the tip barely touching Ellison's throat. "Captain Cutthroat dares anything he likes, mate."

Georgina choked and clamped a hand over her mouth.

For the first time, even Albert had doubts. He watched Clay warily.

Clay nearly smiled. Good. Maybe if everyone believed he was insane, he could scare the killer into confessing.

He glanced at his brother, who stood behind the others.

Morgan was grinning like a simpleton.

Casting him a warning glare, Clay focused on the oldest Chatsworth. "Sit."

Ellison dropped onto a settee.

Lowering his weapon, Clay studied each of them in turn, then at last returned his attention to his brother. "Bowman?"

Morgan appeared confused, then he caught on to Clay's game. He straightened. "Aye, Captain?"

"Take the others to the cargo hold." He swung his cutlass toward Albert. "But leave the peacock."

"No!" Katherine wailed. "Do not touch him, you filthy madman!" She started for him, nails bared.

Ellison caught her around the waist. "Katherine, stop before you get us all killed!"

Clay was surprised by her outburst. She'd always held herself in such rigid control. He nodded to Morgan. "Take them."

When the door closed, he returned his attention to Albert. "So, you thought to fry the duke and his wench, eh, laddie?"

Albert stared at him, then regained some of his confidence. "Your game won't wash with me, Your Grace. I know you're not insane."

"Do you?"

"Yes, and I didn't set the fire. I was with Miranda. Ask her. She'll tell you."

Although Clay's expression didn't change, he was disturbed. He'd swear Albert was telling the truth, but there was only one way to find out. He strode to the door and flung it open, bellowing for the benefit of the others, since he obviously wasn't affecting Albert. "Bowman! Bring the black-haired wench."

A moment later, Miranda and Morgan rushed into the room. "Here she is, Captain."

Miranda's eyes were filled with amusement when she faced him, but she tried her best to appear frightened. "Yes, Your Grace?"

Curling his lip, he glanced at Albert. "Were you with him tonight?"

Miranda swallowed. "Er . . . yes."

*The damned imp. He'd told her to stop playing those dangerous games.* He gently pushed her toward Morgan. "Take her to the library. I'll take care of her later."

He gestured with his sword toward Albert. "Take him to the others and bring the Becker woman."

As they walked out the door, he saw Miranda feign confusion and heard her ask loud enough for the rest of their guests to hear, "What's the matter with him?"

"You know there's no talking to him when he's like this," Morgan lied, going along with the game. "He's out of his head."

"What brought it on?" Miranda asked, effectively hiding the humor in her voice.

"The fire. It was because of a fire on the *Black Wind* that he went mad in the first place. He was trapped in his cabin while the ship was burning around him."

Albert gave a choked cough.

Clay smiled at Morgan's incredible imagination.

"We'd heard the tales of his madness," Miranda said, "but I didn't believe them . . . until now. How'd he escape?"

There was a pause, then Morgan rumbled, "His bowman saved him. Come on, let's go. He's waiting for me to bring Mrs. Becker to him, and I don't want to set him off on a rampage. He's liable to kill someone."

Amber had nearly worn the carpet to threads by the time Miranda returned to the library.

"What's happening? Where's Clay?"

Miranda sat in a chair at the long table, then buried her head in her arms. Her shoulders began to shake.

Alarm rushed through Amber. "What is it? What's wrong?"

She lifted her head, and Amber saw that she wasn't crying, but laughing. "C-Clay has g-gone completely in-insane."

*What?*

At the expression on Amber's face, Miranda burst into another fit of laughter, then at last shook her head and wiped the tears out of her eyes. "Oh, Amber, he's not really crazy, for goodness' sake. He's pretending, hoping to force whoever set the fire into confessing."

"Where is he? Where are my friends?"

"In the cargo hold."

"Where's that?"

Miranda grinned. "I believe the study is serving as his 'cargo hold' at the moment."

Amber thought on that for a moment. "Do you think the others truly believe he's gone mad?"

"Would you like to see for yourself?"

"Could we?"

"Of course we can." Miranda bolted out of the chair and slammed the heel of her hand against a book in one of the shelves. Immediately, an entire panel swung outward.

"Another secret passage?"

"Another?" Miranda appeared confused, then her eyes brightened with understanding. "Ah, I see."

Grabbing the candle from the table, she darted into the musky corridor. "Come on if you want to watch."

Gathering what was left of the skirt of her night-dress, Amber hurried after Clay's whimsical aunt.

When they reached one of many alcoves in the passage, Miranda stopped, then handed Amber the candle and opened a small square panel. "This is behind the sideboard. The glasses and spirits are always arranged to leave the room visible. Here, take a peek."

Amber leaned her head close to Miranda's and looked through the opening. A small gasp escaped when she saw Clay looming over Georgina.

Miranda clamped a hand over Amber's mouth and shushed her.

When Miranda took her hand away, Amber pressed her lips together, but she didn't take her eyes off Georgina. Clay had better not do anything to upset her.

Her cousin stood in front of Clay, her lips quivering, her hands knotted tightly. "I swear to you, Your Grace, I didn't start that fire. I would never do anything to hurt Amber."

"You expect me to believe that, wench?"

"Please, you must. Amber is like my own child. I raised her from an infant."

"But the blond wench isn't your child, is she?"

"Yes. I mean, no. Please, let me explain."

He crossed his arms, his hand still gripping the lethal-looking cutlass. "The tide's turning, maid. Make it quick."

Her gaze fixed on the blade, and she swallowed, then began talking rapidly. "My own unborn child died two weeks before she was born, and I knew I'd never have another." She wrung her hands. "Men don't marry 'soiled women,' and that's what I was. I fell in love with our stable boy, Thomas, and conceived his child. He wanted to marry, but my father refused. Finally, I was forced to tell Father about the babe."

She shuddered and wrapped her arms around her middle, her eyes still on the cutlass. "Father became enraged and went after my Thomas. He beat him to death with a whip, then cast me out in shame. My Thomas was dead, and I was ruined."

Tears trickled down her thin cheeks. "Out of the goodness of his heart, my cousin's husband, William, gave me a home and a place to raise my child. But the babe came early and was too small to survive. My last link with Thomas was broken. I nearly went insane. Only Amber's birth and Amber herself kept me intact. It was as if the Lord had given me another chance. In my heart Amber *is* my child. Please, you've got to believe I'd never do anything to harm her."

Amber felt tears sting her own eyes. She'd heard vague stories about Georgina's fall from grace, but she'd never known all that had happened.

"Bowman!" Clay bellowed.

Morgan immediately opened the door. "Aye, Captain?"

"Take the maid below while I ponder her words. And bring me the doxy with the sharp tongue."

Amber slammed a hand over her mouth to stop another gasp. Her godmother would faint dead away if she knew she'd been called a doxy.

The moment the door closed, Clay spun toward the sideboard. "Damn it, Miranda—*and Amber*—if you're going to watch, be quiet."

"Sorry," Amber whispered.

Miranda grinned. "Your performance is wonderful."

"Wait til you see my next one," he warned. "The one where I lock my lovely aunt in her room and feed her bread and water for a week."

"You're getting snippy, Clayton."

"I'll make you think snip—"

The door opened, and Morgan ushered Katherine into the room.

Amber dragged her gaze from Clay.

Her godmother held her chin high, but she couldn't hide the fear in her eyes.

Clay intimidated her even more by swinging his cutlass slowly from side to side. "So, wench. Tell me where you were when a blaze was put to the companionway."

Katherine clasped her hands in front of her and straightened her shoulders. The head scratcher hanging from her wrist swayed with the movement. "Since I have no idea what time the fire started, Your Grace, I could not possibly tell you."

A muscle ticked in Clay's jaw. "An hour ago, wench. One hour."

Katherine raised her chin. "At that time I believe I was in my bed, resting quite comfortably."

Clay laughed wickedly and moved toward her, his hand tight on the cutlass. "Nay, wench. That won't do. Could be a lie, easy as not."

"I do not make a habit of lying."

"But once wouldn't hurt, eh?"

Katherine's eyes blazed. "If you think I am capable of hurting that sweet child, then I suggest you run me through with your wretched sword, and be done with it. Surely, no pain could be greater than being accused of such a heinous crime."

Clay studied her for several long seconds. "You know, lady, I think I almost believe you."

He bellowed for Morgan again and instructed him to take Katherine back and bring Ellison.

"Well, what do you think?" Miranda whispered.

"I don't know. I didn't hear what Albert had to say, and I believe Georgina and Katherine completely."

"Albert was with me."

Amber swung toward her in shock.

Miranda sighed. "It's not what you think."

Amber didn't know what to think, and she wasn't about to make an embarrassing remark. Instead, she posed the question that had been nagging her. "Where's Robert?"

"Overseeing the cleanup of the fire."

Amber started to ask if she'd be able to return to her room tonight, but the appearance of her godfather stopped the words.

Ellison strolled into the parlor looking quite poised, but the loose skin quivering below his jaws gave him away. He was extremely nervous.

Clay held his cutlass up and ran his finger along the sharp edge, his eyes on Ellison over the blade. He looked so sinister that Amber actually shivered.

"So, mate. You are the last. What tale will you tell, I wonder?"

Ellison gripped the lapels on his robe and lifted his wobbly chin. "About what?"

Clay's eyes narrowed dangerously. "Don't jest with me, mate. You won't like the consequences. I know you despised the gold-haired wench's father. Mayhaps you despised her, too. Enough to see her dead."

"That's preposterous. I adore that child. She's been the only bright spot in my miserable existence—and much more of a daughter to me than Albert's been a son." His wig slipped to the side, and he straightened it. "But you are right about me despising William. I did. If he was alive, I still would. That bastard took everything I ever loved away from me. My wife and my son."

"Nay, mate. Does not ring true. You had both under your own roof."

Ellison expelled a harsh breath. "Oh, yes. They were in my home, but neither belonged to me. Albert was William's son, and Katherine only had room in her heart for the man I'd once called friend. I possessed them, but they were never mine." The bitterness in his voice gave Amber chills.

Clay narrowed his eyes thoughtfully and studied Ellison for a score of seconds. "Where were you when the blaze started?"

"In the kitchen with the servant, Bowling. We were indulging in a game of chess."

Clay arched a brow. "I understood that one of the pieces was missing from the game."

"I'm . . . quite aware of that. We used a portion of a biscuit in place of one of the white knights."

Clay gave his words thought, then returned the cutlass to his side. "I will speak with the duke's man. But hear this, mate. If I learn you have lied, I'll run you through and pin you to the wall with me blade."

After Morgan took Ellison to the others, Clay motioned her and Miranda into the room.

To Amber's surprise, Miranda pushed on the wall in front of them and it opened, swinging the sideboard to one side.

"Well, what's the verdict?" Miranda asked, walking to the fireplace to warm her hands.

"What's yours?"

Miranda shrugged. "Personally, I don't think any of them did it."

"What about you, Amber? You know them better than either of us. What do you think?"

Amber sat down on a settee and drew the tattered remains of her nightdress around her legs, trying to keep her gaze on his face and not the way he looked in those enticing clothes. "I'm not sure. Something one of them said or did didn't set right with me, but I can't grasp what it was."

"Think. Damn it, Amber, *think.*"

"Clayton, stop," Miranda ordered. "She's trying her best to remember, and your bullying is only making it harder."

"Fine!" he roared. "In the meantime I'm going to make sure nothing like this happens again." Whirling around, he stormed out.

241

Amber felt a trickle of fear. "What do you think he has planned now?"

"I don't—"

"Bowman!" Clay's bellow carried through the door. "Take the wenches to the first mate's cabin and the blokes to the cabin boy's quarters. Lock them in and feed them rations until this matter is settled."

Amber was horrified. "He can't be serious."

Miranda bit her lower lip and stared at the door. "I'm afraid he is."

# Chapter 19

"We found where the lantern came from, Your Grace," Bowling announced as he walked into the dining room carrying a second platter of fluffy breakfast eggs.

Clay set his fork beside his half-full plate and leaned back in his chair. "Where?"

"The storage closet. Several candles and a single lantern were missing."

Clay felt like smashing his fist through the table. He glanced at Amber and was relieved to see that she seemed unaffected by the mishap. She'd spent what was left of the night in his aunt's room—with Miranda heavily armed. Still . . . "Thank you, Bowling. That will be all."

When the butler departed, Morgan edged his chair a bit closer to the window behind him and washed down a bite of scone with his tea. "Whoever it is, is smarter than we've been giving them credit for."

"Why do you say that?" Robert asked around a mouthful of melon.

Amber, who had still eaten very little, tilted her head, apparently curious to hear Morgan's summation.

Morgan shrugged one of his massive shoulders. "If you think about it, I mean *really* think, you'll see what I mean. Take, for instance, the fact that all of the accidents could have been caused by either a man or a woman. The day of the carriage accident, according to what you told me, Clay, all four of Amber's friends were near the conveyance. Whoever damaged the axle made sure they couldn't be singled out."

He swirled the liquid in his cup. "It was the same when they put the poison in Amber's tea at the inn. The room was filled with any number of people who could have done the deed."

Clay nodded. "There is an exception, though. That day on the beach, when the top of the cliff gave way, Albert had a sound account of his whereabouts." He glanced at Miranda. "Our beloved aunt."

"I still think that was caused by nature," Amber voiced.

"So do I," Miranda seconded. "I simply can't imagine one of the guests having enough strength to dislodge an entire cliff."

"All right," Morgan said, waving a dismissing hand. "Let's forget the cliff for a moment. Recall, instead, the day Amber was nearly drowned in her bath. Everyone was dressing at the time, so none had a solid alibi—and the gloves that were used came from the garden, where any of them could have snatched them during the day."

Robert popped a strawberry into his mouth and chewed thoughtfully. "What about the fencing accident? Do you think it truly *was* an accident?"

"Yes," Clay affirmed. "The blow from my sword knocked Albert's from his hand. I was as much to blame for that as anyone." He glanced at Amber, again experiencing the knot of terror he'd felt.

"Then that only leaves the fire," Morgan surmised. "And, of course, it happened at a time when everyone *should* have been in bed, but they weren't. Albert was with Miranda, and Ellison was with Bowling." Morgan leaned back in his chair. "The way I see it, it has to be one of the women. As I mentioned, all the attempts could have been executed by either gender."

Clay gave it careful thought and decided that Morgan could be right. "Miranda? Did Albert leave at any time while you were with him last night?"

"No." She frowned. "Wait. Yes, he did. He went out for firewood. Because of the foggy chill, I'd used more than normal."

Amber's head snapped up. "He was in your room?"

"Yes, and contrary to what my skeptical nephew thinks, there was nothing romantic happening. Albert and Ellison had had a row, and I found Albert in the courtyard, ready to drown himself in alcohol. I could tell the moment I saw him that he needed help." She shrugged. "So I helped."

"How long was he gone?" Clay asked.

"Perhaps ten minutes."

"Long enough to collect wood *and* start a fire," Robert deduced.

"Your Grace? Lord Chatsworth had cause to leave the chess game for a few minutes also."

Clay whipped around to see Bowling standing in the doorway. It never ceased to amaze him how the man could enter a room so quietly—and know every damn word that was said in the house. "When?"

"Shortly before the fire. He excused himself to—" Bowling glanced at Amber and Miranda. "Er—to . . . well, I am certain you understand the delicacy of his mission, Your Grace."

So Ellison had answered nature's call. That was understandable. It was also damned conveniently timed.

"Perhaps we should check the fireboxes in the

rooms. See which one used the most kindling last eve," Miranda suggested.

Clay shook his head. "It wouldn't do any good. The boxes were filled first thing this morning."

Morgan let out a frustrated breath. "So, we're right back where we started. The women have no one to verify their whereabouts, and the men both had the opportunity."

"You know, Clay," Amber said in a small voice. "You may be sued for holding my friends prisoner." She gnawed her lower lip. "I-I mean, my godparents won't sit still for this type of treatment."

"I wouldn't care if they sued me for every shilling I have. Your life is worth far more than any fortune, sweetheart."

A rosy flush darkened her cheeks, and she averted her gaze to Morgan. "I don't think he understands."

Morgan chuckled. "Oh, he understands, all right. And truthfully, beautiful, keeping them locked in their rooms is much better than what he originally wanted to do."

Clay smiled as he took a bite of egg. Morgan and his imagination were at it again.

"What was that?" Robert asked.

Morgan took a sip of tea and set his cup down, pausing dramatically before he spoke. "He wanted to torture them."

Clay almost choked on the egg.

Amber looked horrified.

Miranda and Robert stifled a burst of laughter with their napkins.

Morgan leaned back in his chair and grinned, watching the various reactions.

When Clay could breathe again, he decided that his brother should take up storytelling for a living. He'd make a bloody fortune at it. Setting his napkin aside, Clay rose. "Fortunately, Morgan talked me out of that idea"—he couldn't pass up his own bit of dramatics—"for now."

Amber was staring at him as if she'd never seen him before, and it made him damned uncomfortable. Her opinion of him had just taken another plunge. Well, it was probably for the best. They didn't belong together.

"If you'll excuse me," Clay said, nodding. "Since our guests are otherwise occupied, I'm going to check on the rye crops this morning and notify the buyers when harvest will begin."

"May I ride with you?" Amber asked without a breath of hesitation.

Clay was barely able to hide his surprise. "If you wish, but make sure you wear a warm cloak," he instructed, wondering why this woman kept him so unbalanced and why she never reacted the way he expected her to. She thought he was capable of torture, yet she wanted to be with him. It didn't make sense.

It took Amber all of two minutes to race upstairs, grab her cloak, and sail down again, her cheeks flushed, her eyes bright with excitement.

Then he realized why. Since they'd arrived at Westshire, she hadn't left the grounds. For her own safety, he'd virtually kept her prisoner. Uncomfortable with the wave of guilt that tumbled over him, he slipped a hand over the small of her back and guided her toward the stables, knowing what a toll that must have taken on someone as free-spirited as Amber. Someone who lived for the social life.

Amber felt the warmth of Clay's hand on her spine and tried to squelch a rush of pleasure. Since they'd had their talk about what happened four years ago, she'd realized what a position she'd put Clay in—and how he'd reacted in the only honorable way possible. Now, when she could think about that night without pain, she could see what she'd done to him. How much it had cost him to send her away.

She smiled to herself as she watched him help the groom saddle the horses. She'd been a fifteen-year-old child that night . . . but she wasn't anymore.

She thought about Markland and how badly she and the tenants needed someone strong and knowledgeable to run the estate. Then she thought of Clay. He was perfect. And he would make a perfect husband for her.

Miranda's words came back to her. *Perhaps you should give him a little nudge.*

The mere thought made her cheeks grow warm. To think that she would even consider behaving as she had all those years ago. No. She was a grown woman now. If Clay wanted her, she wouldn't have to *give him a little nudge.*

Her thoughts drifted to last night in the maze, and her cheeks began to burn. She had instigated Clay's behavior, and true to his honor, he'd called a halt before things got out of hand. He was strong in will and honor, where she was malleable as a kitten when it came to affairs of the heart.

Of course, the fact that she was in love with him—and always had been—didn't help. Still, they *were* adults now. If he truly did want her, there was nothing to stop him. They could marry . . .

Her gaze drifted to where he stood tightening the cinch on her new sidesaddle. There was nothing to stop them now—well, once she found someone to take care of Markland. So why did Clay insist on keeping his distance?

The misty gloom shrouding the sky seemed to descend and cloak her in a damp chill.

"Is something wrong?"

Startled, she glanced up to see him watching her. "No. I was just . . . wondering if it was going to rain."

He motioned her over to Sahara Dawn. "It is. I'm just hoping it holds off until we get home."

"How can you be so sure?"

He cupped his hands for her to step into them and mount. "A seaman learns to read the signs. Sometimes the life of his entire crew may depend on his accuracy. He has to know when to pull into a safe harbor and when to stay and take the wind."

"You love the sea, don't you?"

"There are very few things I love, Amber," he said as he mounted his own horse, "and the sea isn't one of them." He bent forward and drew his palm along Mercury's sleek neck. "But horses are my second love."

She couldn't stop the words. "What's the first?"

His gaze met hers, and he watched her for several seconds, then glanced away. "The Colonies come pretty close." He lifted Mercury's reins and nudged him out the stable door.

Leather creaked beneath her as Amber nudged Sahara Dawn into a slow walk. "Tell me about them."

Clay raised his face to the cool wind. "The parts I've seen, mainly in Virginia and Pennsylvania, are breathtaking. But there's one place that stands out above all the rest—an area called the Shenandoah Valley. England is a beautiful country, but it pales next to that splendid valley. The grass is lush and so green it looks like an artist's painting. Wild animals graze openly because they haven't yet learned to fear humans." His gaze took on a faraway look. "And all men are equal, no matter how much or little money they have. There a man's worth is judged by his behavior, not his station."

Amber sighed as they descended the steep roadway leading to a rolling, open valley below. The Colonies were a difficult mistress to compete with. She'd never heard Clay talk with such emotion in his voice, such reverence. If only there was some way they could share it.

But there wasn't. She carried the burden of Markland on her shoulders. She could daydream about pirates and the lush Colonies all she wanted, but it wouldn't change the fact that she was responsible for scores of people.

She again considered Albert. After all, Markland belonged to him, too. Of course, he didn't know that.

"Want to share your thoughts with me?" Clay asked as he drew his mount up next to hers.

"I was just thinking about Markland."

"Well, don't worry about it, sweetheart. I'm sure my steward is handling things well. He's invaluable to me here. Fortunately, his assistant is handling Westshire passably well in his absence."

"Does your steward by chance have a brother who's as adept as he is?" Maybe then Ellison couldn't do too much damage to Markland.

"No. But he has three sisters."

Sighing, Amber guided her mare around a cluster of heather. "You wouldn't consider lending him to me for a few years, would you?"

Clay chuckled. "Miranda couldn't spare him."

"When do you plan to leave for the Colonies?" *And say good-bye to me forever?*

"As soon as your father's murderer is caught."

"What if they're never caught?"

"They will be."

Amber was hoping he'd say he'd never leave. But Clay wouldn't give up that easily. He would find the killer if he had to *torture* everyone who'd been within ten miles of Markland the day of the accident. She smiled to herself when she recalled Morgan saying Clay had wanted to torture her friends. Morgan's imagination was remarkable—and he seemed to forget that she'd known him and Clay all her life. Clay was not cruel . . . at least not in the physical sense, she amended.

"There's the rye," Clay announced with a sweep of his hand.

Amber followed his gesture to see miles and miles of golden fields dancing in the breeze. The slim-leafed spikes grew long beards to protect their precious clusters of rich, golden seeds. She studied the sturdy plants, impressed by their size and color. "How do you control insects?"

"Ash. The field hands sprinkle it over the plants every few months."

She mentally pictured Markland's barley fields, sometimes overrun with grasshoppers and small black-and-white insects the field hands called chinch bugs. "Does it work on barley, too?"

"I don't see why not."

Filing that bit of information away, Amber returned her attention to the fields. "When do you think you'll begin harvest?"

He studied some of the plants closest to them. "About two weeks. When the seeds turn brown. Come on, let's go into the village, and I'll post a note to the buyers. We have a post rider who comes through three times a week."

As she followed him deeper into the valley, she had the strongest wish that he would be the one to run Markland with her.

Knowing it was an impossible wish, she buried it deep in her heart along with all her other hopeless dreams. Dreams that centered on the tall man riding beside her.

# Chapter 20

Clay had watched Amber the entire day. For the first time since the accident that killed her father, she was at ease and relaxed. She smiled often and laughed when the village children's hands left marks on her skirt, making him wonder if he hadn't misjudged her. Any other lady of the upper class would have had a fit of vapors if children had soiled her expensive clothes.

He loved the sound of her laughter and the way her eyes sparkled. The way her smooth cheeks creased near the corners of her mouth.

The trouble was, he loved everything about her, from her stubborn streak to the way she could arouse him with a single glance. Sighing, he led the way out of the village and headed for Westshire.

Yet, as he rode, he couldn't stop watching her. He studied the way she lightly but surely gripped the reins, the way her breasts swayed with the movement of the horse, the way golden curls danced along her smooth jaw and down her back to her waist.

She was such a beautiful woman.

He shifted in the saddle, feeling a pressure in his breeches. Since she'd opened her eyes that night after the accident, he'd been in a state of half arousal. Everything about her cried out to his male body. Fleetingly, he thought about returning to the village, where he knew he could find a willing widow to ease the discomfort Amber had caused. The trouble was, no other woman appealed to him.

Only Amber did.

Again and again, he had to remind himself of his plans for the Colonies. Still, raising thoroughbreds in the lush Shenandoah Valley wasn't quite as appealing as thoughts of making slow, sweet love to Amber Sinclair.

The fabric of his breeches strained, and even the chilly wind couldn't cool his lust. Swearing beneath his breath, he urged his horse slightly ahead of Amber's until he regained control.

"What's that?" Amber asked.

Horrified that she'd noticed his body's response, he whipped around. To his relief, she was pointing at a large abandoned shed nestled in a grove of leafless maple trees. He let out a quiet breath. "It was built for the field hands for shelter from storms and storing equipment until I had a larger one constructed closer to the fields."

"What's in it?"

"The last time I looked, there was a box of broken tools, a few discarded grain sacks, a threadbare sofa, and a three-legged table."

"What do you use it for now—"

A crash of thunder exploded.

Mercury whipped his head up and reared in fright.

Clay hauled back on the reins and tightened his legs as the stallion tossed its head and pranced sideways. Damn, he'd forgotten how easily the animals spooked during a storm.

He'd almost gotten Mercury under control when another explosion ripped across the sky.

The stallion went wild, bucking and spinning in circles, jerking frantically against the reins. He reared up, pawing at air, then lunged forward in such an unexpected burst that Clay lost his seat.

He hit the grass hard and rolled, instantly coming to his feet.

As he stood in stunned disbelief, watching Mercury snort and paw the ground a few feet away, the heavens opened up in a downpour.

"Damn it!" Clay bellowed. "Amber, come on. Head for the shed." He started for the building but stopped in his tracks when he saw Amber's horse loping toward the stallion.

He whirled around.

Amber was lying on the ground.

Fear tore through him with the force of a lightning bolt, and he broke into a frantic run. "Amber!"

Rain pounded down on his head as he bent over. "Sweetheart?"

She smiled up at him, then winced. "I t-think Sahara Dawn got the better of me."

He was so relieved that she wasn't hurt, he closed his eyes and said a quick prayer of thanks.

"Do you think we could go in out of the rain?" Amber asked on a winded breath.

"God, yes. Come on." He sprang to his feet and took her hand to pull her up.

"Wait!" she cried.

"What?"

"I need to get up slowly. I think I hurt my hip." Her voice was nearly drowned out by the rain.

"Which one?" he demanded.

"The right."

Stepping to her left side, he bent and scooped her up in his arms and headed for the dry shed. Water dripped into his eyes and ran down his cheeks.

Once inside, he stood her by the door until he could beat most of the dust out of the sofa with a nearly bristleless broom. After he sat her down, he wiped the water from his face and glanced around for something to build a fire.

He found some flint, an axe with a split handle, and a discarded periodical. His gaze drifted to the three-legged table, and he smiled.

Listening to the constant drum of rain, he took the ax to the table.

Amber dried herself as well as she could with her petticoats while he checked the stack on an old, rusty cookstove to make sure it was clear of debris, then piled the wood and paper inside. When he at last had a fire going and warmth radiated through the damp, chilly air, he lit a stub of a candle and set it on a crate near Amber, then joined her on the rickety sofa.

She was massaging her right hip.

"How bad is it?"

"I can't tell for the pain."

"Maybe I should take a look at it." The minute the words were out, he could have bitten off his tongue. Exposing her bare thigh was all he needed. He shouldn't do it. Damn it, he shouldn't tempt himself.

The decision was taken out of his hands when Amber turned on her left hip and started gathering her skirt up her injured leg. "If it's not bleeding, I'll be fine. But if it is, be prepared to deal with hysteria. You know I can't stand the sight of blood."

Her hysteria would be easier to take than his lust.

Damning himself for his loose tongue, he brushed her hand aside and carefully inched her skirt up her smooth leg.

She winced. "Ow. Right there."

Being as gentle as possible, he folded the material back to reveal a firm bare thigh—and an angry red scrape. There was no blood . . . except the blood rushing to strategic places in his body. "It—" he cleared his throat. "It looks like you'll have a bad bruise, but there's no serious damage."

"The wretched thing feels broken."

There was only one way to tell. By touching her. It was a bad idea. A dangerous one.

Cautiously, he laid his fingers against her satiny flesh. Her skin was so warm, his fingers tingled. Forcing himself to concentrate, he carefully probed the injured area. Her muscles tightened beneath his fingertips. Desire slammed into his lower body, and in that instant, he knew if he didn't start for Westshire right that minute, he was going to make love to her.

He surged to his feet. "Come on, we're getting out of here."

"Is it that bad?"

"What? Oh, your leg. No. It'll be fine."

"But what about the rain?"

He glanced desperately around the room. "We'll use the grain sacks to cover our heads." Not giving her a chance to argue, he gathered several of the dusty bags and dropped them by the door. "Wait here, I'll find the horses."

Her openmouthed expression was his only answer.

The rain had eased some by the time they got home, but they were still drenched. Clay immediately ordered Miranda to help Amber change into dry clothes, then he hurried up the stairs behind them to do the same.

As he dried and dressed, he couldn't keep his thoughts from Amber. He again pictured her out on that old sofa, her golden hair spilling over the arm, her long leg all peaches and cream in the candlelight.

"Damn," he grumbled. He had to stay away from her. Work was what he needed. Hard work. Buttoning his shirt, he headed for the stables.

"I can't seem to shake the chill," Amber told Miranda as Clay's aunt brushed Amber's hair dry.

"Rain has a way of seeping into your bones," Miranda replied. "Especially sore bones," she teased, referring to Amber's bruised thigh. "But a cup of hot tea might help." She handed over the brush. "I'll see if cook has some water on." With a jaunty step to her stride, she sailed out the door.

While she was gone, Amber tightened the belt on her dressing robe, then continued to brush her hair and think about the mishap at the shed—and Clay's odd behavior. Why had he wanted to leave so suddenly? In the middle of a rain storm. Had she done something?

She thought back to the exact moment he'd changed. He had looked at her leg and was examining it with his fingers when . . . Her hand stilled, holding the brush poised near her head. *Her leg.* He had touched her bare thigh, then surged to his feet.

A smile curved her lips. So that was it. He had been afraid to touch her. Afraid of what might happen if he did. Strangely pleased by that, she began to hum as she continued her ablutions.

When Miranda returned with the tea, she announced that supper would be served shortly, so they set about getting Amber dressed. She took great pains to look her best for Clay, but it was all for naught.

He didn't show up for supper.

Nor had he shown up when it was time to retire, and Miranda helped her undress.

"Where is he?"

Miranda handed Amber her dressing robe and nightgown. "Who?"

"Clay."

"In the stables."

She experienced a jolt of fear. "Is something wrong with the horses?"

"No. Just with my nephew."

"What do you mean?"

Miranda trailed her fingers along the edge of the

257

writing desk. "He's trying to work himself into a state of complete exhaustion. For goodness' sake, he's even scrubbing the wooden stall rails."

"Why?"

Miranda glanced at her sharply. "Don't you know?"

"No."

"He's doing it because of you. I know because he's done it before. When you had your row a few years ago, he was so upset over you, he almost worked himself to death trying to forget."

Guilt swarmed Amber, but she had no idea why. "I haven't done anything to upset him."

"Yes, you have," Miranda said gently. "You made him fall in love with you."

Clay was so tired by the time he returned to his room, he was certain he'd drop into a dead sleep the minute his head hit the pillow.

But he didn't.

Thoughts of Amber refused to leave him. They lay there, just at the edge of his consciousness, recalling the way she smelled, the vibrant color of her eyes, the silkiness of her hair, the sound of her voice . . .

"Damn it," he hissed, tossing back the covers. He should be dead to the world. Instead, he was coiled as tight as a new carriage spring.

Well, he knew what would help. Striding across the room, he pulled on his breeches and headed for the secret passage.

Amber's thoughts had refused to let her sleep. Again and again she heard Miranda's words, *you made him fall in love with you.*

Sighing, she sat up on the edge of the bed and brushed the hair out of her eyes, wishing with all her heart that it was true, but she knew it wasn't. Clay wouldn't try so hard to avoid her if he loved her.

A scraping sound startled her, and she whipped her head toward the connecting doors.

Clay was leaving again.

Curious about where he went on his nightly jaunts, she slipped from the bed and drew on her dressing robe, then quietly opened the door to his room.

Moonlight illuminated the huge bed where Clay slept. It lay in a tumble of sheets and quilts. His pillow was dented in the center, as if someone had tried to punch a hole through it.

The entrance to the passageway behind the fireplace stood partially open.

Wondering where he was going, she thought about following him, but hesitated. She was asking for trouble. But her curiosity wasn't so easily convinced. Gathering the folds of her robe, she stole into the passage.

It was as dark as pitch, and she grabbed a wall to guide her down the narrow stairway. When she reached the landing and door to the second level, she wondered if that was the way he'd gone.

A small flicker bounced against the wall of the stairs just below her, and she knew he hadn't.

Hurrying so she could follow his light, she dashed down the steps.

She saw a door that she knew must go to the first story of the manor, but he went beyond that, too. Down and down, until she was sure they were in the bowels of the earth. Fleetingly, she wondered if this was the secret passage to the cove.

Finally, his light began to climb upward, then suddenly, disappeared altogether.

Amber froze. She was engulfed in blackness. A momentary flash of terror swept her, but she forced herself to relax. The end couldn't be too far.

Placing a hand against the cold, dirt wall on her left, she inched her way forward, wrinkling her nose at the odor of musky soil and dust.

She had gone several yards when her foot hit a hard object in the path in front of her. Recalling the way Clay's candle had risen, she knew it must be stairs.

Wondering where they led, she began to climb. There hadn't been any stairs in the passage behind the cave.

When she reached the top, she found a heavy door slightly ajar.

Only blackness lay beyond it.

Cautiously pushing the door inward, she stepped onto a plank floor. She traced the walls with her hands and found shelves and stacks of towels. Was she in the manor's laundry? No, she couldn't be, they'd passed the first floor long ago.

Searching the walls until she found another door, she carefully opened it.

Moonlight from a clear, rain-washed sky spread over muted green lawns, a gazebo, and the steaming pool she knew was in the center of the maze.

Her gaze drifted to where a pair of breeches lay in a heap by the pool, then to Clay in the water.

He had his arms stretched outward, braced on the tiled edges, his head back, his eyes closed.

Droplets of water glistened in his dark hair, on his wide shoulders, and along the mat of silky hairs on his chest. The water line of the pool drifted against his flat stomach, and she almost envied the way it caressed him.

A heavy warmth moved through her, causing her to tremble.

She knew she should leave and allow him the peace he sought, but something inside wouldn't let her, some pagan part of her that ached to join him.

Slipping quietly out the door, she crept to the side of the pool and stood there for several seconds, waiting for her better judgment to take hold.

It didn't.

She closed her eyes and made a silent plea for forgiveness as she let her robe and nightdress fall to the ground next to Clay's clothes.

Silently, she eased into the water and leaned against the opposite bank. The water was so warm and soothing, yet it was barely deep enough to cover her breasts. She dug her toes into the soft, sandy bottom . . . and waited for him to become aware of her presence.

A distant owl hooted. The slosh of ocean waves floated up from the shore. The aromas of broad-leafed hedges, heather, and her own lilac scent mingled with the steam rising into the still night air.

She wanted to go to Clay, to wrap her arms around him, but she just wasn't that brave. In fact, she was starting to feel very much like a fool. She was behaving as she had four years ago.

The thought made her cringe, and she knew she'd made a terrible mistake. But could she get out of the water without him hearing her? Could she make it back to her room without him discovering she'd followed him?

It was a chance she'd have to take. She turned and gripped the edge of the pool.

"Going so soon?"

His deep, resonant voice froze her in place. The harsh pounding of her heart drummed in her ears, and she wanted to disappear. Still, she knew she had to face him. To explain.

She turned slowly. "I'm sorry. This was a mistake I thought I was beyond making . . . again."

His glittering green eyes bore into hers. "No, sweetheart. The first time was a mistake." His gaze lowered to the rise of her breasts above the water. "This time you knew exactly what you were doing." A sensual, very male smile curved his lips. "You knew exactly what you wanted."

She closed her eyes, wanting to deny his words, but in her heart she couldn't. She *had* known what she wanted—for Clayton Cordell to make love to her.

The realization made her shiver.

Something slid up her thighs to her waist, and her eyes flew open—only to find him standing in front of her, his hands on her waist. How had he moved so quickly?

Amber's heart began to beat so hard, she thought it would pound right through the walls of her chest. "Clay, I—"

"No," he whispered. "The time for talk is over." He moved closer, until they touched from knee to chest.

The contact with his naked body sent streaks of heat and cold flashing through her. Dear Lord, she couldn't take the storm of emotions that were bombarding her. She tried to move, to look away, but his eyes held her as firmly as his hands.

"There's no running, sweetheart. And there's no stopping. As much as I've tried to deny it, I know we both want this."

Moonlight flickered over his intense features, over the sculpted shape of his mouth, the heavy rise and fall of his chest.

Amber knew he was right. She *did* want this. She'd wanted it for a lifetime. Her gaze met his, and the burning desire she saw caused her lips to part in surprise.

His gaze fixed on her movement, then slowly, intently, he lowered his mouth to hers.

When their lips touched, sweet warmth rushed over her, and her lashes fell shut. She wanted to cry out at the way his mouth moved on hers so gently, so sweetly. So elusively.

"Touch me, Amber. The way I want to touch you." The thick desire in his voice made her knees weak.

She gave only a fleeting thought to the consequences of his command, then raised her hands to his face, feeling the water trickle down her arm and into the pool. She explored the contours and hollows of his cheekbones and jaw, noticing the lines of strain, the taut cords at the side of his neck. She wanted to ease that tenseness.

Slowly, she placed her hand against Clay's cheek. The feel of his hot, hair-roughened skin sent tingles through her. She closed her eyes and let her fingers discover all the places she wanted to touch, the thick curve of his eyebrows, his straight nose, the firm shape of his beautiful mouth.

The intimate sensations rushing through her were too much to bear, and she lowered her hand.

He didn't seem to mind. Instead, he returned her ministrations with a gentleness that brought tears to her eyes. He ran his fingertips over her forehead and thin brows, her nose and cheek. But when his fingers slid across her mouth, he lingered, his thumb brushing her lips, then parting them to trace her teeth, to touch the tip of her tongue. It was the most erotic sensation Amber had ever experienced.

Clay let his hands fall away, long before she wanted them to.

Still, the knowledge that he would touch her wherever she touched him next made desire shimmer through her. Wishing she were a bolder person, she timidly raised her fingers to his silky hair. The tie was gone, and his loose hair flowed over her hands and wrists, clinging to her. She explored the perfect shape of his head, the tight cords at the nape of his neck, the smooth curve of his ears. Wanting to touch those spots with her mouth, yet afraid to, she stopped torturing herself.

Only a heartbeat passed before she felt his long fingers slide into her hair. He became intent on touching every strand, testing its length and weight, its softness. He gathered a handful and buried his face in it, inhaling deeply. Then his mouth brushed across her ear, lingering to trace the lobe with his tongue.

Amber's breath stuck in her chest, and she felt him smile against her cheek just before he released her.

Knowing the next move was up to her, she hesitated, then gingerly glided her palms down his arms, then into the water and over the length of his hands, tracing each long finger before moving upward to explore the silken hairs on his chest and the hard contours of his muscles.

His male nipples tightened against her wet palms. A rush of air slid through his teeth.

Amber's own breath caught, and she pulled her hands away.

Clay didn't move for several seconds, as if he was trying to gain control of himself, then slowly he took her hands in his. He brought one up out of the water and placed a kiss in the palm, then he drew her fingers into his mouth one at a time, caressing each with the warmth of his tongue.

She had never felt anything so shocking, so wonderfully exciting. She held her breath and savored each delicious sensation.

She was ready to swoon from lack of oxygen when he finally released her, but the dizziness hadn't even cleared from her head when she felt him glide his palms up her arms, then down, then up again to massage shoulders.

Remembering where she'd touched him next, her stomach tightened, and she waited anxiously.

A heartbeat passed, then two, before he slid his hands into the water and covered her breasts.

Sweet pain flashed through her. Heat spread from the pit of her stomach and settled in an anxious spot between her thighs. She squeezed her legs together to stop the sensation, only to have a sharp stab of pleasure pierce her.

He cupped her, kneaded her, and gently explored her aching centers with smooth, wet fingers.

The heat in her lower body flamed.

Immersed in need, she leaned her cheek against his damp chest and placed tiny kisses over his muscled skin and pebbled nipples, stopping to taste the small nubs with her tongue.

His stomach tightened as she nibbled her way along his ribs and across the upper portion of his stomach until she reached the water line, then up again to adore his chest. She could have kissed him all night.

But he had other ideas.

"It's my turn," he rasped in a thick voice. He eased her back. Their eyes met, and his were filled with such need, she trembled.

He kissed her tenderly, then lowered his mouth to her throat.

Her flesh came alive, anxious for his touch, his kiss.

He caressed her spine while he brushed his lips over the rises of her breasts, her shoulders and throat. Then he lifted her up and slowly, tauntingly, kissed his way to her nipple.

The streak of desire that flashed through her nearly made her cry out. His mouth was so hot, so wonderfully gentle.

He drew on her, caressing her peak with his tongue, suckling, stroking, moving his head back and forth as he nursed hungrily.

The pleasure was so intense, she thought she'd die from it. She grabbed his shoulders for something to hang on to.

He lifted her higher and sought her other breast.

When Amber was sure she couldn't take anymore without crumbling into little pieces, he finally set her back on her feet. An intimate smile creased the corners of his mouth. "Your turn, sweetheart."

The cool air touched the tops of her breasts and

made her nipples tighten even more. Her belly quivered, and her hands trembled as she reached for him.

Never very bold at the best of times, she avoided Clay's lower body and slid her arms around his waist. The tips of her breasts touched his chest. Her belly pressed against his hard lower body, and he sucked in a sharp breath. "Jesus."

His half groan, half whisper made her flesh throb. Drawing in a slow, steadying lung full of air, she worked her fingers up his spine, then down, over his solid, well-defined rear end.

His muscles flexed beneath her hands, and she grew braver. Her fingers brushed lightly over the back of his hair-roughened thighs, then the front. Each stroke brought her closer and closer to his rigid manhood.

He caught her hand when it ventured too near.

"No. Not yet." He covered her mouth with his, filling her with the warmth of his tongue as he eased his hands around her waist and drew her fully against him.

Even through the water his flesh was so hot, she was sure he'd char her to cinders. Her knees grew weak, and she clung to his neck. Her breasts tingled where the hair on his chest teased the tips, her belly tightened at the weight nestled against it.

Clay's magnificent hands massaged the length of her spine, the curve of her hips. When he moved to caress her thighs, he carefully avoided touching her wound, but he wasn't so patient when he explored her bottom.

He shaped her, stoked her, and taunted her until she thought she would bite her lip in two. But the worst part, ah, sweet Providence, the worst part was when he drew tiny circles on the insides of her thighs, inching closer and closer to the part of her that begged for his touch, yet never close enough.

"Your turn, sweetheart." His wonderful hands slid away from her body.

Her eyes snapped open, and she stared anxiously into his. Her turn? What was left? Her gaze lowered to the water, to the hard flesh she knew lay beneath, and heat rushed to her cheeks. "I—"

He took her hand and placed it over his pulsing member. "There's nothing to be afraid of."

His length shifted beneath her hand, and she started, then marveled in his strength, his incredible power. Slowly, cautiously, she began to move her hand, exploring the long, unyielding length, the full softness at the base. She brought her other hand up to absorb and test every glorious inch. She loved the satiny smoothness, the straining ridges, the silken dome.

"Amber, stop." He caught her hands. "I can't take any more." He gave her a crooked smile, then reached for her. But instead of touching her as she'd expected, he lifted her out of the water and set her on the edge of the pool. He studied her face, her eyes, her mouth, then he kissed her, long, and deep, and very, very thoroughly.

She was breathless by the time he moved to nibble her ear and throat. His long fingers teased the tender, flesh of her spine, while his mouth again sought her breast.

She was on fire. There was no other way to describe the searing flames that licked every inch of her skin. The scorching heat that burned through her woman's place.

Then he touched her there.

Her whole body jerked at the jolt of desire that shot through her.

All too quickly, he withdrew his hand, leaving her trembling and aching.

She gripped his shoulders. "Clay, *please.*" She needed to be touched by him again . . . in that special way.

"Easy, sweetheart," he whispered against her

breast. "There's much more to come." He nipped at the sensitive area surrounding her nipple, then covered her and nursed lovingly, drawing her deeper into the warmth of his mouth. When he'd taken his fill, he moved lower, sampling the flesh covering her ribs, her side and stomach.

He gently pushed her back until she was leaning on her elbows on the grass, her feet dangling in the water, then he lowered his head back to her stomach. He cherished her navel, dipping into the tiny recess with his tongue. He burned a trail across her skin as he continued to kiss her hips, the tops of her thighs, the responsive insides.

Her heart was laboring so hard, Amber feared it would collapse from exhaustion. Her arms quivered.

His tongue circled higher on the inside of her thigh, moving ever closer to her woman's place. She became frightened by the sensations that were clamoring inside her. She couldn't let him do this. It was wicked. It was . . . "Oh . . . my . . . God," she groaned as he covered her with his mouth.

Alien sensations tumbled on top of her from every direction. She was being buried alive. Her head fell back. She dug her fingers into the grass, but nothing could stop the maelstrom caused by the slow sweep of Clay's tongue, the teasing strokes and playful jabs. The deep, urgent thrusts.

Her insides were going to explode. She could feel the pressure building. Higher and higher. Nothing could stop it. Nothing could prevent her from shattering into a million pieces.

Then it came. A blinding flash of pleasure that was so intense, it tore a scream from her throat. Her arms collapsed, and she fell back on the grass. Her spine drew into a bow. But he didn't stop. He lifted her bottom and plunged deeper with his tongue, refusing to release her from the landslide that would surely carry her to death's door.

Finally, *finally,* the last shimmer rippled through her, and he let her go—only to join her on the grass. "There's still more, sweetheart. Still more . . ." He rolled her beneath him and nudged her legs apart. His mouth took hers as he rubbed his sex erotically against her throbbing place.

Incredibly, another spark of desire ignited, then grew with each seductive movement as he gently tested her opening, entering the tiniest bit, then withdrawing, then penetrating again, a little deeper each time.

He stopped and eased back until only the smooth tip touched her. "Hold on to me, sweetheart. Hold on tight."

Trustingly, Amber slid her arms around Clay and buried her face in the curve of his neck. She knew what was coming. Georgina had told her what to expect. Bracing herself, she felt him give a shudder, then take a deep breath.

He thrust sharply.

Pain ripped through her, and she buried her lips in his shoulder to keep from crying out. Sweet heavens, that hurt.

He didn't withdraw, but he didn't move either. He was simply waiting. The instant the pain passed, and she relaxed her muscles, she realized what he'd been waiting for.

Carefully, he began to move inside her in slow, arousing circles. As her body became accustomed to his size, he grew bolder, more intense. He lifted her bottom with one hand, while his mouth fiercely sought hers.

He drove into her, deeper, harder, forcing the new, wild sensations upon her again. Air strained to get into her lungs. A coil of pain-pleasure tightened in her abdomen, then burst free in an explosion of delicious, heart-pounding, mind-numbing pleasure.

It went on forever, fed by the provocative movements of his body, the urgency in his deep thrusts.

Through the pulsating spasms she felt him stiffen and shudder. A deep, harsh groan rumbled up his throat, and something wet and warm spilled into her belly.

An instant later, he slumped, his chest slick with water and perspiration, his heart thundering against hers, his breathing ragged and heavy.

The waves still rumbled from the shore, and the scent of hedges and heather still filled the air.

But Amber knew she would never be the same. She had taken the final step into the world of womanhood, and she had never known such complete satisfaction. Not only had Clay given her the greatest gift she'd ever received, she knew he would soon give her another, even better one.

He would ask her to become his wife.

# Chapter 21

Clay stared out across the maze, ignoring the chill that swept his naked flesh. How could he have been such a fool? How could he have let his guard down so readily. And *how* would he now face the consequences?

His gaze drifted to where Amber was struggling into her nightgown. He knew he should offer to help her, but the rage inside him was too great. He'd probably strangle her.

He closed his eyes. Damn it, he couldn't blame her for what happened. It was his fault. *He* was the one who lost control when he saw her in the pool. He was the one who should have let her go when she wanted to, should have called a halt to the madness. And he was the one who would have to make it right.

He'd been in love with her for as long as he could remember. Surely being with her every day, hearing her laughter, seeing her eyes light with happiness would be worth sacrificing his dreams for the Colonies.

Thoughts of England and the *ton* rose, but he determinedly put them aside and faced her. "Amber, I'm sure you're aware of the consequences of our actions and what we have to do to make it right."

Her fingers stilled on the belt of her robe, and she turned to look at him. "Was that a proposal?"

"Yes."

Confusion clouded her lovely features. "A grudging one?"

"No. A sincere one. Damn it, Amber. I just took your innocence. I have no choice. It's my duty—"

"No choice? *Duty?* Is that what it is?"

"That's not what I meant."

"Isn't it? Then tell me, Clayton, do you truly *want* to marry me?"

"If things were different, but—"

"The answer is no."

"What?"

"My answer to your proposal is no." Grabbing the candle and flint on top of his clothes, she whirled around and ran toward the passage.

"Damn it, Amber." He scrambled into his breeches and went after her. But the second he entered the passage, pitch black surrounded him, and he had to stop, then feel his way along the corridor. "Amber!" he called out. "Come back here!" But she didn't answer, and there was no light at all ahead. She must have run to get that far ahead of him. "Damn her."

Amber was so angry, she could have broken a tree in two with her bare hands. Locking the connecting doors, she threw herself on her bed and glared at the ceiling. How gallant of Clayton to sacrifice himself in marriage to her. *Because it was his duty.* She slammed her hand against the feather tick. Curse it all, when was she going to stop breaking her heart over him?

"Right now," she hissed. "Right this minute."

Heaving herself from the bed, she jerked open the

hall door that had been unlocked since her companions were confined and rushed down the stairs to Miranda's room. She'd stay there until the murderer was caught and she could leave. And if God was willing, she wouldn't see Clay again.

By the time the sun rose, Clay had been almost out of his mind with anger. He'd spent nearly the entire night waiting for Amber to return to her room.

When she hadn't, he'd gone looking for her—and found her in Miranda's room.

He paced his chamber. She refused to see him. Refused to even talk to him, and damn it, Miranda wouldn't let him in. He'd tried several times throughout the day. For what? Miranda was as stubborn as Amber.

He stalked out onto his balcony and gripped the rail, his gaze on the maze below. At the thought of what happened there last night, some of his anger cooled. Amber had a right to be angry with him. He'd hurt her.

Again.

He needed to make it right, but his aunt didn't understand. She was trying to protect Amber. She didn't know about the terrible mistake Clay had made. Clay hadn't realized it himself until the wee hours of the morning, when his worry about Amber had turned to gut-wrenching fear. He couldn't imagine life without her. It didn't matter if they stayed in London. He'd adapt, just as he had on the Captain's ship. And having Amber at his side would make it all worthwhile.

But he had to have the chance to tell her.

A door inside his room opened, and Clay whirled around to see Morgan strolling toward him.

Certain he knew about his trouble with Amber, yet not wanting to discuss it, Clay said the first thing that came to mind. "How are our 'guests' faring?"

Morgan's mouth quirked as if he knew exactly what Clay was doing. "Not well, I'm afraid. Katherine has threatened to sue you for so much money your great-grandchildren will owe her, and she's demanding laudanum for the headaches caused by confinement." He smiled. "I thinks she's making a list of all the wrongs you've done her to give the magistrate."

"What about Amber's cousin? How's she holding up?"

"I think she's a mass of nerves after spending so much time locked up with Lady Chatsworth. She bursts into tears if you ask her what she wants for supper. And the men aren't faring much better. Ellison looks as if he's pulled most of his hair out, and Albert has taken to pacing. I think he's ready to start tearing the walls down."

Feeling a prickle of guilt over his cruelness, Clay tried to think of a way to ease their confinement. "Maybe Miranda could take some yarn and needles to the women, and Robert could play a hand of whist with the men to keep them occupied for a while."

Morgan leaned against the rail. "Father's not here. He went to exercise the horses with Franklin—and Miranda won't leave Amber." He turned and gazed out over the maze. "How long do you plan to keep them locked up, anyway?"

Clay massaged the nape of his neck. "I wish I knew. But one thing's for sure. After all Amber's been through, I'm not going to place her life in danger again. I'll keep them prisoners until I figure out who's responsible, or one of them breaks down and confesses."

"Who do you think did it?"

"I lean toward Albert. He has the most to gain from both deaths, and I'm fairly certain that he knows about William being his sire."

"My money goes on the cousin," Morgan said. "She's too quiet, almost too far above suspicion."

Clay studied him. "So are we to assume that Katherine and Ellison are innocent?"

"No. Just at the bottom of the list."

"There's still the possibility of an outsider," Clay pointed out.

"I used to think that, too," Morgan admitted. "But not anymore. Amber received a post from her friend Sara, who Father thought might be responsible. She's in Bristol at a relative's. Besides, Westshire is guarded like a damned fortress. No one could—or *has*—gotten into the house undetected, unless, of course, they knew about the secret passages—which is highly unlikely."

"So we're right back where we started."

"It would appear so."

"I don't—" Clay's eyes widened as a thought hit him like a bolt of lightning—a thought that should have occurred to him days ago. He spun on his brother. "Have Miranda gather the servants in the ballroom. If she objects to leaving Amber, tell her it's a matter of life or death. I need to talk to them."

"About what?"

"I'll explain later."

"But—"

"Morgan, go. And bring the stable hands and groom."

"What's going on?"

"I think we're about to learn the identity of the killer."

Not wanting to alert Amber until he knew the answer to his question, and praying she'd be safe in Miranda's room, Clay headed for the ballroom. If he was right, he'd either know the killer's identity within minutes, or he'd at least have narrowed it down.

The servants and stable hands were nervously awaiting him as he walked in.

His first inclination was to assuage their fears. His second was to get right to the point.

He studied each of them in turn, then posed the question uppermost in his mind.

"Which one of our guests knows about the secret passages?"

Amber was so tired, she felt that she could sleep standing up. She hadn't slept at all last night. She'd been too upset.

But even through her anger, she wondered if she was being unfair to Clay. After she'd thought about what he said, she remembered when she asked him if he wanted to marry her, he'd said, *"If things were different . . ."* What things? If she wasn't being stalked by a killer? If he was settled? What?

She really needed to know what he was going to say. They'd had a terrible misunderstanding last time. It wasn't going to happen again.

Rising, she walked to the mirror hanging over Miranda's bureau.

Poo flapped his wings as she passed his cage on Miranda's desk. *"Awk.* Man overboard. Man overboard."

Smiling at the bird, she glanced at her reflection—and nearly groaned out loud. She was a mess. She couldn't talk to Clay or anyone else looking like this.

Knowing Clay had summoned the staff to the ballroom, she slipped out Miranda's door and headed for her own room. She'd be glad to get out of her sleeping clothes—for all the good they'd done her. She hadn't had any sleep.

Yawning as she strolled into her room, she made for the armoire and lifted out the green gown she'd received for her birthday. It made her feel good, and she needed that badly right now. After laying it across the foot of the bed, she sat down to remove the slippers Miranda had lent her.

A heaviness pressed down on her shoulders. Good

heavens, she was tired. Her whole body felt like one giant lead weight.

Eyeing the pillow beside her, she pressed her cheek into the softness. Maybe if she rested just for a few seconds . . .

A low, raspy scraping sound startled her. Blinking, she sat up and shoved the hair out of her eyes.

The room dipped, and she gripped the edge of the mattress to steady herself. Good heavens, her head felt like it was too big for her shoulders. She lifted a hand to massage her tired eyes.

"Are you tired, child?"

She whipped her head up. "Katherine?" Her tired mind tried to focus, but it was too fuzzy. "What are you doing here? Where's Georgina?"

"Why, I am visiting my goddaughter, of course, and your cousin is sleeping quite comfortably at the moment—with the help of a little laudanum."

Laudanum? Amber shook her head trying to clear it. She couldn't have heard right. No. Clay must have released her and the others from their rooms. "Did Clay find out who's been trying to hurt me?"

Katherine moved to the foot of the bed and placed a hand on one of the massive posts. The head scratcher hanging from her wrist swung. "Not yet. But I am certain he will before long. That is why I am here."

Amber wished she could think straight. Nothing Katherine said made sense. "What do you mean you're here because Clay will soon learn who killed . . ." Then it hit her—what had been nagging her since Clay questioned everyone in the parlor. Katherine had never denied starting the fire. Amber's skin tightened. Oh, no.

Katherine gave her a smile like she'd never seen before. It was a demented, evil smile. "Your intelligence never fails to amaze me, child."

Amber jumped to her feet but couldn't maintain her balance. She staggered and stumbled into the washstand. The white ceramic pitcher tumbled over the side and crashed to the floor. Water and bits of porcelain splattered the bottom of her chemise.

"Now look what you have done," Katherine scolded.

Her gaze settled on Amber, and a chill went clear through Amber's bones. Katherine's eyes were empty. Vacant. "W-Where's Clay?" Amber asked, already knowing the answer, but she knew something was very wrong, and she wanted to keep Katherine talking.

Katherine took the head scratcher off her wrist. "Below. Gathering his servants in the ballroom."

"Why?" *Oh, Clay, please hurry up here.*

The older woman gripped the head scratcher with both hands and pulled it apart to reveal a thin, sharp dagger. "He is trying to learn which one of us knows about the secret passages."

Panic squeezed Amber's chest. Oh, dear God. Not Katherine. "W-What are you doing with that?"

She glanced down at the weapon as if she hadn't realized she held it. Then her eyes took on that strange light again. "It is to end your life with, child."

Amber's knees almost buckled. She grabbed the edge of the stand to keep herself upright. *"Why?"*

"For Albert, of course. You are the only obstacle standing between him and Markland. He is entitled to it, you know. He is William's firstborn and heir. Markland belongs to him."

"But you said yourself that my father included Albert in his will."

Katherine's slim fingers curled around the hilt as she shifted, bringing her a step closer to Amber. "The original will, yes, but William was going to pen a new one as soon as he married Sara Lawrence. Did you know that?"

Amber edged a step toward the double doors. "No, no. I had no idea."

Katherine stealthily stepped to one side, effectively cutting off any escape Amber might have attempted. Amber was cornered between the fireplace and washstand. "He did it because Albert was a disappointment to him. William claimed our son was a wastrel who would never amount to anything. He did not understand why Albert behaved so badly, why he took to imbibing spirits and frequenting the clubs. William did not understand that Albert was rebelling because of Ellison's indifference to him. Ellison had shut Albert out of his life the day he learned of Albert's true parentage."

"But what has that got to do with me?" Amber cried.

"Your father was shutting him out, too. I could not allow that. Nor could I allow William to marry that Lawrence woman and possibly bear yet another heir. My son deserves Markland and the earldom. It is his birthright."

"But Albert doesn't want to run Markland. I asked him to. He refused."

"He refused your proposal," Katherine corrected. "He could not possibly marry his own sister."

"He knew?"

"Yes. He told me the night of the fire. He had overheard Ellison and me arguing about his birth when he was ten years old. He has always known. And if it had been anyone but you, he would have taken Markland at any cost."

"I don't think he wants an estate as much as you think he does."

Katherine laughed, not a nice laugh. "How little you know about my son. You could not know of the times Albert would sneak into Ellison's study when he was away to pore over the estate's books. Or how he read every piece of literature available on the rasing and care of grain, the current prices and market, or how he would ride out to the fields and check the crops for insects and growth, or how he would toil in the fields himself when the field hands would get behind. He had such wonderful, bright ideas."

No, Amber hadn't known any of that. She knew Albert wanted an estate, but she had no idea it was to that extent.

"Albert will have his dream, Amber. And you are the only thing standing in his way." She advanced a step.

Amber backed up, right into the wall. "I-If you planned to kill me, why did you push me out of the way of Albert's sword that day in the courtyard?"

"I did that for my son. He would have never forgiven himself if you had died by his sword. He would have gone mad, and everything I had done would have been for naught." She stepped closer. Too close. "You should have died in the carriage accident or at the inn."

"You put poison in the wineglass, but how did you know where I'd sit?"

"Oh, child, you are so easy to read. Did you not think I noticed the discord between you and the duke? I knew you would choose to sit beside me rather than him." She shrugged. "If not, I would have 'accidentally' knocked over the goblet." Her empty eyes stared into Amber's. "You should have died that night or, at the very least, in the bath or during the fire, but you did not."

Amber grasped for anything. "What about the cliff? How did you dislodge it?"

"I know nothing about a cliff."

It *had* been a genuine accident, Amber realized.

Her gaze lowered to the blade in Katherine's hand. But this wasn't. Anxiously, Amber's gaze darted to the door, praying that Clay would somehow appear.

"He cannot help you," Katherine said, as if she'd read Amber's thoughts. "It will take him some time to sort out that one of the cook's boys told me about the passages." Her gaze softened. "Unfortunately, you will be dead by the time he does."

"They'll know you did it."

"It does not matter. Only Albert's happiness matters."

A rush of terror climbed Amber's spine. She was really going to do it. "He'll hate you for this," she cried frantically.

Katherine hesitated, blinking, as if her rational brain was trying to absorb Amber's words. Then she stared vacantly. "Do not try to poison my son against me. It will not work. He will understand the depth of his mother's love."

Her eyes took on a feral gleam, and she raised the dagger.

Amber swung her arm with all her might, and hit Katherine's hand. The blade flew from her grasp and skittered under the bed.

Katherine let out an insane shriek and dove at Amber.

They crashed into the wall, then tumbled to the floor, Amber trying desperately to keep Katherine's nails from her face.

She grabbed Katherine's hair to the side, and they rolled to the foot of the bed, but the move caused Amber to strike her head on it.

Lights burst before her eyes, and she swung her arms wildly, trying to keep Katherine away.

Hands closed around Amber's throat. Vicious hands that dug into her tender flesh.

She clawed at the hands, trying to dislodge them. She couldn't breathe!

The pressure increased, and her chest began to burn. She twisted her head from side to side, trying to pry Katherine's thumbs away from her windpipe.

She was too strong. The insanity gave her inhuman strength, and in that instant Amber knew she was going to die.

Hysteria seized her, and she swung her arms savagely. Her hand caught on the green dress and pulled it over them. Fire burned across her lungs, and the room started growing dark.

She grabbed a handful of dress to shove in Katherine's face. Her hand touched something hard. The gold dagger Clay had given her was in the pocket of the dress! Oh God. If only she could reach it!

There was no time—she could feel herself slipping into darkness.

With the last ounce of her strength, she released the dress and balled her fist. She swung as hard as she could at Katherine's head.

The force of the impact caused Katherine to lose her balance and roll to the side.

Sweet air rushed into Amber's lungs. She took several great gulps, then grabbed for the dress and scrambled away.

Frantically, she searched for the opening to the pocket. Her hand closed around the hilt of the knife just as Katherine lunged at her.

Amber brought the knife up, but Katherine was too quick. She dodged and caught Amber's wrist and turned the knife toward Amber's throat. Her back was against the desk, and Katherine's weight had her nearly bent over backward.

Katherine's eyes blazed with insanity as she brought her other hand up over the dagger and used her full weight to press down.

The point of the dagger inched closer . . . closer.

Wildly, Amber bucked and twisted until they toppled to the floor. They struggled, kicking viciously, each fighting urgently for control of the blade.

Then it happened.

The point of the dagger sank deeply into her flesh.

Clay stared angrily at the cook's boy, Thomas. "Who did you tell, damn it!"

The boy took a frightened step back, his eyes wide. "I-I-"

"Clayton, don't frighten the child, or you'll never learn anything," Miranda said gently.

Clay turned to glare at his aunt and opened his mouth to tell her to stay out of it. Pain ripped through his gut.

*Someone was going to die today.*

Shock held him frozen in place. Then the pain tore through him again. "Noooo!" he roared.

Miranda jumped back, shocked.

Morgan's mouth dropped open.

Clay charged toward the hall.

When he got to Miranda's room, he didn't take time to open the door. He stepped back and kicked it in.

Wood shattered and the metal lock skittered across the floor.

Clay tore through the opening with the viciousness of a wild man—and came to an abrupt halt when he saw no one was there.

The pain sliced through him again, and he nearly went to his knees. "Amber! Oh God. Where are you?"

Her room.

Like the madman people claimed him to be, he flew up the stairs and burst into Amber's room.

He came to a skidding halt and stared in frozen horror.

Amber lay sprawled on the floor beneath Katherine.

Bright crimson seeped from between them and dripped onto the floor.

Clay was too paralyzed to move. To even think.

Then something moved.

Katherine climbed to her feet and stood up with her back to him.

Terrified, his gaze lowered to Amber, to her closed eyes, to the blood saturating the front of her gown. No. Oh God. *Please, no.*

Suddenly Katherine crumpled back to the floor and rolled onto her back.

The gold dagger he'd given Amber jutted from the woman's midsection.

Numbly, he stared at the weapon, then he heard Amber's quiet weeping.

He nearly wept with relief. Fighting the threat of tears, he dropped to his knees beside her and pulled her into his arms. "I'm sorry, sweetheart. So sorry." He stroked her hair and cheek and spine, reveling in the warmth that filled his arms.

Amber began to cry harder, and through her broken sobs she told him everything. About Katherine's insanity, and her obsessive love for Albert.

Clay didn't know what to say. Didn't know what to do. So he just held her—and thanked God she was alive.

# Chapter 22

"Have they gone?" Morgan asked as Clay walked into the parlor.

"Yes. Ellison and Albert have taken Katherine home for burial."

"How's Amber?"

"Hurting. She loved Katherine."

Morgan leaned back in his chair and downed the rest of the port in his glass. "So what happens now?"

Clay tried to ease the discomfort in his chest by massaging his neck. "Amber and I will marry and move to London."

Morgan was silent for several seconds, then his eyes met Clay's. "Why?"

"Why will I marry her? I think that's pretty obvious. I'm in love with her."

Morgan rose to his impressive height and loomed over him. "Why London? I know you detest that wretched hellhole. All of England, for that matter."

Clay wasn't in the least intimidated by his little brother. "Amber's a part of London. I can't take her away from it." He stared directly into Morgan's blue eyes. "The Captain did that to our mother and lost her within a year. I'm not going to let that happen to Amber and me."

"So you're going to live in London and be miserable for the rest of your life."

"What's the alternative? Living without her?"

"Have you talked to her about it?"

"Why? So she could vow to go anywhere with me, then leave me within months to return to the social scene?"

"You could come back with her if that happened."

"No. It'll be easier all the way around if I just buy an estate near London and raise my thoroughbreds. Amber will be happy, and I'll be doing what I love."

"In a place you hate."

"I told you. I'll adapt."

"Adapt to what?" Miranda asked, strolling into the room.

"Why would you buy an estate?" Morgan continued as if their aunt hadn't spoken. "What's wrong with Markland?"

"Nothing. Amber plans to give Markland to Albert and petition the king for his true title."

"Adapt to what?" Miranda repeated.

Clay refused to get into this conversation with his aunt. "Where's Amber?"

"Packing. She plans to return to London tomorrow. Now exactly what are you going to adapt to?"

Clay sighed and gave Miranda a kiss on the cheek. "Married life." He winked. "But I guess I'd better go talk to her if that's going to happen."

Amber knelt on the floor in front of the armoire, staring at the contents of her secret chest. Since that night four years ago, she'd only looked in it a few times in the last years to place Clay's still-wrapped gifts inside and just a few days ago, when she straightened the contents. She'd kept her treasures in there since she was a child. Mostly the things Clay had given her. Silk hair ribbons from China. A jade statue of a monkey from Indonesia. A wooden doll from the Sandwich Islands. A miniature ivory castle from Africa. Children's gifts.

She picked up a wrapped package he'd sent to her when she was sixteen. She'd been too hurt to open it when she received it, so she'd simply tossed it in her chest and put it out of her mind.

Blinking back tears, she carefully untied the ribbon and parted the linen covering. A delicate gold necklace, set with lovely diamonds and amber stones, winked in the morning sunlight. An exquisite diamond pendant hung from the center, surrounded by thin loops of gold and tiny amber stones.

She fingered the jewels, then turned the pendant over. A small inscription was printed on the back. Just two words.

*Forgive me.*

A tear trickled down her cheek. He had tried to make amends with the first 'grown-up' gift he'd ever given her. With trembling fingers, she put it on, loving the feel of the smooth gold resting over her heart. She could never love anyone as much as she loved him.

"Amber?"

At the sound of Clay's voice, she turned.

His gaze lowered to her throat, and something indefinable entered his eyes. "Miranda tells me you're planning to return to London tomorrow."

"Yes, I am."

"Is that where you want us to marry?"

Pain wrenched her heart. "Clay, I'm not going to marry you."

He didn't even flinch. "Why not?"

She set the linen wrapper aside and rose, crossing

her arms over her middle. She couldn't face him, so she stared out the glass doors. "I won't allow you to wed me because of some misplaced sense of honor."

He came up behind her and cupped her shoulders. "Sweetheart, I do a lot of things in the name of honor, but marrying for the sake of propriety isn't one of them."

He nuzzled the hair draping the side of her neck. "I want you to be my wife now and always. I'll build you a home on the outskirts of London and—"

"What?" She spun around so fast she bumped into him.

"I said I'll build—"

"Why?"

He smiled crookedly. "You have to have someplace to live."

"Why London?"

He framed her face with his hands. "Because I know it will make you happy. And that's all I want, Amber. Your happiness."

Something inside her melted. "What about your happiness? What about the Colonies and your thoroughbreds?"

"I'll still raise thoroughbreds."

He was willing to give up his dream for her. But why? "What if I said I want to go to the Colonies?"

He lowered his hands and stepped away. "No. You wouldn't be happy there."

"I wouldn't?" As far as she knew, she'd be happy anywhere with him.

"No. It's a new nation, sweetheart. They don't have the social set there like in London. There are a few parties, of course, but in the Shenandoah Valley there are no balls or operas or theaters. It's a wild country, sometimes a brutal one."

"What has that got to do with anything?"

He rubbed the back of his neck. "Amber, stop the pretense. I know how much you love the social scene.

Hell, every time I'd return to London these past years, you'd be off to some social function. Your father told me about your coming-out ball and how popular you were, how you'd received invitations from every corner of England, how you'd done your damnedest to attend every one of them."

"Yes, I did," she admitted. "And I see something else. You want to build me a house near London so I can continue to be the social butterfly you think I am? Is that right?" Her hands curled into fists, and for the first time in her life she wanted to swear. "You *pompous jackass*. Did it ever occur to you that I attended those wretched functions because I was trying to avoid you? That I wanted to drown myself in frivolous conversation so I wouldn't think about you?" She wanted to kick him. "For all I care, the whole of London could burn to the ground, and I wouldn't give a blasted shilling to help rebuild it. Stop grinning, you jack—"

He kissed her, long and hard.

When he finally released her, he was still smiling. "If I take you to the Colonies, will you marry me?"

"Only if you *want* to marry me, not because of honor or duty."

"Oh, I want to, sweetheart"—he pulled her into his arms—"more than you'll ever know." He kissed her again, this time very gently. Those beautiful green eyes stared into hers. "I need to make some arrangements before we go. Will you wait for me here at Westshire?"

She'd wait in the rain if he asked her to.

That thought came back to haunt her a month later, when Clay still hadn't returned.

He'd set off that same afternoon, vowing to return in a fortnight with a surprise for her. She hadn't heard a word from him since.

Even Miranda and Georgina were concerned.

Miranda was certain something had happened to him, and Georgina feared he'd set out to hurt Amber again.

Morgan diligently stuck by his brother, saying he must have run into difficulties with the arrangements or he'd already be back.

Amber was beginning to agree with Georgina. Surely, if that had been the case, Clay would have sent word. And if he'd been hurt or injured, *someone* would have notified them by now. No. Clay had apparently changed his mind. After all, not once had he told her he loved her. Not once.

Feeling as if the weight of a boulder lay on her chest, Amber headed for her room to pack—for a second time. But this time, she ignored her secret chest. Clay had hurt her one too many times. When she returned to Markland, she would see it destroyed.

Swiping at the tears stinging her cheeks, she packed her trunks and laid out a traveling dress for the next morning. She would have one of the grooms take her to Middlesbrough, where she would find public transportation back to London.

Changing into a chemise, she packed away her gown, then ran a brush through her hair. Leaving the implement and a ribbon on the bureau for use the next morning, she climbed into bed and blew out the candle.

The sooner she went to sleep, the sooner she could go home. At the thought of Markland, she thought of Albert. According to the king's messenger, Markland now belonged to her brother, but she was sure he would welcome her. Allow her to live there until she married and moved into a home of her own.

She closed her eyes, visualizing rolling green hills like the ones Clay had described in the Shenandoah Valley, but quickly pushed them aside. No. She wasn't going to think about him or the Colonies ever again.

Determined not to think about what could have

been, she pulled the cover up to her chest and willed her mind to clear.

A low, ominous scraping sound startled her.

Old terror rushed to the surface, and she drew the quilt up to her chin, staring wide-eyed into the darkness.

A shadow moved, and Amber's heart nearly exploded in her chest.

The figure stepped into a beam of moonlight, and she saw him—saw the long cutlass dangling at his side, a gold earring glinting in his right ear.

It was Clay.

She nearly wept with joy. He'd come back for her.

Still, she wasn't ready to forgive him for making her worry. She sat up and tucked the quilt in around her. "What do you want?"

His breath rasped heavily. "Ah, me pretty, you know what Captain Cutthroat wants." His voice lowered to a purr. "Your lovely thighs wrapped around mine."

Wings of desire fluttered through her, and she had a hard time holding on to her composure, but she tried to play his game. "But I am betrothed to the duke of Westshire."

He laughed wickedly. "That *pompous jackass?* He wouldn't know what to do with a beauty like you." He moved to stand beside the bed. "But I do." He swooped her up into his arms and tossed her over his shoulder.

Amber burst out laughing. "Clay, wait!"

"Silence, wench!" He marched into his room, then into the passageway and down the steep, dark steps.

It was all Amber could do to keep from laughing at his theatrics.

When they at last emerged into the light, they were in the secret cove, and the *Black Wind* was rocking gently in the water just offshore.

Without a word, he strode to a longboat, and

stepped inside, still holding her draped over his shoulder.

Sighing, she rested her cheek against his back and enjoyed the sound of his beating heart.

Cheers from the *Black Wind's* crew went up as the longboat drew alongside the ship.

Clay didn't release her nor did he speak as he carried her past a sea of grinning faces and down a short flight of stairs to a large room.

When he lit a candle, he tossed her on a big, soft bed, then towered over her. "So, wench. My bowman tells me you planned to attempt escape on the morrow."

She could tell by the look in his eyes, he was serious. Giddy with happiness, yet knowing she had to explain herself, she kept on with his game. "Yes, I was. You see, the man I love went away for only a fortnight, but a month passed, and he didn't return. Didn't send word. He never told me he loved me, and he was actually forced into proposing, so I feared he'd changed his mind."

Clay frowned. "I was late returning because I had a devil of a time gathering my crew, and what do you mean I never said I love you? Bloody hell, woman. I've said it a thousand times in my heart."

"I can't see into your heart."

He closed his eyes and arched his head back. "What a damn fool I am." Then he met her gaze with all the love there for her to see. "I love you, Amber. And I want you to be my wife for no other reason."

"Curse it all, Clayton, I've been in love with you since you swaggered into my life when I was five years old. You know nothing would make me happier."

"You couldn't be any happier than I am, sweetheart." His eyes brightened with love. "And if you want a London wedding with all the finery, that's what we'll have. Or if you want to be married this night by a crusty old sea captain, it shall be. The choice is yours."

Amber studied Clay's handsome face, loving him with every fiber of her being. "The London pomp would be nice"—she touched his beautiful mouth—"but it would take much too long. Marry me tonight, my roguish captain, and take me home to the Shenandoah Valley."

# Let
# *Andrea*
# *Kane*
## romance you tonight!

*Dream Castle* 73585-3/$5.50

*My Heart's Desire* 73584-5/$5.50

*Masque of Betrayal* 75532-3/$4.99

*Echoes In the Mist* 75533-1/$5.50

*Samantha* 86507-2/$5.50

*The Last Duke* 86508-0/$5.99

*Emerald Garden* 86509-9/$5.99

*Wishes In the Wind* 53483-1/$5.99

*Legacy of the Diamond* 53485-8/$5.99

-------- Available from Pocket Books --------